ABOVE HIM THE MOUNTAIN GROANED SOFTLY, PROTESTINGLY

After a week of excavation, Brennan seemed no nearer to his goal. Still, each succeeding day he dug deeper, filling his artifact boxes with shards and pieces of metal, and Carlisle envied him.

Carlisle stood up, preparing to head back toward the camp. What would he do, he wondered, if the archeologist's efforts *did* produce some hidden, earth-shattering information? CALIFUR, after all, warned of a period of great danger, a danger epitomized by this very dig. Dusting snow from his boots, Carlisle started downslope.

"Brennan!" Jancy's voice came over the comm net as a triumphant yell.

"What is it?" Down below in the ruins Brennan stopped working, looked vaguely west.

"There's a chiseled-out cavity here—right into the rock. Dirt's fallen in. Snow, too." There were muttered words too low for Carlisle to hear, and then an exultant cry from the girl.

"It's █████████████████ back in there. There's █████████████████ute, I'll get it out . . ."

A cra█████████████████ ears, followed by a slow █████████████████

Edward A. Byers

The Long Forgetting

BAEN
SCIENCE FICTION
BOOKS

THE LONG FORGETTING

This is a work of fiction. All the characters and events portrayed in this book are fictional, and any resemblance to real people or incidents is purely coincidental.

Copyright © 1985 by Edward A. Byers

All rights reserved, including the right to reproduce this book or portions thereof in any form. Sections of this book have appeared in different form in *Analog Science Fiction/Science Fact*.

A Baen Book

Baen Enterprises
8-10 W. 36th Street
New York, N.Y. 10018

First printing, September 1985

ISBN: 0-671-55980-X

Cover art by Paul Chadwick

Printed in the United States of America

Distributed by
SIMON & SCHUSTER
MASS MERCHANDISE SALES COMPANY
1230 Avenue of the Americas
New York, N.Y. 10020

To Hugo—Who Started It All

Acknowledgements:

Ben Bova, Joe L. Hensley, Adele Leone, Betsy Mitch-
ell, Ray and Nancy Schandelmeier, Stanley Schmidt,
Lola Trude, The Vicious Circle, Greg and Patty Weakley.

Before the Beginning

We are creations of our times, as surely as the times are our creation. No one asked to be born in the 10th century B.C., or in the days of Caesar, or when Tamerlane ruled from the Euphrates to the Ganges.

And certainly, no one asked to be born into the time of the Fugue . . .

It began quietly enough, at the very fringe of Man's frontier. A communique from a moon observatory was interrupted in midsentence, severed as though by a knife.

The observatory was sufficiently distant that it took two years for the alarm to reach another human outpost, and three more before the news became a datum to be reckoned with.

Peregrine was the first populated world devastated by the Fugue. Situated on the far edge of a spiral cluster, home to a fundamentalist group of Abyssinians, Peregrine specialized in the manufacture of folk handicrafts and the husbandry of goats.

A message escaped Peregrine, the only thing to do

so. In a voice both plaintive and prophetic, the speaker left behind a footnote for future historians.

"Something is happening. . . !"

All the habitable worlds of a Class IV system named Burfour's Reach, a hegemony consisting of four planets and eleven moons, were the next victims of the Fugue.

A docking commander, shipping produce and medical items to Burfour through a stargate link, suddenly noticed a logjam building up on the conveyor. When it reached nuisance proportions, he delegated one of his loaders to investigate. His loader did not return, and the commander, dismay segueing into suspicion, called the local gendarmerie.

Three volunteers entered the stargate and vanished. Though their orders were explicit—to return immediately—they did not.

There were mechanical devices that could go where Man could not. Several of these devices, called COmPUtes, were shunted through the stargate. Cameras inside their alloy carapaces whirred as they trundled along. After a suitable time they retraced their path, eventually activating the stargate at Burfour's end and returning from whence they came.

What the cameras revealed was revelatory.

Reporting to the chief of staff for sector affairs was one James Kilroy Spencer, a field investigator assigned to study the Burfour phenomenon. He carried with him a case containing a pictorial synopsis of what was only slowly becoming known as the Fugue.

The chief of staff and his aides sat stiffly while Spencer set up a display monitor. When he was ready, Spencer said, "These pictures were taken, via COmPUte, on one of the planets in the New Dublin system. It is about two light weeks from Burfour." Without commenting further, he sat down and flicked the switch.

The screen showed a man dressed in a military jump suit carrying an automatic weapon.

"His name's Whitney," Spencer murmured to the chief of staff. "A convict. This is immediately before he went through the Gate."

"He volunteered, I suppose."

"That's right. For commutation of sentence."

"Is he wearing a camera?"

"No. We're recording it on both sides. Watch."

Whitney was clearly nervous. Clutching his weapon, he sidled toward the arched entrance of the Gate. A moment or two later, positioned in the center of the transfer chamber, he snicked off the weapon's safety catch and adopted a stance that was half a crouch.

Passage to the New Dublin system was instantaneous. The COmPUte cameras at the other end of the Gate picked Whitney up the moment he appeared. They zoomed in close.

"My God! His face!" The words were wrenched unbidden from one of the aides.

Whitney's facial muscles twitched, slackened, realigned themselves. The jaw thrust forward a little, the nose flared. A frightened beast stared dumbly out of Whitney's eyes.

There was a space of three or four seconds, then the convict made an inarticulate cry. The automatic weapon fell from nerveless fingers, clattered noisily on the parquet tiles.

The chief of staff looked around at Spencer. "What in hell is going on?"

"Wait," Spencer said grimly. He pointed toward the screen. "The cameras have a thousand-meter radius of operation. We followed Whitney right out into the streets."

The convict was moving, loose-jointed at first, then with more control, as though he were learning to walk all over again. A close-up shot showed a vacuous expression, a rope of spittle descending slowly from his half-open jaw. Whitney entered a corridor leading to the building's loading docks. There was evidence of wreckage, some of it caused by machines running amok.

Beyond the docks lay New Dublin. The city bore an air of emptiness, of desolation, like a latter-day *Chi Chén-Itzá*.

It was not, however, entirely deserted. An ominous growl of anger and terror met Whitney's appearance as he made his way out of the Gate complex. There were a dozen men and four women crouching in the shadow of a wall—dangerous, filthy, dressed in tatters of clothes and glaring like jackals.

Whitney made it another two meters before the first rock struck him. The convict howled and made as though to back away. In a flash the others were on him, hurling him to the ground, rending his flesh with sharp stones and broken bottles.

"Jesus!" The chief of staff turned half around, looked at Spencer with horror in his eyes. On the screen, bits and pieces of Whitney were hoisted in triumph, then carried off as trophies.

"It happens like this wherever the Fugue hits," Spencer said, turning off the monitor. "Entire worlds . . . whole populations. Intellect is lost, leaving only a kind of brutal cunning."

"My God, man! This Fugue—what the hell *is* it?"

Spencer shrugged, unfolded a map, laid it on the table. "This shows a portion of star-scape with three outer-edge galaxies. Only a few of the planets out there are populated." He pointed to the bulging gaseous side of one of the galaxies. "This is where the Fugue was first detected—a world called Peregrine. Further in is Burfour's Reach; still further the New Dublin system."

"Something attacking us?" the chief of staff asked in frozen tones.

"Maybe. Maybe not."

"How fast is it moving?"

Spencer looked uncomfortable. "*Apparent* movement is point nine four of the speed of light, but it seems to be accelerating. Apparent angle is on a plane going thusly." He drew his finger in a slashing line across the edge of the map.

* * *

Tigrisov was the name of the world. It was located three light-weeks from Burfour's Reach.

The woman hiding in the weed-choked ravine was naked except for a tattered blanket. It was night, but not too dim to see. Two men, their hands gripping crude clubs, were working their way toward her. One of them wore half a shirt, the other nothing at all. From afar came cries of other members of the pack.

The woman scanned both banks of the ravine, then rose and clambered up the slope that was least steep. Stones and clumps of earth broke loose and fell noisily to the bottom. There was a cry of triumph from one of the men. He sprinted forward, arriving just as the woman attained a small ledge four meters up.

There was no further ascent possible. The ground above her and to both sides was flat cliff-face. The ledge itself was narrow, and tapered to a point after only a few steps.

The woman tried to crouch, make herself small. With a howl of delight the naked man attempted to scale the slope. His club made him unwieldy, however, and he made it only halfway to the ledge before he slipped back.

The man with half a shirt did not try to reach the woman by climbing up the bank. Instead, he seated himself on a large stone, put down his club, and surveyed the female just above him with a speculative air. After perhaps a minute he bent double, picked up a fist-sized rock, and shook it at the female.

The naked man had given up after three assaults on the steep bank. He lay panting, eyes fixed on the ledge above.

The rock from the half-shirted man struck the woman on the right hip. She yelped and scrambled along the ledge toward its narrow end. Halfway there she slipped, almost but not quite recovering her balance. She fell, scraping a leg on the rough stone.

The half-shirted man caught her when she hit the bottom, delight evident on his moon-shaped face. He made guttural noises in the direction of his companion and hauled the woman upright.

Though cannibalism was widespread, this female would be spared. She was young enough to find a place within the pack.

Several months after Spencer reported to the chief of staff, Lord A. F. Trane held a news conference attempting to bring into perspective the difficulty of rescuing worlds in the immediate path of the Fugue.

Trane: Locus physics dictates capacity of any stargate. Masses above five hundred kilograms distort the Gate field and result in temporary 'wavering' of material transported. That means our rescue attempts are limited to three or four persons per Gate sequence—figure twenty-four per hour.

What that means in practical terms is more than a little dismaying. It's analogous to what was said about a certain country several centuries back: 'If the population were to form a line four abreast and walk through a doorway, the end of that line would never be reached.'

Gentlemen, the Fugue is going to catch one hell of a lot of people. (*Pause*) And it's accelerating!

Question: How about those that have already been caught? Will we ever be able to rescue them?

Trane: Maybe, if the Fugue is a merely transitory phenomenon. If not . . .

Question: If not?

Trane: I don't have an answer. Let's hope that it *is* transitory.

Question: How fast is it accelerating? It can't go faster than the speed of light, can it?

Trane: That is supposed to be the ultimate limit. If it is, then most of us will be safe. At light-speed it would take thousands of years for it to sweep across the galaxies. There's only one catch.

Question: What's that?

Trane: The Fugue is a freak. It doesn't follow the

laws of physics. That being the case, it *might* accelerate past the speed of light.

Question: What happens if it does?

Trane: Um. Depends whether the ratio of acceleration is arithmetic or geometric. If it's arithmetic, we'll still have time—centuries—to study it, discover how to control it.

Question: But what if it's not? What if it's geometric?

Trane (Smiling faintly): Then we should all look for a hole to hide in. No place in the cosmos will be safe from it.

Question: Do you think we'll find out what the Fugue *is*?

Trane: Given time, my friend, Man can puzzle out just about anything. Question is, will we have the time?

The Fugue: No one could describe it, reproduce it, or predict that once gone, it would not come again. It was like a vast hellish scythe, leaving a mindless darkness behind it. A true Dark Age—one that lasted 840 years.

By the time the Fugue passed and the first stumbling *Homo sapien* had, with simian curiosity, crept beneath the bulbous shell of a 2nd Class Teaching Machine (nuclear powered) much of Man's works had crumbled into ruin. *Viva Ozymandias.*

Man being Man, it was likely inevitable that his new-found knowledge be put to something worthwhile. The first man founded a religion.

There were records, albeit scant and unsubstantiated, that the Darkness was the result of two Gods warring in the universe. On one side was Setsen Dai, The Shining Light. This creature, perfect in nature and benign toward every living thing, was responsible for the passing of the Fugue and for Mankind's rekindling of intellect.

His opposite was an avatar of evil. He was called simply Kirst, and was the embodiment of darkness. His two demon pets were Pain and Suffering. He had ruled his dominion for eight centuries. Now Setsen Dai had driven him away.

It was a good, solid religion. It had its saints, its martyrs, its prophets.

And it had its heretics.

Book One

Chapter One

Corthun was a dull pebble in a black pocket, a planet on the edge of nowhere.

There was, however, a molybdenite mine near her southern pole. Its entrance was located on a steep rise on exposed gneiss, beneath a high dark sky. There were forbidding granite walls to the north and east, and a cold brisk wind blowing out of the southwest.

A mining road, merely a track after twelve centuries of disuse, wound between several massive monoliths. A man, dwarfed by the stones on either side, walked jauntily down the track's middle, following the curves in the roadbed. He was on the thin side, tall, with whitish-blond hair. He wore a go-to-hell grin and he was armed.

A faded name plate on his metallic gold suit said his name was Pierce.

Halfway to the mine the road detoured. Pierce studied the secondary track carefully. It was smaller and less inviting than the primary. Finally, shrugging, he broke off down the detour.

The track ended abruptly forty meters farther along.

There was a bare rock face, and beneath it a kind of gully that slanted downward until it was lost in shadow. Pierce prowled along its edge, finally squatted on his haunches and stared down into the depths. At last he grinned and said a single word: "Midden." The sound startled him, and as he turned away he laughed.

Following the track back to the main road, Pierce turned again toward the mine. Half a kilometer farther on, he found what remained of a metal shack and a few assorted pieces of mining equipment. He poked and pried through the piles of oxides, cursing softly, and moved on to the mine itself.

The adit was four meters high, three across. It led into a stygian darkness that succumbed only reluctantly to the light Pierce wielded.

Sixty meters into the shaft the ceiling had collapsed, blocking further progress. Pierce examined the fallen blocks of stone carefully, frustration evident on his thin features. He determined that the rock fall had occurred centuries before, when the shaft supports became mere metal skeletons, lacking any true strength. If he somehow got through *this* block, he supposed, more such falls waited in the shaft beyond.

He left the mine and spent the remainder of the brief day exploring the surrounding terrain. He possessed instruments that detected masses of metal, but the instruments only led him to more crumbling oxide piles.

He drycamped where the steel mine shack had stood, munching a meager ration of food and staring disheartenedly up at the stars. He slept, out of habit, with his weapon in his hand.

In the morning, Pierce examined the upland area, then hiked eastward following a dry riverbed. He found no hint of human occupation.

Noon found him once again at the mine's entrance, the corners of his mouth drawn into a fierce scowl.

From impulse, he followed the mining road back to

the secondary track. Turning up it, he trudged through the tracks he had made going and coming, the dust seeming unusually thick and heavy.

Again he examined the gully, shining his light into its depths and checking the dials of his detectors. He sat down at last on the gully's lip, dangling his legs over the edge, his eyes showing an open contempt for the danger involved.

Sitting thus, his eyes chanced to **fall** upon a mound of rubble three meters to his left. Pierce stared at it for almost a minute before realizing no arrangement of stones like *that* happens in nature.

Clambering to his feet, he approached the mound, started clearing rubble, lifting stones, and rolling them away from the gully. Ten minutes was sufficient to show him that the mound was a burial site, and that its occupant had long since leached his/her bones into the soil.

What remained in the burial cavity was a small metal case, its surface etched by time. Pierce tugged tentatively at the lid. Amazingly, the pressure of his fingers alone was enough to break it open.

Inside was a sheaf of plastic pages and a photograph. Pierce picked up the photograph and held it in a hand that was suddenly frozen. Breathing stentoriously, he replaced the photograph and lifted out the sheaf of pages. There were words filling up each page, though some of them were faint.

Pierce sat down on what remained of the stone mound and began to read.

Chapter Two

Monsignor Charles Carlisle, wearing the green robes and woven metal belt of the Morganite Order, pushed open the door of the Gate Authority, removed his stiff-brimmed hat, and gave his name to the cleric sitting behind the desk. Then he sat in an uncomfortable plastic armchair and tried to relax. Only one other person was waiting, a short, unsmiling matron. The cleric, himself short and broad-featured, looked up at infrequent intervals. Each time Carlisle smiled, his fingers gently kneading the coarse woolen fabric of his habit.

"You're outbound where, Monsignor?"

"Pio-Tan," Carlisle said. He produced several official forms, each displaying prominently the seal of his Order. Each was signed and countersigned.

"Pio-Tan, umh—" The cleric sucked his lower lip and consulted a directory. Then he looked at Carlisle suspiciously.

"That's LUO—Limited Use Only."

"There's an archeological excavation going on

there," Carlisle explained. "When the field results are in, it's expected to be cleared for colonization."

"But for now, it's LUO," said the cleric without humor. A small sign on his desk said his name was James Luther. Almost absently he picked up the metal-embossed plate and polished it on his sleeve. He sighed, as though Carlisle had thwarted some long-cherished personal taboo. Eventually, however, he initialed each form and placed them in a slot marked *Travel—Expedite.*

Carlisle waited another fifty minutes before he was called to enter the Gate.

Far down in the valley there was the rhythmic thudding of huge wings. Their echoes bounced off the granite cliff faces. Carlisle heard them as he plodded up the narrow trail leading to the dig.

He looked up when a shadow touched him. One of the mammoth fly-malcons wheeled above him, its wings bellied out in clouds of brown and white. He made it ten meters from wing-tip to wing-tip. The bird's scimitar-shaped claws glinted in the azure light.

Carlisle continued walking. The Index said birds on Pio-Tan seldom attacked creatures as large as humans. *Seldom.* Carlisle, who had helped write that selfsame Index, knew it for only an approximation of the truth. He wiped his brow. Approximations of the truth seemed to abound, these days.

"The dig? Oh, sure—it's only a few kilometers up the middle of that valley," the priest at the Gate had said. He'd kept his face straight, too, and Carlisle had started out bravely enough, thinking the incline would level out, that the dig would appear around one of the first few bends.

But he had been going on for close to an hour, and the path was growing steeper, leading him toward a green-yellow bluff whose walls were impossibly steep.

"Daiists believe they're stewards of The Shining Light," Carlisle's bishop had once said. "And they hold the caretaking Orders in little regard. Try to keep yourself humble, Charles, when you treat with them."

Carlisle, who had joined the Morganite Order for love of scholarship and service, found the Daiist *hubris* tiresome. After all, weren't *all* the Orders followers of The Light?

Maybe that was true, Carlisle thought to himself, and maybe it wasn't. One thing *was* certain. The Daiist Order coveted the single valuable thing the Morganites possessed—the organic COmPUte called CALIFUR.

The broad flat silhouette of a floater came into view at that instant, swinging through his field of vision in an arc, breaking up his reverie. The floater's pilot waved a languid hand, banked the craft steeply, and descended to a flat spot on the trail ahead.

"You'd be Carlisle?"

"Yes—and God's thanks for stopping!" Carlisle expelled a breath of relief. As he settled himself on the flat bench behind the pilot, he said: "You *are* going to the dig?"

"Sure as hell am—excuse me, Monsignor—name's Kahn. I run equipment in and out between here and the Gate. They said you'd be coming this way." The man, small and brown as a nut, paused and turned his head. His eyes crinkled at the corners. "You shouldn't have come alone, not down here in the valley. A fly-malcon doesn't know you have God's blessing."

Carlisle gripped the support bar on the back of the pilot's seat. "You mean they *do* attack humans?"

"Not singly, but they've been known to hunt in packs." Kahn lifted the floater, angling it upward, applying power. Carlisle clutched the bar tightly, his robes whipping behind him in the sudden wind. Mentally, he made a note: Indexers should not make inferences from individual behavior only.

The dig came into view the moment they cleared the top of the cliff. Carlisle saw a broad expanse of tan-colored plateau, most of it sectioned into small, even plots. Teams of men wielding soil siphons worked in the narrow trenches, spumes of raw earth jetting back over their shoulders.

Kahn said, "Welcome to Crislau. You'll be wanting to see Brennan, I suppose."

"Dr. Hook, yes." Carlisle squinted as they came up on a circle of shelters. There were half a dozen power generators, two other floaters, and a hodgepodge of equipment, most of it protected with weather-beaten plastic skin.

Kahn sat the floater down easily, then swiveled his head around to look at the priest. There was a coldness in his eyes. He said shortly, "A bit of advice, Monsignor. Don't call the Chief 'Dr. Hook.' Not in *his* presence."

"No?" Carlisle returned the man's gaze, then nodded soberly, apologetically. "I'm afraid I have been given some misinformation. The priest at the Gate is Daiist; I am not." His smile was quick, rueful.

Kahn took in the priest's robes, grunted: "I'm not familiar with your Order, Monsignor."

"We are not many, and we do our work, for the most part, in seclusion." Carlisle stood up and exited the floater. "I am a Morganite." He stared past Kahn at the laboring men. "What is it you're digging for?"

"There used to be a village here," Kahn said. "Crislau was its name." He stepped out of the floater, stretched hugely, and gestured for Carlisle to follow him. He headed toward one of the gaily colored shelters.

"How old is it?" Carlisle asked, coming up beside him.

"The village? Fifteen hundred years or so. It was destroyed in a battle."

Carlisle glanced around once again. There were walls still standing, mute skeletons of stone, their surfaces scoured white by the wind.

Kahn stopped abruptly, and Carlisle nearly ran into him. Coming toward them was a big man dressed in the sapphire-blue robes of the Daiist Order. He had an eagle's look about him, a look augmented by his jutting nose and piercing deep-set eyes.

"Oh, Monsignor Carlisle, this is a counterpart of yours. Father Maxwell Stuyvesant."

They shook hands, Carlisle feeling the difference in height intensely. Stuyvesant loomed over him by fully half a meter. The indifferent power in the man's grip was immense.

"A Morganite." Stuyvesant stared at him with something like annoyance. "Aren't you a little out of your way, here on Pio-Tan?"

"Yes," Carlisle said simply. "But I've been given a mission. I'm to see the archeologist in charge here. Dr. Waverly Hooker-Brennan."

"What about?"

Carlisle shook his head. "In all good conscience, those are matters both private and personal."

Stuyvesant was not pleased. He pursed his lips and arched an eyebrow. It was, Carlisle thought with sudden insight, a combination learned in the classroom, when an errant novice had need of instant retribution.

"You have authorization, I suppose."

"Of course." Carlisle removed a rolled piece of plastic from his pocket. It bore the signature of Bishop Poole. He handed it to Stuyvesant, who scrutinized it intently before handing it back.

"Very well. However, Dr. Hooker-Brennan isn't here at the moment. Perhaps you would like to wait in my shelter. The food is nourishing, the wine at least adequate."

Carlisle hesitated. He did not want to offend Stuyvesant. The Daiists numbered in the tens of millions, while his own small Order doubled shifts merely to man the stargates tasked to them. At the same time, he'd rather not be sequestered with Stuyvesant.

Kahn rescued him neatly. Smiling, he turned toward Carlisle, gestured toward the laboring men. "Maybe you'd like to look over the dig. There're lots of artifacts. We don't have names for most of them."

"Yes, thank you." Carlisle nodded and bowed to Stuyvesant. "With your permission, Father."

The nearest trench was a meter or so in depth. The strata in the trench walls changed from red to pale yellow to a faintly greenish color.

"Anyone digging here?" Kahn called out to one of the trench crew.

"We stopped working that area," a burly laborer yelled back. "Nothing there, so far as we could find."

Kahn hopped down into the trench, looked back at Carlisle. "Want to try your hand at siphoning?"

Carlisle's eyes brightened a bit. "No one would mind?"

"Nah—it'll be all right." Kahn strode down the trench, tapped the laborer on his shoulder. "Why don't you show Monsignor Carlisle how to use a siphon?"

"Please," Carlisle said when the two approached. "Just call me Father. I dislike honorifics."

"Sure, Father." The burly man unslung the siphon's heavy coil from around his shoulders, dropped it to the ground in front of him. "My name's Thorson. I've been a siphoner for most of five years." He grinned. "It takes a little getting used to."

Carlisle slid down into the trench. There were steps every ten meters or so but no one seemed to use them. He rolled up the sleeves of his cassock and eyed the soil siphon warily. "What do you do first?"

"Get 'er strapped on," Thorson said. He lifted the siphon, which resembled a tuba, and held it while Carlisle maneuvered his left arm through the hole in the middle and got it settled on his right shoulder. It was startlingly heavy. Carlisle wondered how the diggers managed to work with them all day long.

"Comfortable?" Thorson asked.

"It's fine."

"Good." Thorson winked at Kahn and handed Carlisle the siphon's snout, a ten-centimeter-wide hose with a handle at the top. "To turn it on, you simply flip that switch there," he said, pointing. "The hand grip controls the level of penetration. Set it wide and you'll start gulping up earth at maximum rate. Set it thin and you take off just a few microns. Go ahead, get the feel."

Carlisle flipped the siphon on, was rewarded with a soft *huffing* sound. He squeezed the handle and held the spout against the trench wall. Almost miraculously earth began to disappear, to become a rooster tail of sand-fine particulates shooting out the siphon's nether end.

"What if you hit a rock?" he asked Thorson.

"That's an acoustical vibrating head there," Thorson told him. "It'll chew up rock as easy as you please."

Hefting the soil siphon, Carlisle started deepening the trench. He didn't realize it, but his mouth was stretched in a wide smile.

"Go ahead," Thorson said. "Open it up."

Carlisle squeezed harder on the handle, felt the siphon lurch and start to drag him forward. At the same time, the amount of earth escaping through the exhaust increased dramatically. The effect was a jet that propelled Carlisle up against the trench wall with a *whump*.

"See what I mean," Thorson said, grinning at him. "It takes some getting used to."

Chapter Three

"What do you think, Bren—that ridge looks like a good place to put in some sounders." The man speaking was thick-chested, with carrot-red hair and massive freckled arms. As he spoke he leaned partway out of the floater, pointed with an outsize finger.

Dr. Waverly Hooker-Brennan, who preferred the diminutive of his last name to any other, followed the other man's gaze. The spine of cliffs to their right was a loesslike yellow, gleaming in the sun as if layered in pale gold. Farther along was a stunted mesa; beyond that, a narrow valley. Half a dozen acoustical/visual COmPUtes, sounders, could detail fauna activity with maximum accuracy from the ridge line. It was a good choice.

"Put in six," he said, glancing at the freckled man. Judd Caskell had been his dig foreman for seven years—long enough to anticipate most of Brennan's thoughts on site preparation. Caskell was more than just a dig foreman, however. He was the nearest thing Brennan had to a brother.

"Any bets on what they'll turn up?" Caskell asked.

"Mostly fy-malcons," Brennan answered, smiling. "And that rabbitlike thing—the one the Index's labeled a miffit."

Caskell gave a soft snort, indicative of his thoughts on the Index. He swung the floater to the left and fed power to the grid vanes. The seat slapped them on the bottom as they angled over a rise and down the other side. In a moment a floodplain came into view, its colors rich in umbers, browns, and ochre yellow. An ancient roadbed cut across the floodplain's tip.

"Wonder where that goes," Caskell murmured.

"The sea, probably," Brennan said from beside him. He squinted, his eyes following the almost vanished trace.

When he was 11 years old, Brennan had been given a map of the sky as seen from his bedroom window. It had little meaning until his father pointed out that that wedge of space between the horizon and the broad leaves of a journeyman palm contained almost a thousand worlds once occupied by Man. Brennan's interest was piqued even more when he learned that no trace of that occupation remained, though the Black Fugue had ended four hundred and thirty years earlier.

When he was 17, he chose archeology as his profession, turning down a seat on the board of the Hooker-Brennan Trading Co. To his family's consternation and chagrin, he did not marry. Now, at 38, a slender man of medium height, sandy hair bleached white by too much time under alien suns, Brennan had discovered what had happened on twelve of those worlds. The similarity of their demise was depressing in its sameness.

War.

Plague.

Ritual murder.

Still, there were 988 to go.

"Let's get back to the dig," he said, looking at Caskell.

On the plain they skimmed meter-high grass, the

wind of their passage flattening it into windrows. After twenty minutes of level flight they angled upwards again, and shortly reached the plateau, where the reds and blues and greens of the shelters made a carnival-like appearance.

The archeologist was in his shelter preparing for dinner when one of the dig hands stuck his head into the entrance.

"You have company, Chief."

"Oh, thanks, Riley—who?"

The other withdrew without speaking. Moments later a priest entered, a broad-torsoed smallish man with soft black hair.

"Dr. Hooker-Brennan?"

"Right—and it's just Brennan." The archeologist looked puzzled. "Who are you?"

"Father Charles Carlisle. Of the Morganite Order."

"An Indexer!"

"That *is* one of our duties." The priest looked around. The accommodations were certainly Spartan enough. He indicated a camp chair.

"Do you mind if I sit? Your men have been showing me the excavations. They're wondrous—truly—but climbing in and out—and using one of those siphons has involved the use of muscles long neglected."

"Go ahead."

Gratefully, Carlisle seated himself. He sighed and stretched. Then, without preamble, he said: "Do you know Gustaphson Pierce?"

"Gus? Sure." A vertical line appeared in Brennan's brow. "I went to school with him. He didn't have much of a career. I heard he got into some kind of trouble with the Church—spent some years in a penal colony."

"He was poaching artifacts."

Brennan nodded. "According to the rumors."

"The rumors, for once, were correct." The priest cocked his head to one side. "It is more serious than that now, though. That's why Pierce demanded somebody come to you."

"Why?"

"He's dying."

The archeologist stroked his chin. Gus Pierce was a maverick. He'd been drummed out of the Archeological Society. And, although Brennan himself had abstained from voting, his sympathies had been with the Society.

"He was caught after hours, looting a museum," Carlisle said, looking up at Brennan. "He fell trying to escape and almost eviscerated himself on a pike fence. The damage is irreparable."

Brennan clenched his jaw. "And he requested *me*? Why?"

"Only God and Gus himself know that." Carlisle gave a minute shrug and squared his shoulders.

Brennan went to the shelter's entrance, stood looking out. He said, honestly, "I have no idea why Gus would want to talk to me. We weren't close—quite the opposite; he probably hated my guts." The archeologist turned and shook his head. "He was bright enough, sure—somewhere in the upper tenth of his class. But he always insisted on taking shortcuts, risks. He scratched through, somehow—don't ask me how. But traditional avenues were closed to him."

Carlisle said wryly: "He chose *un*traditional avenues."

"Where is he?"

"There is a hospital on Geste that can maintain life at the cellular level. We moved him there."

"Then he's in no danger of dying," Brennan pointed out.

Carlisle put on his hat, removed it again, placed it uncomfortably on his lap. "Gus is aware of the situation. And he wants no part of institutional life. He wishes to die."

"Can he do that?"

"The Church must permit it," Carlisle said with professional caution. "However, he stopped the process a few weeks ago, and asked for you."

Brennan cursed beneath his breath. "*If* I went, how long would it take?"

"Two weeks only, perhaps three. There's a Gate quite close to Geste. I'll accompany you, of course; red tape would be minimal."

Brennan turned again to look out of the shelter. Caskell was leaning over one of the excavations, his ruddy face intent as he talked to the men.

"Give me a day or two," he said at last, turning toward the priest. "I've got to go over the scheduling with Judd." He stopped and raised his eyebrows. "Gus'll last that long, won't he?"

The priest smiled. "Of course. He has nothing to *do* now but wait."

Climbing into the floater three mornings later, Brennan took a last look behind him at the trenches crisscrossing the plateau, and at his men working them. Judd Caskell, his hat doffed so that he might wipe his brow, waved reassuringly.

"Your crew seems to work instinctively," Carlisle murmured, impressed. "They almost don't need supervision at all."

"Some of them have been with me for ten years and more," Brennan replied, giving the other a smile. "We know how to excavate lost civilizations."

"All set, sir?" Kahn turned in the pilot's seat, checked to make certain Brennan's suitcase was properly stowed, and waited with raised brows.

"All set," Brennan affirmed. A moment later the craft lifted, drifting slightly as a crosswind hit it. Kahn corrected the motion with a deft touch and the vehicle picked up speed.

"Judd said you put in a full day sifting one of the middens," Brennan remarked, turning to look at his companion. "Even the men were impressed. Did you find anything of interest?"

Carlisle's answering smile was full of the wonder and awe characteristic of newly hatched archeologists. It was predictable. If digging in dirt was contagious, then turning up objects thousands of years old was nothing less than enthralling. "We were down about a meter and a half," the priest began with ardent enthusiasm. "We hit a resistant shell. Inside were these . . ." He thrust his hand inside his robes and produced a chipped green sphere, its size no larger than the end of his thumb. "There were about a dozen of them. No one knows yet what they were used for."

Brennan examined the glass sphere with a shake of his head. "I've seen them before, but colored a bit differently." He grinned abruptly. "Did the crew give you this one?"

"Why, yes."

"And they said not to tell Judd?"

"Yes." Carlisle's normally open face grew clouded.

"It's illegal to take any unregistered artifacts off a dig site," Brennan pointed out. "Though something like *this* isn't particularly serious, it could still be sticky if it were found on you."

Carlisle stared at the glass sphere in the hollow of his hand, a flush spreading slowly across his features.

"Don't worry about it," Brennan said with a laugh. "We'll give it to the priest at the Gate. He'll register it and you can take it through on clerical dispensation."

"I showed it to Father Stuyvesant," Carlisle said ominously, staring straight ahead. "He said nothing about registration." He paused for five seconds, and then, chagrined, looked at Brennan. "Thank you for telling me. I should have thought before I accepted it." He replaced the spheroid in his pocket and faced front, watching the hills dissolve into flat terrain. Ahead, well within sight now, was the Gate.

The priest on duty was one neither Brennan nor Carlisle had seen before. The paperwork was routine, kept, as Carlisle had promised, to a minimum. While travel between unrestricted worlds was commonplace and uncomplicated, the outer worlds remained strictly controlled. Now, stepping into the brown and red transmission chamber, Brennan experienced a moment of prescience, as though an animal with centipede's legs were walking down his spine. The blue sky of Pio-Tan vanished abruptly, replaced by the scruffy closeness of a receiving terminal.

"Korff's Station," Carlisle said, gesturing around at the peeling walls, the cracked and rutted floor—eight centuries of neglect. Terminals off the beaten path tended to be dismal places.

"What if there's no shuttle available?" Brennan asked, peering around. The station seemed nearly deserted. "We could be stranded here for days."

"We won't be." Carlisle urged his companion down a corridor. "I have the use of a Church shuttle."

"Really?" Brennan almost stopped. He looked puzzled. "Aren't you going to a lot of trouble for a simple thief?"

"Umh, yes," Carlisle answered, assuming the air of someone with a troubling secret. He took the archeologist's arm. "Come on. I'll tell you about it on the way."

The shuttle *Alonzo* was built like a tug. It was square and unlovely and not given much to comfort. Still, somebody had shown enough foresight to put aboard several bottles of beer. Eighteen hours out, Brennan found himself seated in the navigator's chair, glass in hand, studying the priest's round face.

He said, "Tell me about Gus."

Carlisle stepped away from the port, glanced idly at the COmPUte-controlled 'black box' that was the shuttle's guide, and sat down facing Brennan in the pilot's chair.

The humor departed from his mouth. In a curiously neutral voice, he said, "When the Black Fugue ended there were huge areas that were uninhabitable, whole star systems contaminated, awash in radiation, poisoned with corrosive gases."

"The Cone," Brennan said, sipping beer.

"That's right—the Cone. The Church quite properly proscribed the area."

"Is that where Gus went?"

"We think so." Carlisle took the hem of his habit between his fingers and began to fold it into tiny pleats. "He found something—found it and hid it."

Brennan digested that for a long moment. Poaching was a game a lot of people played with the Church. Some had gotten wealthy—there was so *much* out there. But no one had been stupid enough—or desperate enough—to go into the Cone.

"You think he's going to tell *me* what he got?"

Carlisle cleared his throat. "That was the impression. He would talk—but only to you."

The archeologist stared at the liquid in his glass, then put the glass aside. "Why is the Church interested? What could be so important?"

"Because it has something to do with the Church itself," Carlisle said, interrupting him.

"What?"

"We don't know." The priest sighed and shrugged. "But we know *that* much because when he was caught, just outside the museum, he had old records on him— maps, solidographs, a few tapedexes."

"It's crazy," Brennan muttered. "Gus was never a religious man."

"But if he *has* found something," Carlisle said urgently, "we've got to know what it is."

"Setsen Dai's halo?" There was an ironic sparkle in Brennan's eyes.

"Joke if you want," Carlisle said grimly. He stood up and went to the port. After a moment he turned back, smiling a conciliatory smile. "All we ask is that you *talk* to Pierce. That much, no more. Even if you don't believe ..." The priest trailed off, looking at Brennan, his face almost comic.

"Just talk?"

"Yes. Just talk."

"Sure," Brennan said after a moment's reflection. "Why not?"

The cellular incubation chamber on Geste was an airy rectangle. There were only three glass columns occupied—two by patients awaiting skin grafts, the third by Gustaphson Pierce.

"He can't see you or hear you," Carlisle said, looking at the man on the other side of the glass. "The column is filled with preservatives and electrolytes with a refractive index of zero."

"Then how can we communicate?" Brennan asked.

The priest stepped to the wall and flipped a series of switches. "Through an organic 'bridge' COmPUte."

With a last look at Pierce, the priest withdrew. Brennan found a chair, dragged it in front of the column, and seated himself. The near-cadaver seemed indifferent to his presence.

Pierce was tall, with leaden skin, hair that was nearly white, and a death's-head grin. The grin was Pierce's trademark, and he'd bear it to his grave.

Brennan said, "Hello, Gus."

"Hook?" Pierce's lips hadn't moved. The voice came from a speaker hidden in the base of the column.

Brennan's lips tightened. He'd had his share of schoolyard brawls, bloodied more than a few noses. He loathed that name. Leave it to Gus to dredge it up again.

He said dryly, choosing his words, "Hell of a way to end a career, Gus. They said you impaled yourself on a fence."

The cadaver laughed eerily. "Tore up everything, sliced right through the spinal cord. It took them over an hour just to get me off that spike."

"What were you after, in the museum?"

"Information."

Brennan smiled grimly. "Religious histories, pre-Fugue apocryphae? Come on, Gus."

The voice chuckled sepulchrally. "I was looking, specifically, for a world."

"One in the Cone?"

"No, not there." Pierce stopped, as though hesitating to go on. At length he said, "I can see you, Hook. They have scanners on top of all the columns."

Brennan squinted upwards. "So?"

"I thought you might have gotten fat by now. Soft. I'm glad you haven't."

"Go to hell, Gus."

The chuckle again. "Don't get me wrong, Hook. I still don't like you—never did. It's only that I admire someone who has finally made it. You're what—third or fourth in the field? Talent and drive you have, as well as brains. Too bad you were always too damned ... *establishment*."

"Nothing wrong with the establishment," Brennan murmured. "You *can* work inside the system."

"Not when it ties you up at every turn," Pierce protested with vehemence. "Restrictions ... regulations ... Church policy. Church—!" Pierce spat the word. "Parasite is more like it! They're sucking the blood right out of me. You, too, if you got in their way."

Brennan had never seen Gus so worked up. He said nothing, let the silence build between them.

"Hook?"

"They call me Brennan these days," Brennan said, a bit tersely.

"Ah. Sensitive, I see. That much of you is still human, then."

"Why did you send for me?" Brennan asked wearily.

"I take it the social niceties are over," Pierce said. "Very well. I sent for you because I found something— something big. You can't guess how big." The cadaver's voice took on a triumphant tone. "So big it's going to raise eyebrows all over the quadrant."

"There are other archeologists. Why pick me?"

"Because I *dislike* you." Brennan could swear Gus was sneering. "Besides, you have power. Contacts. You're famous. You can get information I would have to steal."

"I won't do anything if it's illegal," Brennan said, lacing his fingers together.

"Don't worry. This will be legal enough."

"What is it, then?"

"I want you to look at two artifacts. Then make up

your mind. They could be the find of the century."
Pierce broke off for a moment, then resumed. "It's
too bad they can't be registered."

Brennan was curious, but his face remained impas-
sive. He sat staring at the columned figure. "I'm
already working a dig, Gus. It'll be another six, eight
months at a minimum. I don't have time to go on
wild goose chases."

Pierce clucked his tongue roguishly. "You won't
pass this up, Hook. You'd regret it the rest of your
life. Besides," and the voice dropped an octave to a
loud whisper, "I tricked a Church functionary into
running the artifacts through CALIFUR. They came
back with authentication numbers of 82 and 84. When
was the last time you have any *that* high, hmmm?"

In spite of himself, Brennan was impressed. He
stirred in his chair, stretching his legs and staring at
the puckered scar that ran halfway up Pierce's abdo-
men. CALIFUR was one of the few remaining intuitive COmPUtes. It was used almost entirely by the
Church to authenticate pre-Fugue documents. A finding of 60 percent was considered good, a 70 out-
standing. Any document rated above 75 percent was
unquestioned as to authenticity.

"If they're that good, the Church would have to
accept them," Brennan remarked. "Why not make
them public, see if the Church will register them?"

"You fool! They wouldn't register them—they'd restrict them."

"What are they, Church artifacts? Holy items?"

"No, not really." Brennan could sense a hedge in
the other's voice. "You have to *see* them, Hook. Then
you'd understand."

Brennan shook his head. "You're wasting my time,
Gus. I'm not interested in Church relics. Get a clerical archeologist—there *are* a few." He smiled. "Hell,
you might even go down on the Church scrolls as a
great man."

Pierce was unbelieving. "You won't even look?"

"That's right."

"Damn you, Brennan. Wait a minute, I know something you'd give your right arm for."

Brennan stood, approached the switches.

"Stop! Damn it, man—I'll tell you!"

Brennan waited, one hand raised halfway.

"One of the artifacts—it's a picture of an *alien!* An *alien*, Hook, you hear me?"

Brennan froze, his eyes widening as he stared at the cadaver.

"I mean it—a goddamn *alien*."

"Where'd you get it?" In spite of himself, Brennan's voice was strained.

"The Cone. Way out on the edge. Look at it, Brennan, *look* at it. *Then* tell me you're not interested."

"Don't try to suck me in, Gus. Whatever you have is unregistered. If I get tangled up in that I could end up like you—a blackmarketeer."

"Afraid of getting dirt on your shiny white suit?"

"That's right."

"My sister has it," Pierce said, his voice low, almost whispering. "On Duvalle. She's with the Endless Sabbat. Go and see her, Brennan."

"*Damn* you! Give it to the Church."

The near-corpse generated a peal of raucous laughter.

"Why are you doing this?" Brennan asked, looking through the column of glass. "You couldn't hate me *that* much."

"Because you're a symbol," Pierce answered him, his voice mechanical and cold. "You're the *system*. Going to see what you're made of, is all."

"You picked the wrong man, Gus."

"We'll see," said the cadaver.

There was a long silence, broken finally by Pierce. "That Morganite priest, the one they call Father Carlisle. Watch out for him, Hook. He's smarter than he looks." There was a snort. "Hell—he caught *me*!"

"I'm not going to Duvalle. I won't have to worry about the Church."

"You'll go," Pierce grunted. "Just to see if what I say is true." He paused a moment. "My sister's name is Jancy. She doesn't know what she has. I just asked her to hold a package until I, or someone I send, contacts her—."

With a savage movement of his hand, Brennan slapped the switches closed, shutting Pierce off in midsentence.

Standing in front of the column, Brennan felt cold. He shivered, then muttered sourly to himself, "Goddamn it, Gus. What the hell have you started?"

Chapter Four

"Perhaps Pierce wouldn't talk to him after all," said Bishop Lawrence Poole. He cleared his throat and sat down in the overstuffed chair he kept beside the fireplace. Then, looking up, he examined Carlisle with the patience of his accumulated years.

"Perhaps." Carlisle was pensive, eyes troubled. "It's possible, I suppose. He has certainly not talked to *us*."

"But?"

Carlisle smiled fleetingly, shrugged. "Dr. Brennan seemed uncharacteristically evasive. He said that Pierce spent most of the time insulting him."

Bishop Poole poured himself a small dram of 40-year-old brandy and offered some to his protégé.

"No, thank you," Carlisle demurred. He had been sitting, and now he rose. Hands clasped behind his back, he paced back and forth across the room.

"What is it?" Poole asked. "What's bothering you?"

Carlisle stopped pacing and sat again. He glanced over at Poole and managed a faint grin. The old man always knew when something was churning in the back of his head.

He said, "I felt an affinity for Dr. Brennan—his work, his scholarship. It's something I can't explain, exactly."

"You liked him."

Carlisle hesitated only a moment. "Yes, I did—I do."

"But you think that he might be lying about Pierce."

"I hope I'm wrong, but I fear I'm not."

Bishop Poole sipped his brandy with obvious enthusiasm. "Tell me why you think he's lying."

Carlisle shifted minutely in his chair. "I checked the wattage drained off by Pierce's column during his visit. It suggested a longish conversation, not a simple spate of insults."

"Anything else?"

"The fact that Pierce asked for him at all. He surely would not request his presence simply to excoriate him."

Poole sighed, looked longingly at the bottle of brandy, then put it away and turned to his subordinate. "I'm afraid that's all pretty thin, so far. You don't have anything else?"

"I've saved the worst for last. I checked the Church logs on Pio-Tan. They show that within a month of his return he Gated for Duvalle."

"Ah . . ."

"He has no close relatives on Duvalle, and no friends, to my knowledge."

Poole took a deep breath, scratched at his gray pate. "I suppose you cross-referenced Pierce's records."

"I did," Carlisle said, nodding. "Duvalle is the base of operations for the Endless Sabbat." He paused a moment for effect. "Pierce's sister is a member."

Poole stood up, sagged a little as though a dizzy spell had caught him. He said, "Follow up on this, Charles. Keep an eye on Brennan. It may be he's headed for trouble."

"My Lord." Carlisle rose also, concern for the older man evident on his face.

"I'm fine," Poole muttered. "Age is the only thing wrong with me." He grimaced abruptly, put a hand on Carlisle's shoulder. After a second or two he straightened and made for his bedroom.

Carlisle went out on the terrace, looked up into the twilit sky. The colors were indigo and steel. Leaning on the terrace railing, Carlisle felt the first stray zephyrs of evening.

"You *want* too much," Bishop Poole had told him many years earlier. "You want to know, and see, and unravel all God's mysteries." It had been the mildest of rebukes. Unrepentant, Carlisle knew he was right.

He remembered discussing the aspects of God with the old man. Then, Poole had been a Monsignor, with more time for a young man with questions.

"Can Setsen Dai ever take on human form?" he asked once.

"He could, but why should he?" was Poole's reply. "The Shining Light is perfect as he is. To make him less is to diminish him. Making him human would diminish him to the point of nonexistence. You surely wouldn't wish *that* on him."

"How do you see him?" wondered Carlisle. "As radiance? As a globe of saffron light?"

"Look around," Poole said. "See those sunbeams falling on the table? Those are part of Setsen Dai. He *is* light."

"And Kirst?"

"Imagine the deepest and blackest hole in the universe," Poole responded, putting his arm around Carlisle. "Down there *things* move. Terrible things. Those things are Kirst's minions. He lives down there, dreaming of the time when he can come out and defeat The Shining Light."

"Does everything have to have two parts—black and white, good and evil?"

"The cycle seems to be endless," Poole said. "Now run along. It's time for evening prayers."

Standing on the terrace, remindful that Poole was dying, Carlise wondered if infirmity and its attendant ills were simply aspects of Kirst. Poole would have thought so, he suspected.

He thought about Brennan. Was *he* an agent for The Shining Light? Or was he guided by something darker? He hoped the archeologist would choose the former. He had felt a kinship there.

Chapter Five

Duvalle was legend before the Fugue sheeted it with nonremembrance and desolation. Now, a sunlit oasis adorned with slums and human offal, it had become legend all over again.

Its stargate was located exactly at ground level, an occurrence so rare it had given a new name to odds-making.

Some on the planet were rich. Some were poor. Because it was on the main Gate routes of two star systems, Duvalle teemed with custom.

On a world like Duvalle, many things were possible.

Number 46 Salacia was an archway leading into a series of corridors. Chants welled and ebbed from cells within. A young man in flowing white robes came from an inner room, passed through the doorway, almost stumbled as he bumped into the slender form of an outworlder.

"Excuse me."

"Excuse *me*," Brennan said. "I'm looking for Jancy Pierce."

The man shook his head. "Not here—she's got a performance today."

"What does she do?"

"She's a Dysip Breather—and a damned good one, too."

The term rang a bell in the back of Brennan's head, but that was as far as it went. He said only, "Where is she giving it?"

"The Wall, where else?" The man stared at Brennan, half turned away.

"The Wall?"

"The Zacatal Wall. Ask anyone." The man waved airily and walked away, robes fluttering behind him.

It was easy enough for Brennan to find; it was visible from almost any place in town. The Wall was a mortared construct twelve meters high plastered with placards and graffiti. Beggars and street entertainers were everywhere. At one end, where stones had loosened and sections of the Wall were slumping into nondescript piles, Brennan found Jancy Pierce.

He didn't know what to expect—a female version of Gus, perhaps. She was not that; she was instead only a trifle shorter than he, with short platinum curls and burnt-bronze skin.

She was seated cross-legged with her back to the Wall. In front and half a meter to her left was a bearded oldster wearing thong sandals and a loose tunic. She had attracted a semi-circle of twenty to thirty tourists.

"This is Rocker Van Terss," Jancy said, smiling toward the old man. "He's from BF912. For those of you dating from the present, that figures out to be a little over two millennia."

"She's right, you know," Van Terss said, sweeping the crowd with hawk-bright, unblinking eyes. "In my time, I couldn't even have *imagined* anything like the Fugue."

Someone in the crowd giggled, and the old man scowled.

"What did you do back then?" Jancy asked.

"Humph. I was a Dysip."

"Which is to say?"

The oldster sighed gustily. "Must I go through this cockamamie recital every time you spirit me up?"

"But you do it so *well*," Jancy returned smoothly, winking at the crowd. Her mouth curved in a sunny smile.

"Really?" Somewhat mollified, Van Terss half turned in his seat, crossed his legs, peered left and right. "A Dysip in the original sense was a teacher, a communicator, a *guru*. Some of the early ones sat by water courses. It is said they could join their spirits to it."

"How did they do that?" someone wanted to know.

"Damned if I know," the old man shot back irritably. "I never understood any of that *merde*."

"Then you're not one of the early ones?" that same someone said.

"Do I look crazy?" Van Terss drew himself up. "I'm an odds *savant*, is what. High rollers used me to take on the house."

"So you syndicated yourself," Jancy prompted.

"That's right." Van Terss scratched his bare leg. "I got myself put on a Dysip COmPUte." He grinned. "Then I retired."

"How?" Jancy asked, grinning slightly herself. "I mean—how do you get put inside a Dysip cube?"

Van Terss gave the girl a shrug. "Two or three sessions in a transphasic-memory tank, an *emph*-grid inventory, and maybe a couple of retakes. Then *voila!*" He paused and gave a sour grimace. "Damned expensive, though."

The sun appeared over the broken edge of the Wall, and Van Terss's left forearm disappeared. The part of him remaining in shadow took no notice.

Jancy stirred. "Time to go, Rocker."

"I was just starting to enjoy myself," Van Terss said testily. "Who are you bringing out now?"

"Don't be jealous," Jancy said. "I think Su Lui."

"That bitch!"

"Ta ta, Rocker." Jancy seemed to take an extra deep breath. Without preamble Van Terss ceased to be.

Su Lui, a Dysip from BF214, proved to be an extraordinarily gifted dancer, her repertoire consisting of unabashedly erotic *schottisches*. When her act was through, the tourists drifted off in ones and twos. Jancy began collecting the coins they'd thrown on the ground.

"Miss Pierce?"

She glanced up but did not stop her movements. "Call me Jancy. Do I know you?"

Brennan introduced himself, ended up saying: "Your brother never particularly liked me, but he must have mentioned my name on occasion."

"You're right about that," Jancy said, the tone of her voice saying that was an understatement. She scooped a couple of COmPUte cubes off the ground and stowed them in a voluminous pocket. Van Terss and Su Lui. Then she stared at Brennan thoughtfully, plucking at her lower lip with thumb and forefinger. "Have you seen him?"

"On Geste," Brennan admitted.

"The Church!" Jancy said bitterly. "They've been hounding him for years. And now they've finally got him." Her eyes had gone icy.

"He went into the Cone," Brennan said, keeping his tone even. "And he brought out some artifacts— the ones he gave to you."

"He told you that?"

"Yes."

"You're the one he called the *wunkerkind*, aren't you?"

"He used to call me that at college," Brennan murmured, ill at ease. He shrugged and looked at his hands. "It was always meant sarcastically."

"Some of the time, but not always," Jancy corrected with a crooked grin. "He did admire you a little—secretly."

"Not Gus!"

"You didn't know my brother very well," Jancy interrupted, her voice terse. "He had to take assignments no one else wanted, sweep up after people he knew were his inferiors; he was never very good at it." She gave him a sidelong glance. "He never included you in that group."

"No?" Brennan shifted uneasily. "Maybe that's why he wanted me to see the artifacts."

"Probably not," Jancy said, wrinkling her nose. "Gus is a devious son of a bitch. He'd have his own reasons."

An hour or so later they were seated on cushioned mats in Jancy's austere quarters.

"Gus said he wanted me to have this if anything happened to him," Jancy said, digging out a battered archeologist's case. "At the time, I didn't think anything about it."

Brennan put the case on its side and released the hasps. Inside were two packets, each bearing the ornate CALIFUR seal.

"Eighty-two point three," Brennan said, picking up the first packet and pointing to the authentication number emblazoned on its front. "He didn't lie about that."

Cracking the seal, he drew forth a Forster thin-gel photograph, so old its edges had whitened and begun to decompose. Hand shaking slightly, he raised it to the light.

"What is it?" Jancy asked, watching his face.

Brennan let out a deep breath and placed the photograph almost reverently on top of its envelope. After a moment he sat back.

"It's important, isn't it?"

Glancing at the girl, Brennan nodded. "I can't tell you *how* important. It's a photograph—*of an alien!* Do you know what that means?"

"No, what?"

Brennan spoke in a breathless monotone. "There have been stories. Rumors. Most of them in pre-

Fugue literature, of course." He stopped and pointed at the artifact. "But never tangible proof—until *this*."

"It's not very clear," Jancy said, looking at the photograph. "When was it taken, at night?"

On the back of the envelope were site coordinates. Brennan scanned them briefly, looked at Jancy disbelievingly, and laughed. "Not when—*where*. It was taken inside a molybdenite mine."

Confusion flickered in Jancy's eyes.

Brennan laughed again. "Someone—or some*thing*— was stealing ore out of the mine. The mine owners put in a security camera. What they got was . . . *this*.

He looked again at the photograph. Though admittedly, it *was* a little on the fuzzy side, enough detail remained to show the alien's wide, expressive eyes and the strangely articulated limbs. The creature was furred—pale gold—and bipedal. The trunk of its body looked massively muscled.

"What's that over its shoulder?" asked Jancy.

Brennan looked more closely, then abruptly grinned. "It's a sack," he said. "He had to carry the ore in something."

The second envelope had the second-highest authentication number Brennan had ever seen: 84.106. Once, when he had been an assistant at Trospro's prestigious university, a professor had presented him with an aged copy of the Daiist doctrine. CALIFUR had given the document an 86.05. At the time, Brennan had been properly awed.

Now he broke the seal, removed a thick sheaf of plastic sheets.

"Were they both discovered together?" asked Jancy.

"Yes," Brennan said, glancing at the site coordinates. "They were found at a grave site about half a kilometer from the mine entrance."

In the original document the words were faded, the words difficult to decipher. CALIFUR had conveniently provided a verbatim printout.

"Would you like some tea?"

Brennan gave a start, belatedly realized Jancy was

talking to him, her mouth quirking in amusement. She had risen and was rattling pans in one corner of the room.

"Yes, please." He looked again at the manuscript. "Shall I read it aloud?"

"Uh huh." The girl looked at him. "One lump or two?"

The Story of the Helm Maiden

Artifact. Location site: Corthun. Date:
　　Af456/04/03. 00.01% Re-creation. 00.01%
Repaired. Material: 95.78% Hydrocarbon
compounds. 03.20% Trace metals. 01.02%
Other.
　　[Authentication Rating: 84.106%]

It was four o'clock in the morning when my cousin
Amanda woke me. We went to the *aréne* through
pelting rain, lightning off to the south strobing like
gunfire. Sorbonne weather for sure. Inside, shedding
water, Amanda deVere looked at me, at my drowned-
rat expression. She stroked soggy hair out of my
eyes.
　　"You want to be a Helm Maiden, Virgy?" she asked.
I held my breath. "Yes."
　　"You know your mother objects."
　　"Still," I said hoarsely. "Father . . ."

Amanda shook her head. "Your father is dead. And it makes no difference that he wore silk and leather. It is your mother who must be convinced."

"If he were alive he would sponsor me," I said.

"Of course." There was a pause before she spoke again. "He was one of the good ones. And he died as Helm Masters should—on duty. But now there is Frieda . . . and you're but thirteen." She paused again before nodding in the near darkness. "*I* will sponsor you. That is why I came. But it takes work, you know. Much work—endless work." She turned on one of the spotlights, illuminating the center of the arena floor. Her cloak fell away, revealing structured body armor. "Watch," she said. She activated one of the mock-lifes, a six-legged creature the size of a small pony. At the end of each leg were tubular stingers. Amanda adjusted the settings so the thing bobbed and weaved like a punch-drunk bantamweight. "It can kill at this level," she said quietly, and moved to give it room.

The mock-creature immediately began to stalk her, the lenses of its eyes glowing darkly, its legs making sharp clicking noises on the floor.

Amanda circled, her motion controlled precisely by the placement of arms and legs. It smacked of choreography, and only later, when you saw the steel spurs and hand spikes, was it apparent that it was something else.

The moment burned itself into memory, an imprinting as sure as a baby chick for its mother. Amanda, her helm and armor glowing softly in the cone of light; Amanda, lithe, supple, stinging death at the end of her fingers. *Helm Maiden—Ai!*

The mock-life made its attack at the far side of the arena, scuttling like a mad tap dancer to cut off Amanda's retreat. But she did not retreat; she feinted left, and then her movements became blurs too subtle and too many to follow.

In the first moments she crippled the thing, shearing away two of its legs. She stood back, studying it, then moved forward for the *coup de grace*. It tried once more, feebly, to attack, but Amanda was too fast, her movements too sure. When it was finished she left the remains on the arena floor and came toward me.

She said, "If that seemed easy to you, don't be deceived. The mock-lives have been programmed to learn from their mistakes—someday I may lose one of these fights."

"Never!"

She smiled at my vehemence, then waggled her eyebrows to make a joke of it. She removed her helm and placed it beneath her arm. It was made of silver and iron. From its peak flew a blue streamer.

She said, "I will talk to your mother. She tends to be obstinate, but I've never known her to be intractable." She removed her gloves, tucked them into her belt. "It *is* what you want, isn't it? Be sure of that."

I met her gaze, grinned then, and nodded. "Yes," I said. "It's what I want—more than I've ever wanted *anything!*" On impulse I took her hand in both of mine, and squeezed.

She squeezed back, and grinned, too, her mouth turning up at the corners in shared delight.

"Come on, then," she said. She shook herself free. "It's back through the rain for us. And you have to dry yourself and get to bed. It won't do for Frieda to catch us making plans she's not consented to."

When I climbed into bed half an hour later I took with me a medallion my father had worn. It was simple iron, with a device on it of stylized wings. I was told that it came from the early years of the Order, when Helm Masters were still indentured to kings, and not yet powerful in their own right.

Those first Masters, dedicated to (H)onor, (E)ducation, (L)iberty, and (M)orality, had served their lieges well. Many times the fate of empires rode on their shoulders.

A century afterwards they broke away as a separate Order, adding Helm Maidens to their ranks. They were still few, both Masters and Maidens, but that was because they chose their new members carefully. In the present day they served as guardians, scouts, and interstellar troubleshooters.

I look more like my cousin Amanda than I do my mother. In fact, Mother alone, of all the deVeres, is the smallest, softest, most neutral-seeming. And it doesn't help that her wardrobe consists only of white surplices and matching hoods. Of course she's a deVere by marriage only. Most of us are like Amanda: tall-ish, slender, auburn-haired, with the typical long face and green eyes. I'm like that, too, except I'm skin-nier, and have no breasts to speak of.

My mother is a disciple of The Shining Light, which explains her surplices, her retiring manner. It's a contemplative religion that dotes on "inner under-standing." And it's a fringe group, pacifistic, low-key. The disciples on Sorbonne number less than 30.

"The Fugue line passed Barnard's star during the night," Amanda announced at breakfast. "That cross-checks its acceleration rate. Seven point two percent of speed-of-light." She took in a mouthful of eggs and raised her eyebrows at us both.

"I thought they had determined that already," Mother said mildly. She scarcely looked up.

"They had," Amanda said. "But this ties it down—there hasn't been a variance in over a year."

The Fugue—the Black Fugue, they call it—though, of course, it's not really black. It is, in fact, no color at all. What it is is an ever-expanding line of . . . well, not light exactly, but *something*, that is passing through the universe—or through which the universe is passing, no one is really sure which. It used to frighten me, before I realized that at its present ve-locity the Fugue wouldn't reach Sorbonne for almost eighty years. Time enough then to get worried.

The effects of the Fugue are pretty well established, though there is some disagreement on the fine de-tails. Simply put, it causes ferality in intelligent life.

Which, of course, includes humans. More succinctly, it means a loss of higher-level logic, a retreat to primitivism. It means, in fact, an abrupt plunge into a mental Pleistocene. No guesses yet as to cause. God, maybe, or some higher physics, depending on your view.

"Have you thought any more about Virgy's future?" Amanda asked, switching subjects. She had taken a two-month furlough to be with us, a furlough that was nearly (and much too soon) half over.

It was Mother's notion that while I might not be a good candidate as novitiate to The Shining Light, I *was* reasonably bright, and ought not to waste myself in aimless pursuits. She sipped tea while she thought over the question.

"I'm going to enroll her in the Academy at Laerdes," she said finally. "I know several of the faculty there."

I opened my mouth to protest but Amanda threw me a *shut-up* look. Her brows drew together. "Is that what *she* wants to do, Frieda?"

Mother smiled and gave me a fond look. But then she spoiled it by saying: "When I was thirteen, I was certain I knew what I wanted to do with the rest of my life. But I didn't—and not for many years after."

"But I *know*," I said. My stomach lurched. "I want to join the Order of the Helm."

Mother was silent for a moment, her teacup halfway to its saucer. She set it down finally and gave me a level look.

"Life is full of uncertainties, Virgy," she said, not unkindly. "You would do better—much better—to diversify your talents."

"Meaning what?" Amanda demanded disgustedly. "That life's a crap shoot? Well, hell—there's nothing new in that." She paused. "And anyway, there's no better survival training than what she would get in the Order."

My mother gave a headshake and my heart sank. She said, "The Order would train her to do two things well. Command—and kill."

Amanda snorted. "Don't be simplistic. We're not reflex-trained traffic cops. And of *course* we'll kill—if other options are taken from us."

She was referring to the fact that the Helm Order helped to open up new stargates, pushing the frontiers back. Sometimes, in the course of that expansion, they met creatures inimical to their passage.

Man, as a rule, won those disputes.

Mother listened, hands folded serenely on the table top. Somewhere close by, thunder grumbled and hard pellets of rain rattled the windows. Sorbonne summer.

"Every person has a place that is right for them," Mother said philosophically when Amanda was through. "And every place has its time. If Virgy is to be a Helm Maiden that will come to pass. But I will not sanction it nor . . ." And she stopped in mid-thought and gave a little shrug, her eyes brooding over some uninterpretable inner vision. Almost absently her fingers sought and found her prayer beads. I looked at Amanda in dismay. When Mother put on that martyred gone-away face there was not the faintest hope of changing her mind.

But Amanda didn't know that. She leaned toward me, patted me lightly on the head. She said, "I'm not through yet, Virgy."

The disciples of The Shining Light met each week in the largest *maison*. They sat in rows like identical white partridges and meditated, the men (of which there were nine) indistinguishable from the women. And it was thus, Amanda told me wryly, watching, that they shed their revealed light upon Mankind. Hearing her say that made me uneasy. Despite her cynicism there *had* been a man called The Shining Light.

His real name was Titus Wilde, but his followers changed it to Setsen Dai, which translates to "The Light that Shines." It's all kind of like a legend, though it didn't happen that long ago. Before I was born, of course. Even before Mother was born.

The first stargate was built by aliens. Pan Kirst, the scourge, the man they called the World Assassin, figured out how to operate it, but only Titus Wilde could use it. Mother says that's because it let through only the pure of mind.

As a result, Kirst wanted to destroy the Gate. The Shining Light intended to preserve it. They met on a mountaintop and fought. They killed each other, Titus Wilde giving his life so that Man might have the stars. That first stargate was removed by an engineer named Morgan, cut apart, examined, and copied. Within two decades Man was building his own stargates, displacing the old "sleep-ships" and jumping across the galaxies in 11-league boots.

Titus Wilde's body was removed from the mountaintop and honored, but Kirst's was buried in an unmarked grave. And whatever else Amanda thought, I'd never heard anyone deny that *something* like that happened.

The Disciples revered Setsen Dai for other reasons, least of all for his heroic death. Mostly it was for the concept of *ürolt* love, the love that spreads outward from the heart and mind and encompasses everything that lives. Cosmic love, unreserved and eternal. The Disciples believed in outward love and inward understanding, the twin concepts of The Shining Light.

There was talk at the meeting of the Fugue line. And afterwards, just before going to bed, Mother said she was making a pilgrimage to Doubab.

It startled me. Mother had never been off Sorbonne in her life, except to attend the university—certainly not to a world so obscure that I'd never even heard of it.

I said, "Where's Doubab?"

She removed her surplice and put on a simple nightgown. Her hair was brown, cut short, left uncurled. Streaks of gray were already visible in it.

"That's its real name," Mother said. "The name it was given when it was first discovered. You know it by the name we call it now. The Crown World."

I said, "Oh," and shut up. That I *had* heard of. It was the world of legend, where The Shining Light had died. There was supposed to be a shrine there, a single small memorial cut into the side of a mountain.

"But why are you going *now*?" I asked, and thought about Amanda. Her furlough would be over in another few weeks. If we could not sway Mother in the time remaining, I would never be a Helm Maiden. My throat constricted at the thought.

Mother ran a comb through her hair before answering. "It's the Fugue line," she said then. "It's less than a light-month from Doubab. Unless I go now I'll never see the shrine."

I bit my lip. "Can I go with you?"

Mother put her comb away. If she was surprised she didn't show it. "If you like," she said. "But there's not much there that would interest you. It's only a mountain on a rather dismal world." She paused and looked at me. "And it's winter there."

"Still," I said. "I'd like to go."

She came close and hugged me, smiling, brushing my forehead with her lips. She said, "Of course you can come."

I drew back a step. "And Amanda?"

Mother shrugged, dismissing the subject. "If she wants to. Now go to bed. *Ajol*, my child."

Ajol—it means may you find peace in the universe.

I woke up in the night and lay there, listening to the Sorbonne winds, the occasional sharp roll of thunder. Something was bothering me, burrowing up from my subconscious. Only later did I realize what it was. Guilt—for plotting like a traitor.

It never occurred to me that Amanda might not go. When I found her next morning she was honing the nicked edge of a spur, her hair pulled back into a ponytail and fastened with a gold clasp. She wasn't happy to hear of Mother's plans.

"When is she leaving?" she asked.

"Day after tomorrow," I said. I marveled at the care she gave her task. The spurs were four-inch scimitars of steel. Amanda had used them in her duel with the mock-life, employing them as curving talons to rip and tear. She finished one and laid it gently back into her weapons case, then picked up its twin and inspected it critically.

"I'm not sure," she said, "but I think Doubab is very close to the Fugue line."

"That's why Mother is going," I said. "She wants to see the shrine there. You know. The Shining Light."

Amanda nodded. She peered closely at the spur, detected a minute flaw. She picked up the hone.

"Do you know where Montargis is?"

"Yes," I said. "It's over the mountain. I was there once, at a Disciples' meeting."

"And do you know a woman there they call the Mad Witch of Montargis?"

I shook my head as Amanda laid the second spur gently beside the first. She closed the case and set it by her side.

"There is such a woman. She was wife to a Helm Master." Amanda paused, and then shrugged. "In matters of love we are only mortal." She grinned sardonically. "He died on Dhorpur, about six months ago. His effects were sent here to Sorbonne."

When I looked puzzled, Amanda said, "His weapons case belongs to the Helm Order, Virgy. It should have been returned to us. But this woman ... this *mad witch*—refuses to part with it."

"Oh. And you have been sent to get it?"

She nodded. "The Order knew I was coming here on furlough. They asked me to stop and pick up the case." She gave me a level look. "I must do that, even if it means I cannot go with you and Frieda."

I stared. "You must! Only you can convince Mother that I should not go to Laerdes!"

She bade me sit, and laid a hand gently on either shoulder. "As long as that case rests in untrained hands, Virgy, there is danger of catastrophe. Not of someone actually getting to the weapons inside—that is virtually impossible—but of someone *trying* to get to them." She gave my shoulders a squeeze. "That case . . . and this one," she indicated the one by her side, "are booby-trapped. *Death*-trapped. My first priority is to recover that case."

"And the Mad Witch?"

". . . was not in Montargis until this morning," Amanda said, finishing the sentence. "I asked the mayor to call me when she returned. He did so an hour ago."

I thought about it. "Montargis is not really that far. Perhaps you can go and return in time to go with us."

"Perhaps," Amanda said. She gave me a lopsided smile. "And perhaps you can persuade your mother to delay her trip until the next shuttle."

I sighed. Easier to ask that Sorbonne stop her rains eternal. . . .

That day was a quiet day. And the next. Amanda did not return and Mother packed her bags for the coming trip. I packed too, and wished the clocks would stop—for an hour, for a day.

"Take warm clothes, Virgy. It's cold there; the winds will cut right through you."

"You said there was a hotel," I said in protest.

"A lodge. And apt to be only a shell after all this time. No one lives on Doubab anymore."

I looked at her. "Why not?"

"Because it's a barren world. Drab, unattractive—more a prison than anything else—so say the disciples who've been there." Mother set both of her bags on the floor. "Its only distinguishing feature is The Mountain of the Crown, where the stargate used to be."

She meant the alien one. The first one. There *was* a Gate on Doubab, of course, put there by human engineers.

That night the sleep I got was fitful. I dreamed I killed the Mad Witch of Montargis.

Amanda joined us just as we were leaving the

maison. She looked haggard, but she was smiling, and she bore a second weapons case beside her own.

"You can't have slept or eaten," Mother said, looking at her red-rimmed eyes. "Come in. I'll fix you breakfast."

But Amanda shook her head. "No time. I can eat on the way. The shuttle won't wait."

Mother didn't insist. She adjusted her surplice and picked up her bags.

Amanda turned her head to look at me and gave me a wink. She said, "If you don't stop grinning like that you'll run out of them by the time you're fifteen."

That stretched my cheek muscles more. I said, "How is the Mad Witch?"

"Madder than ever," Amanda said.

Our stargate was located just off the orbit of Sorbonne's smallest moon. Shuttling up to it was the longest part of our trip; it took almost two days. The window through to Doubab was just opening.

Amanda explained to me that everything that has planetary mass has a locus. That's the jumping-off point, the only place where a stargate will work. The trick is in finding it, teasing it out mathematically from the mountains of data that have to be compiled. And because planetary bodies accrete mass all the time from meteorites and space dust, loci have to be refigured continually. They shift.

Those periods right before the shifts take place are windows to other worlds—to loci in other parts of the universe.

Doubab's locus was on top of Crown Mountain.

"Well, it's livable, but hardly the Elysian Fields," Amanda said, coming out of the exit portal. She indicated the rolling edge of low-flung mountains, pointed down into the valley where shadows hunkered like somnolent dwarves. On the mountain a cold wind was blowing, and above, the sky was gray, like freshwashed slate. The faint warmth of the sun was only a tangential glancing force.

Mother gave it a pensive look but made no comment. Her mind was elsewhere. She moved past Amanda and scanned the rock face jutting above us. Her fingers touched the ochre-colored stone in a tentative way. She ignored the wind.

"It happened here, did it?" Amanda asked.

"Yes," Mother said.

"Where's the shrine?"

"Farther down, along the curve of the rockface." She pointed to our left, into the teeth of the wind.

We moved that way. I was cold, and still disoriented from the sudden change of scene. I drew my cloak around me tightly.

Halfway around the curve Amanda noticed the three-foot-wide depression that marched with us. She stopped and knelt and brushed away its mantle of hard-packed snow.

"That's where the Crown rested, before it was cut up and hauled away," Mother said. She had stopped, too, but her eyes did not. They followed the depression line as it curved back against the rock face.

"That would have been Morgan," Amanda said. Morgan was the engineer who had taken the artifact away.

"Yes," Mother said.

We followed the track. At its end was a snowfilled grotto, as humble in its intent as the Disciples themselves. Mother cleared away the snow, oblivious to the cold. Her efforts revealed a bust—the head and shoulders of Setsen Dai, the man known as The Shining Light.

It was a friendly face, and wise, though by no means all-knowing. The eyes were deeply sunk beneath the brow. Taken altogether he looked somewhat like an owl. There *was* power there, though, and something else. Trust, I thought—it was the face of a man you could trust.

Amanda must have thought so, too. She drew off to one side and studied the sculpture through questioning eyes. I knew her to be openly skeptical of prophets and messiahs, with a quick scorn for those who fell under their spell. Yet Setsen Dai's face, with its openness and quiet wisdom, seemed to affect her strangely.

Mother knelt, drew a small bag from a surplice pocket, placed it before the statue.

"What's that?" Amanda asked.

"Tokens," Mother said. "From the Disciples of Sorbonne."

How could one person change so profoundly the way Man thought? And what might they say in future years of Setsen Dai? I examined the statue's face carefully, looked from it to Mother's. She was smiling a little, her eyes softer than I'd seen them in years. Amanda stirred suddenly, her helm gleaming in the half-light, the blue streamer catching the wind. After some moments she lifted her gaze and regarded the surrounding mountains. They were mist-covered, glacial, locked in winter's death-grip. Abruptly, involuntarily, she shuddered, then caught my eye and gave a little shrug.

"Something about this place," she said defensively. "It seems somehow . . . ominous. Spooky."

I felt it, too, and looked at Mother. "I'm cold," I said. "Where is that lodge you said was here?"

"In the valley. Just at the mountain's base." She walked to the plateau's edge, looked carefully, pointed.

The floater we'd brought took us down to the lodge, an empty cold place with a hand-built hearth and huge high windows that looked out on the mountain.

"It must have been a lonely life, running this place," Amanda said. She ran a finger along the mantel and disturbed two decade's worth of dust.

"His name was Rowan," Mother replied. "The man who owned this lodge. Probably he didn't think of it as being lonely."

"That's right," Amanda said after a second. "Kirst was here, wasn't he? He had the company of the World Assassin."

"I suppose so," Mother said. "The trouble is, there's

not a great deal known about Rowan, except that he came from a prison colony. Blanchot, I think it was."

"That was a maximum security prison," Amanda commented dryly. She opened the dampers of the fireplace and turned to look at Mother. "It begins to appear that they were well suited to each other."

Mother shrugged and stared out of the window before answering. "He seems to have been a decent man," she said at last. "Not a violent one, like Kirst."

Amanda and I gathered scrub, and we lit a fire in the ancient hearth. There was a table there in the common room, a massive thing of lead-colored wood. We sat at it and drank tea and pondered our futures, the futures of Man, and the larger Futures that mark the turn of the universe. Sitting thus, before the roaring fire, we watched darkness fall. It came quickly, as though a curtain were dropped suddenly over the mountains. Doubab, it turned out, was very black at night. There was no moon—only a cold reef of stars above and the faint white glimmer of the slopes.

Just before turning in, Mother pinned a calendar up on the wall. It was blocked off in days, showing the windows that lead from Doubab back to the stargate on Sorbonne. There were many of them, but at the eighteen-day mark they began to drop off abruptly. There were only three after that—eleven days before the cut-off point, one at the six-day point, and another an hour before the Fugue line was due to pass over Doubab.

Mother circled the eighteen-day window. She said, "That is our return date."

Amanda brought up my being a Helm Maiden two nights later, but it didn't go anywhere. She let it lie for the rest of the week while she thought out the steps.

"It's like a military campaign," she said. She frowned, but with humor. "Your mother must have weaknesses, soft spots. When I find them I'll know what to do."

I thought about it, perched on one of the posts supporting the veranda. Mother was like that—a redoubt. I looked for weaknesses and it surprised me. I couldn't find any.

There was a building below the lodge, a small rectangular structure with crumbling foundations, broken walls, and scattered timbers. Mother and I explored it. We found inside a rusted mass of analytic equipment and piles of broken plaster casts.

"This is where Pan Kirst lived," Mother said. She crossed to one of the windows and looked out. Standing there, arms akimbo, her hood fallen back, she struck me as formidable, an unshakeable pillar. A fist tightened itself inside my stomach. *What if we could not change her mind?*

The next three days were busy ones. Mother set out to investigate the climbing, twisting trail that led to the top of Crown Mountain. Amanda and I spent our time in the lower valleys, laying traps to catch the weasel-like rodents that nested there. Broiled and spiced, they made good stew, a welcome change from our packaged fare. While we were setting snares, Amanda installed surveillance cameras at the head of each canyon. "Precaution," she said, grinning. "Practice, really—there's nothing here more dangerous than those weasels."

"There were the aliens," I said. "Once."

"Maybe they left someone behind when they left," Amanda said, laughing at me. "That would be a shock."

It was late on the fourth day. I was preparing dinner in the kitchen when I heard a sudden gleeful shout.

"Virgy, come here!" Amanda's voice commanded from the next room.

The routine scan she had made of the surrounding terrain revealed a tiny smudge vanishing up the side of the adjoining mountain. According to the maps, that one was called Maylow, after the captain who had discovered Doubab. Amanda looked at me, eyes gleaming, then stopped the display and ran it backward until the smudge was centered again on the screen.

I said, "What is it? Some kind of bear?"

Amanda shrugged. "There's no way of telling except by going over there to find out. There's something strange about it, though. See the way it goes from shadow to shadow, staying away from the light?"

She ran it again, and I caught a ripple of tawny fur, a flash of white ruff. The creature moved quickly, for all that its gait was lumbering, erratic.

"It's been injured," I said.

"Maybe," Amanda said. She bounced up and strode to the window, hair an auburn swirl. "Get my case," she said, looking out. "There's still light enough for tracking."

"But Mother should be back at any moment. It's dinner time."

Amanda shrugged dismissively. "There aren't supposed to be any bears on Doubab," she said, her voice rising with excitement. "Or *any* large animals, for that matter. It could be we've discovered something new. It would be a shame to miss the opportunity of seeing it up close."

I stared at her. She gazed back. There was the glint of devilment in her eyes, and suppressed energy. She hadn't brought along any of the mock-lifes, and she missed her daily workouts.

I got the case. The one from Montargis was beneath her bed, pushed well back. Hers was on her nightstand, glowing with polish. It was black, like the leather Amanda wore. But there all similarity ended. The surface was slick, and its hinges, if there were any, were invisible. Along the top ran a double row of lizard's bumps, keys to locks Amanda said could not be broken. Inside the case were the spurs and spikes I had seen Amanda use on the mock-life. Much else, too. Implosion sticks, neural gases, repulsor shields—Armageddon in a satchel, so rumor went.

I picked it up gingerly by its carrying strap. It was lethal, Amanda had said. Booby-trapped.

We got off the floater at the base of the mountain. Its noise, Amanda told me, carried too well on the wind. That much was true enough. I suspect, though, that it had more to do with her own freedom of movement than it did with alarming the creature.

The sky was giving up its gray. We climbed into twilight more black than blue. Shadows made long fingers beneath the ridges.

"Stay close," Amanda said. She scrambled up onto a small plateau. I followed, then turned and looked back across the valley. Rowan's lodge was a tiny spark of light against the gathering darkness.

For twenty minutes we climbed upward, the night wind slashing against our faces. It was fast becoming too dark to see. We ascended a 200-foot ramp and came to another break, a long flat triangle of snow and ice. Amanda strode out onto it and then stopped. She glanced back at me. When she spoke, there was exultation in her voice.

"Tracks here, Virgy. Big ones." She knelt in the snow, spanning the impressions with fingers and hands.

I joined her and we looked at the line of tracks going off up the slopes. They were large, and one of them bore more weight than the other. "It's walking upright," I said, before realization hit me. *My God—it must be human! Male, from the size . . .*

A quick glance at Amanda revealed an unflustered exterior. Her eyes were narrowed on the half-arc of ragged stone above us that made a blot against the sky. She did not appear surprised. I wondered how long she had known. Perhaps from the start—it's hard to fool Maidens of the Helm, and *exceptionally* difficult to deceive Amanda deVere.

"There's a cave up there," she said meditatively. "I wonder if our friend is at home."

"Cave? What cave?" I followed her gaze, saw only darkness.

She caught my expression and gave a little chuckle. "Sensors, Virgy. Built into the helm. I can see pretty far into the infra-red—and some into the ultra-violet. There are aural amplifiers, too, if I need them." She pointed. "There's a hot spot about two hundred yards up and to the left." She stood up with a lithe no-effort movement and followed the tracks upward. After a moment I followed, my skin prickling at the thought of myself wearing blue silk and black leather, afraid of nothing, striding as Amanda did, into the unknown.

The way had been used before—and often. The snow was packed down and bore the look of careful maintenance. I peered outward and saw why. The rim broke off abruptly and plummeted into darkness. A false step meant a long and deadly tumble.

"Stay close," Amanda murmured again. She touched me with one gloved hand and I felt the hard ridged outline of her spike. She gestured ahead at solid-seeming rock. "The cave is just ahead, angled off to the left."

I gripped her shoulder. My voice made a squeaky whisper. "Are we going to go in? Just like that?"

"Of course. Do you want to leave now, and maybe let him get away?" She squeezed my arm. I recognized rebuke and felt a quick flush of shame.

There was a covering over the cave mouth, a patch-work of animal hides. Amanda thrust it aside with one hand so that there was enough room for both of us to enter.

The inside smelled—of ill-cured hides, and far more potently, of ripe humanity. Beyond was a small fire, on its far side a reclining figure swathed in fur pelts. At our entrance the figure stirred, then lunged up-right, one hand grasping a wooden staff.

The first thing I noticed were the scars. Impossible not to. They were deep, and many, distorting the entire left side of his face, a fact his beard did not—

could not—conceal. And he was *old*—his bones showed through his flesh. For all that, he looked at us with a certain amount of bravado, his single eye far back beneath his brow. That single eye gleamed.

"Who are you?" Amanda asked, breaking a brief tableau. She moved toward the fire, a dragonfly in darkly glowing armor—*a Helm Maiden*.

"Stop!" the creature snapped, bringing one hand down across the staff. The move could be interpreted either as a defensive maneuver or one preparatory to attack. His hawklike face bore a certain imperiousness of manner that said he was in command of the situation.

Amanda gave him a taunting look and grinned. The old man threw a side glance my way, checked the shadows along one wall, and made as though to duck that way.

Amanda moved to cut him off, but he anticipated her. He turned in midstride toward the cave's entrance and came through the center of the fire, scattering embers behind him. He came toward *me!*

Amanda told me later I dived at his legs, but I don't remember it. I do remember waking up with a lump on my head and a queasy feeling in my stomach. The old man was lying half in and half out of the cave entrance, a dart protruding from his leg.

"You okay?" Amanda asked. She knelt and touched the bruise that was forming on my forehead. When she looked at the fallen man her eyes smoldered angrily.

"I'm all right," I said. I half sat up. "He nearly got away, didn't he?"

I got a short nod for a reply. "If you hadn't slowed him up he might have," she said. She mussed my hair for me and then gave an abrupt snort of chagrin. "I'll give him this—he thinks things through quickly. *Damn.* He drew me in—I should have been prepared for something like that."

She rolled the fallen form over and studied the man's features. In spite of herself she blanched at the scars, the empty eye-socket. Then, with a dry irony, she chuckled.

"Someone—or some*thing*—marked him," she said. "But our boy won the fight." She gave me a meaningful glance and shook her head admiringly. "That little scuffle must have been a lulu!"

"But who is he? No one lives on Doubab."

Amanda shrugged and removed the dart from the old man's leg. "We'll have to ask him when he wakes up," she said. "In the meantime, let's look around, see what we can find."

We did not find much. The cave was about fifteen feet across. There was a short tunnel leading off to another exit higher on the mountain. On a shelf of rock there were clay pots containing dried roots. We also found smoked meat hanging from strings, a large cache of firewood, and several blankets made from skins.

"I'm curious," Amanda said when we had completed our survey. "Why would he live here when the lodge is available? That would have to be more comfortable than *this*." She toed the sleeping mat in disgust.

"Maybe he was afraid," I said.

"Afraid of what? Afraid of whom?"

I shook my head. Doubab was deserted. What, indeed, had he to fear?

The old man came to his senses slowly. He shuddered all over, drew in long sobbing breaths. His hair fell over his face; Amanda brushed it back.

"Who are you?" she asked.

There was fear written on the man's ravaged face. I wondered how I had thought him imperious. He was a feeble old man whose sole thought had been to escape.

He looked at Amanda, then flicked a glance at me. The gnarled hands raised themselves into beseeching hooks. "No war!" he said hoarsely. He looked back at Amanda and said again, more softly: ". . . oh god, no war!"

* * *

Night on Doubab was a tapestry of muted sounds. There was the creaking ice up on the mountains, the occasional fall of snow ledges, the treble cry of small creatures. And, over everything, the rough-honed edge of the wind.

I listened to it all and fed wood to the big fireplace in the lodge, thankful for its warmth.

"Where is he now?" Mother asked. She had listened to us tell of our troglodyte.

"His cave," Amanda said. "He wouldn't come with us willingly, and it was too dangerous to carry him on that trail. Also unnecessary."

"You're not worried that he'll slip away from you?"

Amanda shook her mane of auburn hair. "There's a tracer in him. Subcutaneous. It was in the head of the dart I stuck him with."

"Who is he?" Mother asked, and looked at us both. It always came back to that. Who was he—and what was he doing on Doubab?

Amanda sat down at the big table and helped herself to a cup of tea. Dark Sorbonne tea. "He won't—or perhaps he can't—answer any of our questions. It's as if he doesn't know himself. Maybe he's a survivor of one of the wars they've had in this area . . . or a deserter. The last war's been what . . . fifty years? He'd be the right age."

"What do you think, Virgy?" Mother asked. She looked my way.

I threw a final stick on the fire and joined Amanda at the table. "Maybe he is a survivor," I said, mulling it over. "He's *awfully* old. Old enough for it to be one of the early wars—maybe even the independence one, when we broke away from Earth."

"Nobody's *that* old," Amanda said, grinning at me.

"There's something strange about him, though," I said. "I mean, other than living in a cave. It's funny. Most of the time he seems like a weak and helpless old man. At other times . . ."

"At other times?" Mother prompted.

I said, "It was just an impression I had ... that, even surprised, he was somehow in command of the situation."

There was a brief silence and then Mother said, "Those words he spoke. What were they again?"

"He said 'no war,'" Amanda answered, stirring her tea.

"That was it? That was all he said?"

"That's all," Amanda said. "Do you make anything of it?"

Mother fingered her beads. "It probably means nothing at all," she said. "But *no war* is an anagram for Rowan."

The old man had left the cave briefly during the night, going farther up the mountain and then returning. Amanda showed us the tracer marks on her tracking scope. We discussed it over breakfast.

"You think there's another cave up there?" Mother asked.

"Could be." Amanda shrugged and broke a biscuit in half. She buttered one of the sections and took a bite before carrying the thought further. "He's probably got an entire network of hideouts in the mountain—he strikes me as being the cautious type." She paused and looked at Mother. "You really think he's Rowan?"

"He *could* be," Mother said only. "With Pan Kirst dead and the Crown dismantled, his existence here on Doubab would no longer have any meaning. The records, and they're hazy at best, say that Rowan left this world. But what if he did not ..." She moved her shoulders fractionally and rose from the table. "Come on. Maybe we'll find out from his own lips who he is—and why he hides in caves."

By daylight Doubab was a wilderness of white. The track leading up the mountain was clear, however, and we took the floater all the way to the cave entrance.

Amanda entered first, the spikes in her hands catching light from the early morning sun. There was no danger, though. Rowan—if indeed that was his name— was seated quietly on a flat stone eating the remains of a small breakfast.

"I've been expecting you," he said to Amanda. He seemed almost cheerful. He tossed a bone in the general direction of the fire, gave me a nod, and then stood so abruptly he nearly cracked his head on an overhang. He stared, and I turned to see what he was looking at. Mother had entered just behind me, a ghostly figure in her surplice and cowl, her face hidden by the shadows beneath her hood.

"Who—?" The old man's voice was suddenly a croak.

Mother took a step forward. She said, smiling, "My name is Frieda. I'm a disciple of The Shining Light. *Ajol*, my friend."

"*Ajol* . . ." the other mouthed the word, echoing it as though it were a long-forgotten prayer. Then he sat down again and clasped his hands, not looking at Mother, not looking at any of us.

"That word means something to you, doesn't it?" Mother said. "Where did you hear it? Who said it?"

The only answer was a flicker from the old man's good eye.

Mother went to him, knelt, and took his hands in hers. She showed no fear, no revulsion.

He raised his head fractionally.

"You're Rowan, aren't you? Come to the lodge— your lodge—and let us help you."

"No!" Power there, but almost a reflex.

Mother matter-of-factly examined his face, running her fingers first over the empty eye socket, then down the scarred cheek. I marveled at her courage, her foolhardiness.

"Do you know who did this?"

"No."

"It nearly killed you, whatever it was. They might almost be claw marks. Did you fight some animal here?"

"I don't know." The man's voice was a murmur.

"Does the name Titus Wilde mean anything to you?"

There was a flicker of something, but the old man shook his head.

"Pan Kirst?"

The man's face was a mask, revealing nothing. He shook his head again.

Minutes passed while Mother knelt, studying him. The small fire began to go out. Amanda and I built it up again, using wood from the stacks along the wall.

"You two go on," Mother said finally, rising and coming toward us. "I'm going to stay here today."

"Hardly," Amanda snorted derisively. "You think he's safe, just because he hasn't hit you over your pointy head yet with that staff of his. Well, I know better. He's still unpredictable."

"I won't be harmed," Mother said. She gave us both an enigmatic smile. *Inner Understanding. Outward Love.* She was a redoubt. A pillar. She said, "You investigate that second cave of his. I'll bet there isn't one."

Amanda was not to be put off. She said, "You haven't seen his moves, Frieda. He's good—even for as old as he is. He had to have been a professional."

Mother did not reply, and the silence stretched out into a long beat of seconds. Finally Amanda shrugged and gave in. Too quickly, I thought.

She said, "I did warn you."

"Yes," Mother said.

"Then at least take this." She pushed a silvery object the size of a thimble into Mother's hands. "If you're in distress, simply press down on the top of that. I'll be here in a matter of minutes."

"Very well," Mother said. She put the thimble in a pocket of her surplice.

Moments later, we found ourselves outside the cave watching sunlight sparkle off ice ledges. I looked at Amanda and she gave me a mugging grin. She didn't quite rub her hands together, but there was about her an aura of suppressed glee.

I said, "What are you up to? Will Mother really be all right?" I didn't understand what was going on— what *had* gone on—only that I had missed something.

"She'll be fine," Amanda said with a nod. She put an arm around me and gave my forehead a kiss. "I think, cousin Virgy, that we've found one of those soft spots I was telling you about."

"What do you mean?"

"One of your mother's weaknesses is that old man in there."

"Rowan?"

Amanda nodded. "If that's his name."

"You said he was unpredictable."

She gave my arm a reassuring pat. "Only so that Frieda will keep her guard up. Actually, he has enough residual tranquilizer in him to keep him tame for a week."

There was no cave above. There *was* a lookout point, though, where Crown Mountain could be seen, and the valley below.

Mother spent the next several days in the cave. Rowan wouldn't or couldn't live in the lodge; something about it seemed to terrify him. He did not protest a beard trim, a bath, and an eyepatch, though, and he began to look decently human.

I went up Maylow once and found Mother teaching Rowan the precepts of The Shining Light.

"Your mother will make him a disciple, if she can," Amanda said, laughing, sitting on a fallen log below the lodge. She had her weapons case with her, and now she opened it, turned half away so that I could not see the combination she used on the lizard bumps. She took out a hunting boomerang, gave me a look, then stood up and jammed a stick in the ground at her feet. She threw the boomerang, and it sailed around a clutch of small trees before returning. It struck the ground two feet to the side of the stick; Amanda shook her head in disgust. "Close, but not close enough. I must have misjudged the wind." She picked the weapon up and held it, preparatory to throwing.

"He seems to understand everything she was saying," I remarked. "And he was agreeing with her on most of it. Maybe he's heard it before."

Amanda let her arm fall, so that she was holding the boomerang by one long vane. "He's been lonely for a very long time, Virgy; that makes him vulnerable. And your mother has not had a cause like this one in all the years she's been a disciple. After all, he's Rowan—he knew The Shining Light!" Amanda paused and looked at me with devilment in her eyes. "That makes *her* vulnerable, too, of course. So we'll watch, and learn—and bide our time." She straightened and threw the boomerang. We watched it arc out, skim the leaves of the trees, and disappear. Moments later it came into view again, a flashing curved windmill. It bounced once, then sliced through the stick Amanda had jammed into the ground. Satisfied, she picked up the weapon. She said, "Have you been keeping track of the days?"

I hadn't. I calculated quickly on my fingers, then said in astonishment: "Tomorrow is the eighteen-day window. We're supposed to go back to Sorbonne."

Amanda nodded. "Your mother told me last night she was delaying her return until the six-day window. Rowan, it appears, is reluctant to leave Doubab."

I thought of the Fugue line and felt the first twinges of unease. What if . . . what if . . . a lot of what ifs. I felt infinity breathing on my neck.

"I want you to use that window tomorrow," Amanda said, putting the boomerang back into its case. "Go to one of the university worlds. Find out everything you can about Rowan. I have a feeling that information is going to prove most useful."

"What about you?"

She gave me a grin and shook back her hair. "I'll keep an eye on things here," she said.

Amanda took me to the top of Crown Mountain next morning, and while we waited for the Gate to become operative, I went to look at the shrine. Setsen Dai looked impassively out upon the snow-covered slopes, his Puckish mouth twisted as if at some monumental joke.

"Time," Amanda called, glancing at her chronometer, and I walked back to stand beside her. She gave me a quick hug and a smile, and nodded toward the Gate. When I entered it I looked back, and inexplicably, I shivered.

The trip was uneventful. One moment I stood on the wind-blown heights of Crown Mountain, and the next I was on the stargate circling Sorbonne.

Laerdes was the closest university with full records of Doubab and the time before. I went there, nodding my head at irony rampant.

Apart from weaker gravity, it was a lot like Sorbonne. The sky leaked, and I was wet before I made the cover of the library overhang. I looked around, saw students everywhere, some of them my age, some older. It didn't look like a bad place, really—but it wasn't the Helm Order.

Inside the library, I sat at a computer console and summoned up the past.

There were no true records of Rowan before his time on Doubab, though there were tie-ins with fraud schemes and certain other low-level criminal activities in the Colony Worlds. There were no pictures; it seemed he had an aversion to cameras. The sole solid link appeared to be Pan Kirst. There was a friendship there of long standing.

Of Kirst there was more—a great deal more. Thirty years earlier, Earth was ascendant, the outworlds in thrall. Kirst had been a tactician in a war of independence. He'd been responsible, personally, for the destruction of at least a score of worlds. World-Assassin, in truth!

Where he and Rowan chanced to meet remained a mystery, but meet they had. Rowan had shown up on Doubab a year after war's end. He'd built the lodge and taken in tourists while Kirst worked at translating the alien language.

I read on, and somewhere between the first day and the third a chill began to grow in the pit of my stomach. When it got too big to carry around I stopped and bit my lip and wondered what Amanda would do in my place. Then the thought came to me—perhaps I was wrong.

I left Laerdes and wandered. I used the stargates. I went from cold and bitter worlds to salty sunlit ones, but my chill did not leave me.

In the end I went back to Doubab.

Amanda wasn't there to pick me up so I walked down, the hills glowing around me with reflected light.

I clumped into the lodge, expecting to see Mother or Amanda or both; it was nearly lunch time. There was no one there, though there *was* stew cooling in the kitchen.

I knew where Mother was. I knew where Amanda was likely to be.

Teaching.

Hunting.

I walked to Maylow.

Halfway up to the cave I looked back across the valley and saw Amanda heading toward the lodge on the floater. I waved, but she did not see me.

When I reached the mouth of the cave I hesitated, breathing in the sharp mountain air. I didn't know for sure what I was going to say, nor how I was going to say it.

It was dark inside. The fire had burned itself out, leaving only the glow of banked embers. I closed my eyes while they adjusted. Then I opened them—and felt myself go rigid.

Mother! Oh, Mother! I saw first the feet.

Four. Bare. Feet. And the blanket lying loosely over them . . .

Mother—what have you done?

My tongue clung to the roof of my mouth. I said something, an inarticulate sound that magnified itself and made an echo in the cave. The forms within the blanket stirred. Mother sat up, saw me for the first time. Her eyes widened, and she stared, but she said nothing. The old man sat up, too, his nakedness white and loathsome.

"He's *Kirst!*" I said finally, strangling on the words, snarling with fury. I pointed an accusing finger at the old man's torso. "His body was never found! He never died! Mother—you've been making love to your own prophet's murderer!"

Mother's face took on expression, then lost it. Thunderstruck, she looked at the figure beside her and then back at me. One hand sought her prayer beads. An inner turmoil was addressed, argued, lost. She leaned forward, one pale breast breaking free of the blanket.

She said, "He's Rowan." Her eyes pleaded.

I shook my head. "No, he's not. I've just come from the library computers. I've seen Rowan's obituary. He died a dozen years ago—in the Colonies."

The old man hunched forward, pathetically scrawny, his single eye blinking furiously.

He said, "I don't *want* to be Kirst! I want to be Rowan!"

"Of course you do," I said scathingly. "But you're not. You're Kirst, the World-Assassin. I saw pictures of what you did to those planets—to Earth. I saw *you!*"

Mother gasped. "You recognized him?"

I hesitated for only a moment, but it was enough. I said, "He was different then, of course. Younger, without a beard, without injuries. But it was him!"

Mother sighed. She said, "But you're not certain—not positive. You can't be." She sat for several seconds, thinking. Finally she stood up unselfconsciously and began dressing, pulling her surplice on over her head and pushing her feet down into her boots. Then, with great tenderness, she bent and touched the old man's head.

"I know you can't be Kirst," she said. "He was an

evil man, and he died a long time ago, on Crown Mountain."

My voice descended into strained whispers. "What are you doing? He *is* the scourge, Mother. What proof do you need? Shall I ask the spirit of Titus Wilde?"

She turned and struck without warning, her hand cracking against my jaw like wood on bone.

"We'll talk of this later," she said. "At the lodge."

I was stunned. By reflex I turned and stumbled out of the cave, my eyes blinking at the sudden light. Below I saw Amanda careening toward me, her pennant flying straight back in the air wash.

It was night, black Doubab night. I slipped out of the lodge with the case I'd taken from beneath Amanda's bed. I followed the tiny triangle of stars that formed a wedge above Maylow.

When I got to the cave I walked in without announcing my presence.

The old man was awake. He stared at me.

I gazed back at him, anger rising through me all over again, making my arms tremble.

I said coldly, "Why do you live in this cave? Why don't you want to leave Doubab? What is it you're afraid of?"

He shuffled his feet and looked away indifferently.

"I'll tell you what you're afraid of," I said. I licked my lips. "You're afraid to face yourself—afraid of what you'll find. And you won't leave Doubab because they have ways of proving who you *really* are. Then there would be no doubt at all!"

He stood up and crossed to the cave's entrance, pushed aside the patch work of skins, and looked out at the enveloping darkness. After a moment or two he turned his head to look at me.

"Your mother has been telling me about the Fugue line," he said. "I've been thinking about that. Does it seem to you that it's a natural occurrence?"

The change of subjects caught me by surprise. I said, "What do you mean?"

He shrugged lightly. "What if the aliens sent it? *Because* we're using the stargates."

I felt cold. I said, "That's profane—*you're* profane! Why should the aliens want to do that?" My voice was thick with contempt. I might not believe everything Mother did, but when he attacked Setsen Dai he attacked her.

He was silent. Then he said, "Why, indeed? Perhaps to stop Mankind from invading the stars."

I said hotly, "You're mocking Setsen Dai—and his gift. What do *you* know, anyway?"

He let the patchwork of skins fall and resumed his seat by the fire. He shook his head wearily. "I'm too tired to mock anybody. It was simply an idle thought— the maunderings of an old man's mind."

I suddenly remembered why I had come. I took the case from my shoulder and sat it down against the ochre stone.

His gaze flickered over it. "What's that?"

I said, "There's proof in that case of who you are. Rowan or Kirst or simply a crazy man. Open it—if you can."

He suddenly smiled, at what I did not know. It was a painful smile, full of irony, full of knowledge unfathomable. He said, "Is there a key to it?"

"A combination. Something based on primes, I think. I watched Amanda open it once. She touched these two first." I pointed to two of the lizard bumps.

He looked at me again, his gaze full and questioning. "You favor Amanda," he said finally. "And I think I know her pretty well by now."

"Yes," I said. "I'm going to be a Helm Maiden."

He looked at the case again, then his gaze flickered between it and me. The muscles of his throat tightened.

"Thank you, Virgy," he said at last.

I left the case at his feet, and came away. Kirst was a tactician, a genius. It was he who had defeated Earth's battlefleets. It was he who had found the secret of an alien tongue. If the old man opened the case he was Kirst.

If he opened the case he was dead.

The case was still there in the morning, and it looked as though it had not been touched. The old man simply gave me a shrug when I picked it up.

"Coward!"

"I suppose so," he replied. "But you were right. The truth is, I simply don't want to know." He went on eating breakfast, his single eye warily watching me.

When I got back to the lodge I found Mother and Amanda arguing. It was the six-day window. Only one remained after this one, at less than an hour before the Fugue line cut across the orbit of Doubab.

"I'm staying here," Mother said. "With him."

"With Kirst?" Amanda's lips twisted. She stared unbelievingly.

Mother's face was smooth, serene. It had recaptured the tranquility I had made vanish the day before. She said, "Even if he *is* Kirst, I will stay with him."

"But you doubt he is?"

She nodded. "I do. But it really no longer matters. He is a human being and a disciple, and his hurt goes deeper than you can imagine. I will stay with him because he needs me."

"And Virgy?" Amanda asked bitterly. "What of her? Will she no longer need a mother?"

Mother sat down at the table and began to make herself a cup of tea. "You spoke of making her a Helm Maiden," she said after a time. "Perhaps that would be best, after all."

I felt a rush of blood to my head. *Helm Maiden!* I was to be a Helm Maiden!

"You won't change your mind?" Amanda asked.

"No. And you'd better go. Your window will be opening soon."

"There's one more, if you *do* change your mind," Amanda said.

Mother took my hand, kissed me, then pushed me away. "Yes, I know," she said to Amanda.

The last I saw of her was as she sat there, sipping tea, her hood drawn up around her face, her mouth firm and solid and full of peace.

Helm Maiden—

Remembering, I felt shaken, bowled over by blurs from the past. And at the same time diminished, unable to deal with them. I swallowed against the dryness of my throat, looked up, saw Baltair's sun shining overhead, felt its heat against my face.

"*Attention!*"

I drew more erect. The awarding of Helms was beginning.

When it was my turn, Amanda made the presentation. She gave me a nod, then a smile, and adjusted the Helm when I donned it. I touched the controls, sent it quickly through infrared and ultraviolet, saw colors chase themselves in writhing patterns across the side screens.

"Congratulations!" Amanda said. She gave my hand a squeeze.

You favor Amanda, Rowan-Kirst had said on Doubab. *And I think I know her pretty well by now*. And he had looked inside my soul, his single eye unblinking.

Yes, he had known me, that crazy old man.

And suddenly tears streamed down my face, uncalled for, uninvited. I could taste their salt on my lips. Amanda looked at me, touched my cheek with a wondering fingertip. She seemed strangely moved.

I could not tell her that it was not for silk and leather that I cried—cried at last. But for a frozen mountain on a doomed planet on the other side of the Fugue line. *What must they be, hunched in their cave?* I had never cried for her before, and I might never cry for her again. But I did now.

Ajol, Mother! Oh, Ajol . . . ajol. . . .

*   *   *

There was a brief silence when Brennan stopped reading. He put down the manuscript, looking wonderingly from it to the Forster thin-gel. He tried, unsuccessfully, to contain his excitement. *Damn! Damn!* Gus had been right! *Either* of the artifacts would have been a bombshell. But taken together—!

Jancy seemed as stunned as he. She said, "The Church is going to have real trouble, Brennan, when this is made public."

"*If,*" Brennan posited shortly, and there was silence again.

"That kid," Jancy remarked after a space of 10 seconds, "was a real brat." She got up from the mat where she'd been sitting and refilled Brennan's mug. He sipped the hot tea gratefully, his mind in turmoil.

"That's what Gus was trying to locate, wasn't it?" Jancy asked. "The location of that planet."

"Yes," Brennan said. "Doubab." He stood up, went to the narrow window that afforded a view of the square outside. Looking out, he said, "Gus was right about the Church, too. If they had this, they'd probably suppress it. Kirst and Setsen Dai as *people* . . . that's explosive!"

"But they *don't* have it," Jancy pointed out. She gave Brennan a conspiratorial grin and plumped herself down on the mat again. "*We* do."

"It was obtained illegally," Brennan said. He shook his head. "Pirated goods—unregistered. If they're found on us we'd be the same as Gus."

"Black marketeers, you mean."

"That's right." Brennan glanced once at the girl, then knelt on the mat and slid the artifacts carefully back into the case. With something like relief he passed the case to Jancy. "Have you got a safe place for these?"

"Sure." The girl looked at him, holding the case against her breasts. "What're you going to do, Brennan? *Use* these . . . or turn them over to the Church?"

Brennan had been asking himself that same question. *Damn* Gus! He'd baited the trap with the one thing he knew Brennan—or any archeologist—would give half his life for. Brennan thought of Gus, his half-dead corpse floating motionless inside the glass column. He managed a grudging smile. The man's *mind* was still working, anyway; Gus would laugh at the rules right into the grave.

As though she had read his mind, Jancy said, "Gus picked you because he respects you, Brennan—and because he thinks you can *win!*"

"Maybe," Brennan returned sourly. "And maybe he picked me because I'm simply the one he hates the *least*."

"But it's still true. If *anyone* can get these registered, it's you. You've risen to the top of your profession—using *their* rules. You're brilliant, wealthy, and have contacts everywhere it counts." She paused long enough to put the case down and approach him. "Gus had nothing—*has* nothing. He *needs* you."

"I haven't made my mind up yet," Brennan said, returning the girl's stare. "But one thing's certain. When I do, it won't have anything to do with Gus. He made his choices . . . and I'll make mine."

The girl's mouth tightened. She said hotly, "Then hell, Brennan—do it for yourself. Gus won't care. And I won't, either."

Which was probably true, Brennan mused. The end result would be the same.

Two hours later he Gated for Pio-Tan.

Chapter Six

Itano possessed two moons. The larger, Cero, was a subdued solid presence in the night sky. Sylvia, the smaller, brighter moon, would not become visible for another hour. Standing on the balcony of the monastery mission, Monsignor Carlisle watched Cero slide resolutely toward the western horizon. Warm though it was, he wore a coarse woolen habit with voluminous sleeves and monk's cowl.

There was a cadenced knock at his door. Carlisle reluctantly gave up his vigil of Cero to answer it.

"Monsignor?"

"Yes?"

"I'm Mayhan. I have the report you ordered."

Carlisle examined the other man briefly. Mayhan was dark, narrow-faced, and wore his silver technician's habit without élan. Bored, Carlise thought. Tending CALIFON, CALIFUR's little sister, must entail a certain amount of tedium.

"Go ahead," Carlisle said.

Mayhan helped himself to a seat on one of the room's bolsters. "You've got yourself a big fish."

"Really?" Carlisle suppressed a sigh and sank into an armchair.

"Uh huh. Name—Waverly Hooker-Brennan," Mayhan said, looking down at a printout. "Scion of the Hooker-Brennan Trading Co. Has a doctorate in archeology, a double masters: astrophysics and mathematics. He's past president of the Archeological Guild, served a term as John Wright Fellow at the University of Trospro. He ranks fifth on Rattison's list of influential scientists." Mayhan looked up. "He's published a raft of papers, all of them dealing with pre-Fugue civilizations."

Carlisle's fingers slowly pleated the hem of his cassock. "I know most of that," he murmured, nodding. "What about his psycho-persona?"

"Nothing there. He's active-detached, non-avoidant." The technician looked up again from the printout, shrugged and grinned. "He's so tied up in his work he hasn't taken time to develop strong relationships, except for those in his own dig teams."

"But there he generates loyalty—and respect," Carlisle said, letting go the pleat. "I know—I talked with his men."

"He's method-oriented," Mayhan went on, scanning his sheet. "A perfectionist. Even a little rigid."

"That's his training. It's fortunate, I suppose . . . it means he's predictable."

"CALIFON thinks so," Mayhan said smugly. "She's got him down to a T."

Carlisle pursed his lips. His face took on a pinched expression. He said, "Given that a black market artifact came into his possession, would he keep it?"

"No."

"No?" Carlisle sat up a little in his chair. "Even if there wasn't any danger in doing so?"

"He'd turn it in."

"And if it had a high intrinsic value?"

"Wouldn't matter. He'd try to register it."

"Sure?"

"CALIFON is sure," Mayhan affirmed shortly.

"How high is the rating?"

"Sixty-two point oh four. Forensic high range."

"Umm. But with room for error," Carlisle muttered, looking down at his hands. "If the thing is valuable *enough*."

"Even then," Mayhan insisted. "Hooker-Brennan isn't interested in money."

"No? What is he interested in?"

Mayhan gave the other a crooked smile. "Knowledge. He's driven by it. That's why the rating isn't higher."

"You mean he *would* break the law—for knowledge?"

"If he did at all."

Carlisle stirred, his fingers exiting the cassock sleeves to drum softly on the chair arm. "Could CALIFON predict Brennan's actions if he were to . . . go astray?"

"Within reasonable limits."

"What does that mean?"

Mayhan shrugged, spread his hands. "The behavioral baseline we've developed gives us a fifty-five percent bulge—plus or minus three percent. We can pinpoint any major moves, probably." He stared pointedly at the priest. "It would help, of course, to know what we're looking for. What it is that makes Brennan so important."

The other parried the comment with a shrug. "It may be that he is not. If it turns out that he *is*, though, I'll need answers fast."

"We give twenty-four hour service," Mayhan answered. He gave a faint grin. "You know our motto: CALIFON never sleeps."

Twilight was the gray of pearl. Fog streamers clung like spider webs to the street lights. High above, Sylvia was a bright orb Carlisle could cover with his two hands joined together.

As a boy, Carlisle had often seen such mists, rolling in off the Bay of Delancy, on his birth world. They had seemed magical to him, then, bearers of a special promise.

There had been a monastery near the bay shore, a huge bastion of hewn stone. From it each morning had issued a phalanx of near giants, young men clad in cotton tunics the color of blood. Hidden in the rocks overlooking the shore, Carlisle watched them train, his breath caught somewhere deep inside his chest.

They were Titans. Soundless, timeless, they sprinted over the sand, covering more than four kilometers each morning. The last leg of their exercise passed directly beneath Carlisle's hiding place. Peering down, the boy looked for hard breathing, some sign of effort on the part of the apparitions. But there never seemed to be any. Finally, with a mystical calm he found wonderful, they vanished into the surging fog banks obscuring the monastery trail.

They were Peacemakers, he learned later, the law-keeping sub-sect of the Daiist Order. The Teeth of God.

He remembered seeing one of the Peacemakers in the village square, waiting to escort a Church dignitary to the monastery.

This one, like all Peacemakers before and since, was close to 200 centimeters in height. The ideal (in archaic measure) was six feet, six and six-tenths inches. His dress was an overcloak of blue metal mesh, beneath which gleamed the sub-order's traditional black weapons belt.

"Clear the way!" The giant looked at Carlisle and waved a languid hand.

"Can you *really* fly—all by yourself?" Carlisle whispered in awe.

The giant's eyes were the same blue as his mesh overcloak. Twin beacons, they stared down at the boy without emotion.

"Can you?" Carlisle asked again.

The Peacemaker did not respond, and for a time the boy thought he had not heard. After a moment, though, the man's huge form seemed to grow larger still, until it towered over everything around it. Belatedly, Carlisle realized the Peacemaker's feet were half a meter off the ground.

The aura of fable engendered that afternoon remained with Carlisle until he was a novitiate in the Morganite Order. There, to his disillusionment and dismay, he was told the Peacemakers, in addition to nonpareil martial prowess, possessed a high degree of hypnotic skill.

After showering and dressing in a fresh cassock, Carlisle took surface transportation to CALIFUR. He descended to a sub-basement meeting room, proffered a signed chit to a guard, and entered.

Two other men were already present. Bishop Poole, his face more haggard than ever, was seated behind a desk, his thin arms resting on its surface. The second man was slender, dressed in unrelieved black. He was approximately 40, with knife-blade features.

"Charles, I don't believe you've met Emil Braganza." Poole waved a hand at the black-clad figure.

"My Lord . . . Mr. Braganza." Carlisle came into the room and seated himself.

"Emil is a licensed blackmarketeer," Poole said.

Being a licensed blackmarketeer meant that Braganza worked for the Church. Though he might traffic in stolen goods, and grow wealthy working both ends against the middle, there was a leash around his neck.

"Does he know?" Carlisle asked, wasting no time on protocol.

"I have told him nothing."

"Then I suppose I should fill him in." Carlisle turned to the other. "Do you know what CALIFUR is, Mr. Braganza? What it's used for?"

"It's a COmPUte." The thin man's voice was a reedy whisper. "The Church uses it to authenticate artifacts . . . sometimes to arbitrate disputes."

"True." Carlisle looked down at his hands. "But it is much more than that. CALIFUR is very close to being sentient. Before the Fugue, it was used to determine the outcome of wars."

"What does that have to do with me?"

"It's *intuitive*. Within limited boundaries, it can predict future events. What it has predicted, Mr. Braganza, is an impending crisis."

Puzzlement was reflected in Braganza's thin face. "Crisis? What crisis?"

"We don't know." Carlisle took a long breath, glanced at his superior before looking again at Braganza. "We *do* know, however, that it's tied to an artifact that was brought back from the Cone."

"Gus Pierce!" Braganza's eyes narrowed into slits.

"Yes, Pierce brought it back. But he won't tell us where it is—or even *what* it is."

Braganza leaned his elbows on the desk. "Give him to me a while—he'll tell." He grinned savagely. "It will be my pleasure."

"Emil was conned once by Pierce," Bishop Poole interjected for Carlisle's benefit. "Still owes him a year's rent on a solar shuttle."

"It's too late for threats, I'm afraid," Carlisle said. He looked sardonically at the blackmarketeer. "His life already hangs by the merest thread. He is beyond coercion." He paused. "What we need to do is to find that artifact."

"Does CALIFUR say what kind of crisis it is?"

Carlisle hesitated. Finally, grinning wryly, he said, "There are several interpretations possible. However, even the most optimistic would not allow for the continued existence of a licensed blackmarketeer."

"Why not?" The man shot Carlisle a worried look.

Softly, Carlisle said, "Because the Church itself will be affected. How deeply, no one can yet say." He paused, looked with speculation at the other. "And blackmarketeers, in the best of times, walk a very thin line."

"I read you," the thin man said sourly. He stood up, sucked at his lower lip. "What do you want me to do?"

"Do what you do best. Cull your museum spies. Check unregistered items coming over the counter. Threaten, if you have to. Pass the word there's big money for a Cone artifact."

Braganza nodded. "What's the deadline?"

"Six to eight months," Carlisle answered, staring up at him. "After that it's all problematical."

"Not much time."

"Enough, if used properly." Carlisle said. "Make certain you make the most of it."

After Braganza had gone, Carlisle removed his hat, laying it gently on the desk's polished surface. "Should we not tell the other Orders?" he asked Poole. "We could enlist their help."

"I talked with the Archbishop only yesterday," the old man told him heavily. "He said *no*."

"But—"

"He fears the Daiists would swallow us whole, use us as a scapegoat. He's a terrified man, Charles. He thinks the Morganite Order could become just a memory in some child's tapedex."

"And you?"

Poole shrugged. "I think perhaps Kirst is stirring. It is his evil that is the cause of this crisis."

"We will find Pierce's artifact," Carlisle stated flatly.

Poole studied the younger man. He said at last, "I'm appointing you my Chancellor until this matter is resolved. And I hope we *do* find whatever it is he brought back. I *pray* we do."

Chapter Seven

Almost all of the excavation work had already been carried out. What remained were the tasks of cleaning and cataloging. Brennan sent most of the men home, retaining only a skeleton crew to keep the site operating.

In his shelter, he sat studying a fragment of Pio-Tan statuary, an exquisite marble hand poised delicately over ... what? A child, Brennan imagined; that was a common enough theme. Above the wrist was a delicate tracery of marble lace, and one of the fingers wore a ring. The hand by itself represented only a fortieth of the entire statue. The rest of it was lost forever ... or perhaps was in one of the boxes stacked ten high above the excavations. The hand was, however, indicative of what the whole must have been. The sculptors of Pio-Tan had nothing to be ashamed about.

Judd Caskell, his massive frame glistening with sweat, stepped in through the entrance and contemplated the artifact.

"I don't remember seeing the rest of that anywhere. Beautiful, though, isn't it?"

"Yes, it is." Brennan returned the sculpture to its box along with the notes he'd made, and closed the top. Swinging around on his stool, he motioned the other to sit.

"How far are we from finishing up?"

Caskell lowered himself into a chair and looked at his friend through bemused eyes. "Ten days—two weeks. We have most of the stuff boxed." He broke into a peal of laughter. "Father Stuyvesant has been so bored the past few days he's volunteered to do part of the cleaning."

"Think you can take over, arrange to have the crates Gated out?"

Caskell looked at him in amazement. "Sure. Where are you going?"

Brennan paused for long moments before answering. At length he rose slowly, placed his hand on the other's shoulder. "Gus Pierce brought a couple of things out of the Cone, Judd. I'm going to try to get them registered."

"It must be big," was all Caskell could think to say. He gave a soundless whistle.

"It is—bigger than anything I've tackled before." Brennan sat down again, reached into his desk drawer, fished out a bottle of cognac. Holding it up, he said, "There are glasses in that trunk—dig out two."

"You sure you want to get mixed up with Pierce?" Caskell inquired, rummaging for the glasses. He found them, held them while Brennan poured three fingers into each.

"I won't be working with Gus." As briefly as possible, he went over the events leading to Pierce's embottlement on Geste.

"It sounds like it could be dangerous," Caskell said. He looked at his friend in alarm.

"It could be," Brennan responded. "But I have to try."

The dig foreman shook his head, growled, "You've always been too smart to get involved with black-market goods. Don't do it."

"You haven't seen those artifacts," Brennan told him quietly. "I have."

"So what the *giff* are they?" the other demanded loudly. "Somebody's bloody crown jewels?"

"If the evidence is to be believed," Brennan continued, "one is from the site of an alien stargate."

Caskell's eyes boggled.

"Pierce didn't Gate to Corthun," Brennan said. "He couldn't—there's no Gate there. I checked the updated listings of the Gate directory."

"So how'd he get there?"

"The closest Gate is on a moon off Daggett. He would have to have taken a space shuttle from there." Brennan ran his fingers through his hair. "It's six months in—and six out. He took one hell of a gamble."

"Why did he pick Corthun?"

"It's the closest planet inside the Cone."

Caskell remembered the glasses of cognac and handed one of them to Brennan. "What *are* the artifacts, anyway?"

"A picture of an alien," Brennan said, watching his friends eyes widen. "A rotten picture, but a picture nonetheless."

"God! And?"

Brennan shifted on his stool. "A diary depicting a confrontation with Pan Kirst—probably the human antecedent to the Kirst myth."

"He hit the jackpot," Caskell admitted, stunned. He paused. "Kirst is supposed to be an avatar of evil. There shouldn't *be* a human antecedent. You sure your artifacts are genuine?"

"They've both been authenticated," Brennan said, nailing down the clincher. "The numbers are too high to doubt."

Caskell smiled grimly. "You're going to step on Church toes, Bren. If they twig to what you're doing . . ." He left the sentence hanging and shrugged.

"I know," Brennan agreed. "If I fail . . . probably a prison sentence—maybe worse."

There were five seconds of silence inside the shelter.

"Blast it! You're going to need help." Caskell looked at his chief with stormy eyes. "Count me in."

"Thanks." Brennan smiled his appreciation, then shook his head. "I can't do that."

"Why not?"

"This is my problem, Judd. Let's keep it that way."

"Hey—wait a minute. What are friends for?"

"Tell you what," Brennan said. "If I need you, I'll send for you. Okay?"

"Um. Okay." Caskell suddenly grinned and raised his glass. "Salud!"

"Salud!" The dig foreman's smile was infectious. Brennan found himself grinning back.

Six o'clock the next morning, Brennan Gated down the stargate pipeline, shuttled across to Geste. His first task was to talk to Gus Pierce.

When he flipped the switches that activated Pierce's cadaver, the least he expected was a cordial greeting. Instead, he got a curse.

"Don't say a goddamn thing, Hook! Go out, get a Private Line COmPUte, tie it into the circuits."

"But—!"

"Do it!" There was open contempt in Pierce's command. "The Church monitors this hospital."

Chastened, Brennan wandered through the shopping stalls of the local bazaar until, eventually, he located a merchant selling privacy COmPUtes. The price was exorbitant, but the warranty seals were unbroken, and instructions for installing it were free.

Presently, Brennan was again seated before the column bearing Pierce's body. Conversation was through the staging links of the privacy COmPUte, making it all but impossible for an eavesdropper to overhear.

"Tell me," Brennan asked Gus, "what makes you so certain they didn't listen to us last time?"

"Monsignor Charles Carlisle," Pierce said promptly, "believes in his God—he's bound by Church precepts."

Dryly, he added, "they might not mean much to some of the others, but they do to him."

"So?"

"So he gave me his oath." There was mingled contempt and wonder in the thief's reply.

"Umm." Brennan crossed his legs, uncrossed them again, leaned forward. "I saw the artifacts, Pierce. I'm going to try to get them registered."

"Why else would you come back?" the other inquired sharply. "How are you going to go about it?"

"I can't do *anything*," Brennan said, "unless what is in the manuscript is true."

"It's true."

"I'm inclined to agree with you. But it won't stand alone—unregistered. There will have to be corroboration, and it will have to be unassailable."

"And legal," Pierce put in with a grunt.

"Yes—and legal. If we had that, they would *have* to register it."

Pierce gave a short barking laugh. "They *can't* register it, Hook. Don't you understand that? It would tear the Church apart. Their God simply a man like themselves—bah!"

"And that's what you're hanging around for, isn't it?"

"Damn right!" Pierce's reply was explosive, harsh. He laughed abruptly. "Got to let people know the Church is built on lies. And you—you're going to do that for me, Hook."

"Brennan," Brennan said after a short pause.

"You got a thin skin, you know? Okay—Brennan."

"I'm not doing it for you, Gus. Get that out of your head. I'm doing it because . . ."

"It doesn't matter," the cadaver broke in. "You're *doing* it." He gave a thin cackle. "Turning the whole damn system upside down."

Brennan sighed. "Have it your way." On another tack, he said, "What did you discover—before they got you?"

There was a rasping sound, magnified by the staging

links. Pierce said, "Nothing. I was looking for Doubab. It has to exist, Brennan—but damned if I know where."

"It's not in the libraries? Not on any of the Gate directories?"

"Would I be *here* if it were that easy?" Pierce flared angrily. "Sure, it may be on one of the old restricted directories, but I couldn't get access to them. I'm no longer a member of the Archeological Society, remember?" His tone was savage.

"I remember. What kind of intelligence does the Church have?"

If Pierce could have shrugged he would have. "They have links into the black market. Snoops. And they pay damn handsomely for information." He stopped for a moment as though pondering the question all over again. Finally he said, "I could have sworn there was no way they could have known I was going to be in that museum. They did, though. Father Carlisle, anyway. Watch out for him, Brennan. He's poison."

"You underestimated your enemy, Gus."

"Yeah." Pierce's voice suddenly rose an octave. "You may need a contact, Brennan. Someone you can trust—in the underground."

"You know someone?"

"Roki Lehngren. He runs a cattle show down in the pits. He's honest enough, though, and he owes me."

Brennan's eyebrows went up. "Cattle show?"

There was a snort. "Blackmarket auction. They go on all the time."

"Where?"

The snort turned into a laugh. "Ever hear of the Endless Sabbat?"

"Sure. They're on Duvalle. You said your sister belongs to them."

"Well, so does Roki Lehngren," Pierce told him. "He has a pit in the catacombs. That's on the other side of the Wall."

Brennan got to his feet. "If I go there, I'll say hello to Jancy for you."

"Don't bother. My kid sister and I aren't that close."

Just before he hit the switches, Brennan turned and looked back at Pierce's cadaver. "Wish me luck, Gus."

"You'd damn well better not muck it up," the corpse returned viciously.

Chapter Eight

The summary that was waiting on Carlisle's desk in the morning read in part:

Fears justified! Dr. Hooker-Brennan left Pio-Tan approx. one month ahead of schedule. Gate records indicate stop at Geste. Brennan had closeted communication with Gustaphson Pierce—monitors blocked by Private Line COmPUte. Brennan now Gating for Trospro. Please advise.

Carlisle poured himself a cup of coffee, then sat down woodenly. He stared out of the window, the cup forgotten in his hand. So, he thought—it has begun.

"Are there orders, Monsignor?"

Carlisle brought himself back to reality with a snap of his head. Fr Jacc and Fr Cols waited patiently near the door, their round faces obsequiously tranquil.

"Yes," Carlisle said impatiently. "Get me Mayhan at CALIFON. And send this message on to Bishop Poole." He passed the note to Fr Jacc.

Carlisle's staff consisted of three: Fr Jacc and Fr Cols from the Library Order, and a single Sister of Bryan. The two archivists were of extreme age, but Carlisle did not consider that a liability. Their knowledge of Archive material was virtually limitless.

The Sister of Bryan was a wispy matron named Kathleen. Her sole task was to afford Carlisle *carte blanche* use of the stargate pipeline. As long as she was with him, Gate priests—even those of the Daiist Order—would log them through without question. A privileged passport, but expensive. Bishop Poole would expect a full accounting when the emergency was over.

When Mayhan's thin features swam up on the viewer screen, Carlisle said curtly: "Brennan went to Geste, from there to Trospro. Why Trospro?"

"University," Mayhan said immediately. "It has one of the largest computers outside the Church."

"To which he has access."

"Of course. He's a member of the Archeology Society. They couldn't keep him out."

"Do we have anybody there?"

"I'll have to check. Probably not, though—we're stretched pretty thin."

Carlisle scowled into the viewer. "Put somebody inside. And activate CALIFON. I want to know every move Brennan makes."

Chapter Nine

The sign on the door said: COMPCEL.

The COmPUte guardian *in* the door said: "Name, please?"

"Hooker-Brennan."

"Title and function."

"Ph.D. Member in Standing, Archeology Society." Brennan slid his chit into the aperture alongside the speaker, then waited two seconds while the door swung open.

He went to the front desk, grinned at the back of the gray-haired lady putting COMP requests into a file.

"Afternoon, Trish."

The woman turned around, did a double-take, then grinned ear to ear. "Brennan! For God's sake—what brings you back home?"

"Missed you, Trish."

"I bet. I wish." She gave his hand a squeeze. "And still not married. I can't believe some young thing hasn't seen what a catch you'd make."

"There's more than one reason to stay in the field," Brennan returned, mock scowling.

"But you can't stay out there forever." Trish rescued her hand as two other patrons walked by. She said more primly, "All right, Brennan. What can COMPCEL do for you?"

"I'm going to make a planetary grand tour. Judd Caskell, my dig foreman, has this crazy notion that Man migrated to the stars using numbers theory. Got some evidence, he says, too. Nuts, huh?"

"Well—"

"Personally," Brennan said, "I think he's wrong."

"But you'd like me to check it out."

"Uh huh. I told Judd I'd look into it."

"This wouldn't be something like PAMPAS, would it?" Trish looked at Brennan with a mischievous twinkle in her eyes.

"Bite your tongue, woman." Brennan grinned at her. PAMPAS was a program Brennan had foisted upon a stuffy zoology professor his freshman year. It delineated the habits of a burro-like creature living in the grassy uplands north of the university.

"How soon do you need an answer?" Trish asked. "COMPCEL is backlogged almost six weeks."

Brennan produced a two-page list of particulars, placed it on the counter. He smiled. "Tomorrow will be fine," he said.

After leaving COMPCEL, Brennan called up an old colleague, Kasim Hobbs. Hobbs had been Brennan's mentor during his university career. Now well into his eighties, the old man still taught, still bristled with an unquenchable life force. His classes, Brennan recalled fondly, were always near-chaotic *events*, crowded beyond capacity.

"There's a 'klatsch' organized for tonight," the old man said, after greetings had been exchanged. "Why don't you come?"

"Same place?"

"Sure. The Brisbane Club."

"I'll be there," Brennan said. "I need to talk to you, Kaz."

Hobbs's lined face showed its delight. "Come early— nine o'clock. The first glass is on you."

The Brisbane Club was behind the university's library, discreetly camouflaged in a rustic time-worn building that went back before the Fugue. Just after nine o'clock, Brennan strolled through the arched entranceway and made his way to the bar.

Students sat around in clumps, arguing heatedly, schooners of beer at their elbows. Brennan smiled as he seated himself. It brought back memories.

He was enjoying his second glass of dark ale when someone sat down beside him.

"It's good to see you again, Brennan." It was Hobbs, a bald sprite whose delighted smile could not be feigned.

"And you." Brennan grinned in return and put his arm around the old man's shoulders. He turned to the barmaid. "Duchess mead for the professor."

"Ah, you didn't forget." Hobbs took a long quaff from his glass when it arrived, set it back down with a satisfied sigh. He said, "All right, Brennan, what brings you back to Trospro? I thought you were happy out in the field."

"I was," Brennan said, and stopped. He looked at his glass ruminantly. "Kaz, what do you know about the two avatars?"

"The Shining Light? Kirst?" Hobbs looked a little startled. "Are we to discuss religion?"

"No."

"Myth, then." The old man nodded, glanced speculatively at his younger colleague. "What aspect did you want to explore?"

"Must the two of them *be* myth?"

"It might be we're back to religion," Hobbs said with a laugh. "Philosophically speaking, they're representatives of the old *yin* and *yang* theory. Is Good a real thing? Is Bad? If so, how are they represented?"

"Couldn't they just be men?" Brennan asked. "Two

men, their deeds blown out of proportion by whatever process is responsible for legends?"

"Um." Hobbs looked doubtful. "Anything's possible. But don't tell that to a priest. Anyway," the old man snagged his schooner and lifted it partway, "it's exceedingly hard to deny that there's *wrong* in the universe."

Brennan ordered a fresh drink. When it was delivered, he turned to look seriously at the other.

"Kaz, I think I've found proof that Kirst and The Shining Light are as human as you and I. Were, anyway."

Hobbs peered up at him. "From the look of you, you found *something*. Have some more ale, my young friend, and tell me about it."

Brennan shook his head. "I can't tell you any more than I have. But . . . I need a favor."

The old man's eyebrows shot skyward. "Well, I must say—you've managed to pique my curiosity. What can I do?"

"I need to hide from the Church."

"Hide—?"

"Disappear for a few days. They most probably have somebody shadowing me."

Hobbs thrust his hands into his pockets, took them out again, put them on the counter. He said worriedly, "You in trouble, Brennan?"

"Not yet."

"This relate to what we've been talking about—the legend thing?"

Brennan nodded.

"Umm." The old man muttered as though to himself. "Well, there's the *magus waltz*."

"What's that?"

"An old theater trick. It'll fool anyone who's not an expert."

"Have you used it before?" Brennan asked.

"No." The old man grinned suddenly. "But I'm a quick study—and a damned good natural actor."

Chapter Ten

Carlisle was getting conflicting reports, and he didn't like it.

Brother John and Brother Leopold, who had been tasked to follow Brennan wherever he went, said he was on Trospro. They'd attended two lectures he had given with Kasim Hobbs and were going to attend another the following day.

CALIFON, on the other hand, said Brennan was gone, tripping somewhere on the stargate pipeline.

"Send a message," Carlisle ordered curtly. "Brother John and Brother Leopold are to verify without question that Brennan is on Trospro."

"Yes, Monsignor." Fr Jacc made notes on a mnemonic recorder.

"Even," Carlisle continued sharply, "if it means confronting him directly."

When the old man had gone, Carlisle punched in Mayhan's number on the televiewer. As the technician's dark features appeared on the screen, Carlisle rasped, "Do a re-check of your last report. We have visual evidence that Brennan's still at the university."

Mayhan looked hurt. "The rating on this went right through the roof. If there's a visual, then it's a trick."

"We're double-checking," Carlisle assured him. "Meantime—run the program again."

Having done all he could for the present to ascertain Brennan's whereabouts, Carlisle switched his concentration to the stack of papers sent via messenger. Brennan's "grand tour" data, obtained from COMPCEL by Church writ. Carlisle would have preferred a more indirect route, but there wasn't time.

Some of it—most of it, maybe—was smokescreen. Had to be. Carlisle leafed idly through half a dozen pages. Quadrant coordinates, Gate windows, system primaries, luminaries, total number of satellites: too much for one person to make sense of; it would have to go to CALIFON or CALIFUR. He ground his teeth. What it meant was that Brennan had something he wanted to hide.

Brother John sat in the first row of the lecture hall, close enough to count the penny-sized freckles on Kasim Hobbs's bald head. To Hobbs's left, eyes sweeping restlessly to and fro, was W. Hooker-Brennan, Ph.D.

Brother John reached inside his cassock, took out a small light bomb of the kind used by Peacemakers to quell rioters. He noted without emotion that Professor Hobbs was fielding all questions. Only occasionally did Brennan speak, when directly addressed by Hobbs.

There was a sudden commotion at the doorway. Brother John glanced back for one brief second, saw Brother Leopold arguing heatedly with a student. Smiling somewhat sourly, Brother John tossed the light bomb onto the dais and covered his eyes. There was a searing flash half a meter from Brennan's chair.

Memo:
Leopold to Carlisle: Brennan not on Trospro. Used a holograph simulacrum programmed for spe-

cific response. In entertainment parlance called *magus waltz*. Kasim Hobbs willing accomplice. Shall we prosecute?

Memo:
Carlisle to Leopold: Why? The damage has already been done. Besides—we don't want to call attention to this. *Check all Gate logs!*

Halfway through the afternoon, a silver-clad emissary arrived from the many-columned edifice that was CALIFUR. He asked for and received permission to see Carlisle.

"My name is Follard, Monsignor," the man said. He stood stiffly, as though he was not entirely welcome.

"Have a seat," Carlisle told him, gesturing with a hand. "Fr Cols, get Mr. Follard some tea. Or perhaps you'd like something stronger?"

"Nothing." Follard remained standing.

"Umm." Carlisle sighed, waved the hovering Fr Cols away. He folded his hands in front of him. "It can't be good news, delivered like this. What is it?"

"The timetable has changed. CALIFUR shows the crisis rate accelerating."

Carlisle suppressed a groan. "How much time do we have?"

"Not more than ninety days."

Memo:
Mayhan to Carlisle: We've got high numbers! I'll bet a bottle of whiskey against a promotion Brennan shows up on Duvalle within forty-eight hours.

Chapter Eleven

The creed of the Endless Sabbat could be expressed in the simplest of equations:

Everybody's entitled to their own damn superstition.

The Sabbat was a movement without a mandate, an idea without a head. It was a rowdy counterculture of hedonists, artists, actors, thieves. And, against the Sabbat's philosophy of nonviolent passivity, the Church could do nothing but grind its teeth. Though headquartered on Duvalle by unspoken consensus, the Sabbat in truth stretched via the stargates to all major population centers.

"Guide, sir?" said one of the Sabbat when Brennan emerged from the Gate. The man was dressed in motley, his face painted with dazzling red-and-white checks.

Brennan couldn't help grinning. "I know my way," he murmured, shaking his head. Outside the Gate-plex he caught surface transportation to number 45 Salacia.

Jancy Pierce was in. She wasn't pleased to see him.

"I thought you'd come back sooner or later," she said, staring at him coldly. "Your priest friends have been following me ever since you left."

"Priests?" Brennan turned up his palms in mystification. Then he cursed softly and shook his head. "I suppose I should have known. The Church has a long arm—and I came here after seeing Gus."

"You mean you haven't told them about the artifacts?"

Brennan shook his head.

She moved stiffly away from him, then turned, puzzlement showing in her green-flecked eyes. "I don't understand you, Brennan. You're too moral to deal with Gus. So what is it—you can't let go? That picture got you? The story that girl told?"

"I'm in," Brennan told her. "All the way. I'm going to try to get those artifacts registered."

"Come on. You said so yourself—the Church can't allow it." The girl's tone was disbelieving.

"Perhaps not," Brennan said. He shrugged, then permitted himself a grim smile. "For *them*, it's a dilemma. For me, it's not. It's simply finding out what really happened." He gave a short laugh. "There's an archaic phrase that seems to fit the occasion."

"Oh? What might that be?"

"*Fiat justitia, ruat coelum.*"

"What does it mean?" Jancy asked, her mouth expressionless.

" 'Let justice be done—though the heavens fall.' "

"And they *will* fall, Brennan, if you bring it off," Jancy said ominously. "Have you told Gus?"

"He knows." Brennan was silent for a moment, looking about the room. He glanced abruptly at the girl, said worriedly, "If there have been priests snooping around, we'd better get a privacy COmPUte."

"Already have one," Jancy told him without hesitation. "They're standard equipment for the Sabbat."

"Umm." Brennan stirred restlessly, got up, paced around the small quarters. He said, "You still giving those performances?"

"A girl has to eat," Jancy said, her shoulders moving fractionally.

"Where did you learn to do that?"

"Dysip Breathing? I was taught by an old woman who died about five years back. She was a lot better at it than I am."

"Really? Then she must have been very good indeed." There was frank admiration in Brennan's gaze. He went to the window and stared out. Turning back, his face was sober. He said, "There's a man named Roki Lehngren. Sells black-market goods at auction. You know him?"

"No. But it's a big planet."

"Gus said he has a pit on the other side of the Wall."

"I've been to a few of the auctions," Jancy volunteered. "I know where they're held."

"Can you find out when the next one is—and take me there?"

The girl sat down on one of the cushions littering the room, tilted her head to stare at the other. "It'll be on the grapevine. There's a lot of traffic comes through here, Brennan. Lots more'n you'd think. I suppose I could take you."

To the left of the trail were deep ravines, their darkness softened somewhat by leafy scrub. Small creatures made night sounds as they scuttled for cover.

"If there are any priests following us, they'd do well to turn back now," Jancy said. She half turned in the darkness, tugged at Brennan's sleeve. "The auctions are not really organized by the Sabbat. They're done by freelance black marketeers, most often, from off Duvalle."

"And I suppose they're none too gentle with interlopers."

"They've never had any trouble. Mostly, I guess, because of the one they call the Frost Giant."

Brennan stumbled over a stone in the path, caught himself before he fell. "Gus didn't tell me about him."

"You can't lie to him, Brennan. Don't try." There was a faint shudder in the girl's voice.

The trail dipped suddenly, and the darkness grew almost full. Brennan followed closely behind Jancy, one hand lightly touching her arm. He was suddenly conscious of her as a woman, felt his body react.

"Steps, here," she murmured over her shoulder, and a moment later Brennan could discern faint lights in the distance ahead.

"We're underground," he said wonderingly.

"Natural caves," the girl returned shortly. "They run for kilometers—in all directions. Don't go wandering off by yourself."

When they entered the circle of lights, Brennan glanced around. The auction was in a pocket amphitheater. Bits of mica and quartz winked back at him from the steep, inward-leaning walls.

There were boxes stacked near half a dozen chalked-off circles. The 'pits', Brennan guessed, that Gus had spoken of.

"Almost fifty buyers," Jancy said, jerking him back to the here and now. "That's a pretty good turnout."

"Where's Roki Lehngren?"

"They haven't started the auction yet. Most likely he's back in one of the tunnels, making a private deal."

Without moving his head, Brennan let his gaze roam the amphitheater. It was not as big as it first appeared, he decided, though the deep shadows made its true dimensions guesswork.

Brennan and Jancy were jostled by several of the crowd, and Brennan spent a moment studying them. For the most part they seemed ordinary enough. Their clothes were dark, inconspicuous, their tones subdued.

"Behind you," Jancy said, tapping Brennan's shoulder. He swung around, saw someone emerging from a pie-shaped wedge of darkness. The man was small, thin, with a wisp of blond moustache.

"You Brennan?" the man asked suspiciously One hand remained hidden within his jacket pocket.

"That's right," Brennan said.

"I'm Roki Lehngren. I heard you were looking for me."

"Gus Pierce said you were an honest man," Brennan said, smiling a little. "Is that true?"

"You know Gus?" was all Lehngren said in reply.

The archeologist gave a curt nod, indicated Jancy with a slight motion. "This is his sister."

The thin man mulled it over for the space of five seconds, staring at Brennan with hard, black eyes. "All right," he said at last, "so you know Gus. What has that got to do with me?"

"Gus said you owe him a favor," Brennan returned evenly. "I'm here to collect it."

Lehngren snorted. "Collect it for a dead man?"

"It's all in your perspective." Brennan's lips twisted in what might have been a smile. "*Gus* still thinks he's alive."

Lehngren smiled coldly, then barked a laugh. "You've got a point. All right. You go see the Frost Giant. If he says you got a favor coming, I'll make sure you get it—for Gus."

Brennan looked around, saw nothing but ribs of shadow. "Where do I find him?"

Lehngren pointed a skinny finger, showing his teeth in a grin. "Follow along that wall to the first tunnel. Take that as far as it goes."

"How will he know we're coming?" Jancy asked. She looked apprehensively at the darkness.

"Don't you worry about that," Lehngren leered. "I've never seen him surprised. Not in fifteen years. No go on—I've got to open my pit." He swaggered away toward one of the chalked circles.

"Have you ever met the Frost Giant?" Brennan asked, as they entered the tunnel and proceeded along it.

The breath hissed in Jancy's throat. "No, but I've heard *about* him."

"And?"

"He was once a Peacemaker," the girl said. "Only he was injured somehow ... terribly, and given up for dead."

"By his own men?"

"That's right. By his own men." Jancy stumbled

and caught Brennan's arm. "They say he hates them now—will do anything to cause them harm."

They came to a series of steps leading upward. The tunnel was wide at this point, and high enough so that Brennan could not touch the ceiling standing on tiptoe.

"There's light ahead," Jancy said, relief in her voice. Their steps quickened. Almost without realizing it, they were in a bowl-shaped cavern, its sides and roof illuminated by some primitive kind of COmPUte.

The Frost Giant was curled up on a small couch that sagged beneath his weight. His eyes were open and directed at Brennan and Jancy, but they did not blink, and he did not acknowledge their presence.

"Oh!" murmured Jancy in a small voice.

Brennan did not know what to think. The man's close-cropped hair was white. His skin showed the pallid whiteness of underground existence, though here and there on his neck and face brown splotches had begun to form.

Slowly, so slowly the effort seemed excruciating, the Frost Giant came to life. He seemed ageless, an immense troll of unusual musculature. The hands and arms of the man were massive, ridged with veins and knots of muscle. His skull was strangely deformed and ugly, smaller on one side than the other; it looked pushed in. Mottled masses of scar tissue spanned his temple.

His eyes, Brennan noted last, were pale blue, the wintry frozen color of glacier ice.

"So," the Frost Giant said. "*You're* the one they're following." His voice was flat.

Brennan felt the hair rise on the back of his head. "Followed—here?" The accusation was like a blow.

"No. To Duvalle," said the Frost Giant. He straightened his torso and popped the knuckles on one massive hand. Staring at Brennan, he said musingly, "It would be CALIFUR, maybe—or one of the smaller ones."

"Huh?"

The Frost Giant licked his lips, and Brennan glimpsed the thick wedge of tongue as it darted out.

"Not your fault. You couldn't have known."

Brennan could think of nothing to say.

"Way to beat it," the hulk muttered as though to himself. "Counter and stymie." He started to chuckle, the sound like stones dropped in sand.

"What are you talking about?" In spite of himself, Brennan was getting angry.

The giant looked up, narrowed his eyes. "Sorry. Sometimes I have to think a long time before I talk." He stopped and licked his lips again. "Because I have only half a brain."

Jancy was pale, her lips a thin narrow line. "The *right* half."

The Frost Giant chuckled again. "Correct. *And* a few million neurons left over from the damaged side—enough to do the caretaking."

Brennan was about to say something but thought better of it. Jancy was doing just fine.

"You said they were following Brennan," the girl said. "You think they know he's here, in the catacombs?"

"Maybe, maybe not." The giant shrugged his huge shoulders. "But against an Intuitive he's *sooo* predictable."

Brennan smiled a strained smile. "What can I do?"

"Maybe fight fire with fire," the former Peacemaker responded slowly. He heaved himself up off the couch. "I'm intuitive, too—what's left of me. Maybe the computer and I, we'd cancel each other out." The chuckle continued, a humorless cascade of sound.

"I want to register two artifacts Gus Pierce brought back from the Cone," Brennan told the other. "The Church will try to stop me."

The Frost Giant folded his arms across his chest and licked his lips once more.

"I can help you. You willing to pay?"

Brennan was amazed that avarice ran deeper than the man's hatred of his own kind. Then he shrugged. If money was all it took . . .

"I'm willing," he said, nodding.

"It will be steep."

"No matter." If necessary, he could draw upon the not inconsiderable resources of the Hooker-Brennan Trading Co. His family would love it—it would give them a long-sought hold on him.

"Agreed, then." The giant smiled for the first time, showing dirty teeth. He unfolded his arms, pointed across the room. "Chairs over there. We got some time, enough to give me a picture."

Presently, as briefly as possible, Brennan summarized the events leading him first to Gus, then on to Duvalle and Trospro. When he reached the point where he left Kasim Hobbs and Gated off-planet, he hesitated for a moment, marshaling his thoughts. "I went to the museums," he said, continuing. "And the libraries. All those places Gus had been denied access to." He paused again, looked at Jancy and the Frost Giant. "There were traces, sure. Reference, footnotes— enough to eliminate thousands of star systems. But *not* enough to pin down Doubab's location."

"So how can Roki Lehngren help you?" Jancy wanted to know.

"Because I *did* get enough to point me in a direction. The information I need is in the Hamman Wing of the Archives. I even have the aisle numbers."

"Nobody gets into the Archives," the Frost Giant grunted, narrowing his eyes. "Only properly assigned priests."

"Not legally, anyhow," Brennan affirmed.

"What's there—in the Archives?" Jancy asked.

"Hieroglyphics," Brennan replied, giving her a glance. "Some sort of alien records. They were found on Doubab."

The Frost Giant sat down again on the couch. After a brittle silence he said, "Roki will help you, Brennan. So will I. But remember the price. Now leave me. I want to think this over."

Halfway out of the cavern they could hear the Frost Giant chuckling again; the sound seemed to come from everywhere.

Chapter Twelve

Monsignor Carlisle did not like his devotions to be interrupted. As he knelt before the altar, he could see Fr Jacc from the corner of one eye. The old man seemed unusually active, hopping from one foot to the other, then turning to see if Carlisle had risen yet. As a consequence, Carlisle deliberately remained longer than he had intended. He said a second prayer for Fr Jacc.

"*Laus Deo!*"

The old man started forward, but then, remembering his place, took a step back.

"*Laus Deo!*"

Fr Jacc remained still.

"*Laus Deo!*"

Carlisle rose, genuflected, and prepared to retire from the chapel.

"Monsignor!"

Fr Jacc had had the decency to wait until he was through.

"What is it?" Carlisle asked with some asperity.

"Archbishop Drayton is waiting for you—in your office."

The Archbishop was a dried-up husk too small for his gold-threaded cloak and emerald raiments. His eyes, however, were bright and calculating.

He waited until Carlisle had kissed his ring. Then he said, "The Daiists know something is amiss."

Carlisle gave an inward sigh. "It was bound to happen, my Lord. Too many things have been happening on too many levels. It was inevitable that something would get out."

"What do you suggest?" Drayton looked at him expectantly, hopefully.

"Tell them," Carlisle said, giving it no more than a moment's reflection. "Only not everything. They'll have to catch up to where we are—and by that time we'll be that much further ahead." He paused, gave a small smile. "In the meantime, our Order can take credit for having given the alarm."

"Umm." The Archbishop considered his counsel, but did not say *aye* nor *nay*. Instead, he asked, "How goes your surveillance of Dr. Hooker-Brennan?"

"As well as might be expected, your Lordship. He has been on Duvalle three days. He lives quietly, for the most part."

"And still we do not know what it is Gus Pierce brought out of the Cone."

"No, your Lordship."

"What of the information obtained from COMP-CEL?"

"We're still working on it. Sooner or later we will find a pattern there—if, indeed, there is one."

The Archbishop stood up and marched about the room, hands clasped behind his back. "You are getting maximum cooperation from Bishop Poole?"

"It's been quite satisfactory."

"And your staff is sufficient?"

"Yes, your Lordship."

Drayton stopped pacing long enough to stare at his

subordinate. "You're probably wondering why I came here unannounced."

"I do admit to some puzzlement, your Lordship," Carlisle replied. He waited, and when no response was forthcoming, he murmured, "I'm sure your reasons were meritorious."

"I've come to consult CALIFUR," Drayton told him. He looked pale. "I want to see if this means the end of the Morganite Order."

"Oh, surely not, my Lord!"

"The Daiists have been hounding us for decades," Drayton complained. "They would like nothing better than to wound us mortally—"

"You mean," Carlisle said, looking up, "if they should use us as a scapegoat."

"Yes."

"But no one knows yet what form the crisis will take. There's no reason to suspect it will fall solely upon the Morganites. It could fall upon the Daiists as well."

Drayton looked somber. "But they are many, and we are few. What would be a minor setback for them would be unmitigated disaster for us."

"And they would have CALIFUR," Carlisle said.

"Exactly," said Archbishop Drayton.

Long after the Archbishop had gone, Carlisle sat behind his desk and contemplated the message Drayton brought. The Daiists were ruthless enough, he granted that. But would they do away with an Order ... to obtain an Intuitive? The answer, he decided, was yes.

Later that afternoon he got a flash from CALIFON:

Mayhan to Carlisle: This is crazy! All I'm getting are low levels of undefined mush. Either something's wrong with CALIFON, or Brennan's vanished into thin air.

Chapter Thirteen

From 3,000 kilometers out, Spyre was beautiful, an oyster-shell goddess traced with lines of blue and green. Circling the planet, like dark stones in a shallow pool, were the Archive moons. Once, in the time lost before the Fugue, there had been five. The remainder of that fifth satellite circled Spyre in a faint ring of stony debris.

"About another hour ought to do it," Roki Lehngren said, glancing out of the spacecraft's front viewport. He frowned. "I sure hope Frosty knows what he's talking about. These moons used to have some heavy defenses."

"Even if they knew we were here, the Library Order wouldn't fire on us," Brennan said. He was seated behind Roki and to his left. His view of Spyre was limited to a single high-albedo arc.

"Could be automatic," the other man maintained stubbornly. "These are pre-Fugue repositories."

"Why would they *need* defenses?" Jancy asked from her seat against the bulkhead. "Who would want to destroy a library?"

"It's too bad they're not here to ask," Roki grumbled over his shoulder. He bent to his controls, hitting buttons with more enthusiasm than skill.

It had been Roki's idea to steal the little mining tug.

"Well, we can't use the Gate inside the Archives," he'd grunted with perfect logic when Brennan objected. "You leave everything to Frosty and me." He shot Brennan a wicked grin. "Besides, *you* can't go around making plans—CALIFUR'd twig in a moment."

Two weeks and three days of travel confined between the bulkheads of the tug had created areas of friction. Brennan, used to making his own decisions, was frustrated and angry. Roki, who was discharging his duty to Gus Pierce and pocketing a large amount of Brennan's money, couldn't have cared less.

Only Jancy had kept the two from each other's throats.

"Which one is Ramman?" she asked now, peering out the port.

"It has two mountain ranges," Roki told her. "And a crater at least twenty kilometers across."

Fifteen minutes later Jancy yelled, "Got it!" and pointed excitedly. Roki grinned in self-satisfaction and trimmed the craft, shedding most of their velocity in the meantime.

When they had achieved a stable orbit only kilometers from the moon's pocked surface, Roki shut down the engines and pushed himself out of his chair.

"I'm going to get a drink," he announced as he floated toward the ship's gangway. "A big one. Then I'm going to get me about eighteen hours sleep."

Perplexed, Brennan struggled with his chair clamp. "Wait a minute, dammit! And then what?"

"Then we wait," answered the vanishing Roki. "That's all—just wait."

"Predictability," Jancy said, her palms flat on the chartroom table, her arms straight. "It's your Achilles' heel. One of the Intuitives has locked onto you like a limpet mine. You *can't* make your own decisions. Gus did—and look what happened to him."

"But *this*," Brennan returned fiercely, gesturing with both hands, "is outright lunacy. We've been sitting off Ramman for almost a week. It's time we did something."

"We are doing something," Roki said from the doorway. He shoved off the archway with one hand and drifted slowly toward them. He caught himself at the last moment by snagging one of the light fixtures.

"What?"

The black marketeer righted himself, pulled up a chair, sat down facing Brennan. "There's another ship due here in about six hours. I spotted him just now from the conn."

"Another ship? Who's in it?"

Roki shrugged. "Frosty keeps some secrets from me, too. Better that way. I think it's our break-in-and-enter man."

"I thought *we* were going to do that."

Roki's lips twisted. "What you think is your business. But what we *do* is something else. We have to keep one step ahead of the Intuitives, don't we?"

This incoming ship was even smaller than the mining tug. But whoever was piloting it was a better helmsman than Roki had proved to be. With minimum maneuvering, the tiny craft placed itself in orbit less than a kilometer from its companion.

Roki contacted it by laser, out of earshot of Brennan and Jancy. The two watched, however, as an hour later, the tiny craft edged in toward Ramman.

Brennan had given the Frost Giant a description of the twisting corridors inside the Archive Wing, writing out in detail where the hieroglyphics might be stored. At the time, he had not seen the point of it. Now, however, as he watched a spacesuited figure emerge from the ship and disappear toward the Archive's outer lock, he wished he had been more explicit.

The tug was not in synchronous orbit. Darkening

shadows on Ramman's surface replaced the mountains' bright relief. In less than 10 minutes the other craft was out of sight.

"What's our orbit time?" Brennan demanded.

"Forty-five minutes," Roki replied. He shrugged. "We *could* pull out to a longer orbit—but why bother?"

"What if he gets into trouble?"

"Look," the black marketeer grinned crookedly before shaking his head, "the longer the plane, the more likely it is we'll be noticed by the Archivists. We're nice and dark here. Anyway," he looked at the other challengingly, "it would take at least forty-five minutes to maneuver into high orbit."

"Why do you suppose we *haven't* been noticed?" Jancy put in. "They're supposed to have some pretty sophisticated detection devices on the Archive moons."

"Frosty said we'd be all right," Roki said. "Besides, there aren't many Librarians. And what few there are are *old*."

"That can't be said of a COmPUte," Brennan stated unequivocally.

Roki shrugged, kicked himself off the bulkhead in a long somersault heading toward the galley. "Just *wait*, Brennan. Things will turn out fine."

Forty-five minutes later, the tug again passed over the Archive Wing's outer lock.

"See anything?" Jancy asked, peering over Brennan's shoulder.

Below them Ramman spun by with agonizing slowness, her colors a mixture of dingy red and loesslike yellow.

"No . . . no . . . wait a minute." Brennan's eyes caught movement on the moon's surface. "There!" he exclaimed, pointing.

A spacesuited figure was striding purposefully away from the Archive's outer lock. Something about it bothered Brennan. Something—

"There's our boy," Roki announced cheerfully from the other port. "He should be in orbit by the time we make another pass."

The black marketeer spent the final minutes of their next revolution getting into one of the tug's four pressure suits. All of them were equally ill-fitting and malodorous. All were covered with gouge patches. "It doesn't look like tug work is all that profitable," the little man remarked with a sour grin. As he hefted his cumbersome helmet, he said, "Just keep everything running as is. I'll be back in no time."

Something had been bothering Brennan, and now it rose up in him like a bubble. Without stopping to think, he moved closer to Roki, lifted him off his feet, and pinned him against the suiting room wall.

"Hey! What's going on?" Surprise froze Roki's features, surprise that turned rapidly to anger.

"You're not going over there," Brennan stated flatly. "I am."

"That's out! Frosty said . . ."

Brennan didn't wait for the other man to finish. In the bulky suit, and without access to his weapons, he didn't present much of a threat. Brennan picked the struggling form up bodily and stowed it in an empty tool locker.

"Goddamn it, Brennan—!"

Brennan cut him off by slamming and dogging the door. Then, ignoring Jancy's wide-eyed look of puzzlement, he dragged a second suit out of its cubicle.

"Have you lost your mind?" the girl demanded. "When you're *this* close to getting what you were after?"

"You can let him out when I've cleared the air lock," Brennan told her, climbing into the suit. "By then it'll be too late to stop me."

"Why are you doing this?"

Brennan started to answer, stopped, shook his head dumbly. "I know it doesn't seem to make sense, but . . . something just didn't fit." He shrugged as well as he was able, slapped the helmet over his head.

Outside the tug, stars hung in bright majestic clusters, too many for Brennan to count. He oriented himself by climbing over the top of the spacecraft.

Through one of the ports he caught a glimpse of Jancy releasing an apoplectic Roki.

The other ship was less than a kilometer away, dark and tiny, its orbit a little below that of the tug. He crossed to it using the suit's four rocket motors and an angling COmPUte that obligingly locked him onto his target.

Approaching the other's airlock, he became aware of an insistent background buzz. His suit detector said something was leaking radiation. He banged a fist on the air lock door, waited an intolerable thirty seconds before the outer shell slid aside.

It took longer than necessary to cycle him through. Brennan thought of using the controls on the wall of the air lock. He was reaching for one of the switches when the inner door rotated open.

The background buzz reached an abrupt crescendo. Brennan grabbed the edge of the inner lock and shot through into the ship, stopping only when he hit the far bulkhead.

The pilot was seated in his command chair, his face flushed, pinched with pain.

"Judd!" Brennan cracked his helmet, kicked off the bulkhead.

Judd Caskell lifted his head only slightly, let it fall back weakly against the chair.

"How, man? Why? Why?" Brennan covered the final few meters in a headlong tumble. Then he reached up, his gloved hands clumsy on his friend's shoulder.

Caskell was hemorrhaging, tiny blood vessels bursting beneath his flesh, making his skin slippery.

"God—why'd you do it, Judd?" Brennan asked again, meaninglessly. His eyes suddenly stung. "That part of the Archives must have been seething with radiation."

"Didn't k-know it," Caskell said, his tongue thick in his mouth. "Suit never indicated trouble." He stopped, breathed deeply. "Got what you wanted,

Bren. It's over there." One massive finger lifted, fell back.

Brennan's glance fell on a sealed carry-all near the air lock. He instantly wished he'd never heard of Gus Pierce, of the artifacts now tainted with his friend's blood. He sailed across the room to Caskell's pressure suit, examined the radiation detector, prying at it with his finger. Up close it was easy to see; someone had cut the wire to the alarm.

It came to Brennan then, as he dropped the suit and turned back to Caskell. The Archivists had not had to guard Ramman. Whatever had destroyed Spyre's fifth moon had left Ramman a contaminated hulk. The agent would be radioactive cobalt, perhaps—or iodine. Something with a half-life measured in millennia. No *wonder* Ramman didn't need defenses.

"Knew it was you," Caskell was mumbling, his face a mask of pain. "Instructions ... all in your scribble."

Brennan cursed with slow-mounting fury. It was apparent, finally, why the Peacemaker required written directions. He'd needed someone like Caskell, a professional. Someone who would recognize Brennan's hieroglyphics.

There was a light blinking on the ship's console—the tug, trying to contact him on the laser link. Brennan ignored it, pushed himself back to the dying Caskell.

"I can help you," the Frost Giant said. "You willing to pay?"

"I'm willing," Brennan said.

"Goddamnit!" Brennan yelled. "Hang on! There's a Gate right here in the Archives. We'll get you through to Geste, keep you alive."

"No," murmured Caskell. He stared through blood-filled eyes. His head abruptly sagged. "It's too late for that."

"The price will be steep," the Frost Giant said.

"It doesn't matter," Brennan replied.

Brennan's fist crashed impotently against the ship's console. He felt helpless rage, an all-consuming anger. Damn! Damn! If he'd known . . . he'd never have paid *this* price.

Chapter Fourteen

Carlisle had reduced Brennan's "grand tour" information to a manageable pile. He thumbed through it, expecting some pattern to jump up at him. He thought he knew the way the archeologist's mind worked and, hidden beneath the surface frustration, he admitted to a certain reluctant admiration.

"You look tired, sir," Fr Cols said, leaning solicitously over his shoulder. "You should rest for a few hours."

Carlisle *did* feel tired, but without giving it much thought, decided to go on. He rubbed his eyes wearily and shook off Fr Cols' hand. The old man meant well, but perhaps that was the problem. Everyone meant well, and very little was getting done.

"What are the numbers coming from CALIFON?"

"Still low level, sir. But Mr. Mayhan is constantly making adjustments."

"Umm." Carlisle bit his lip, held his temper in check. Mayhan, give him credit, had been sleeping with the Intuitive for the best part of a week.

A light began to blink on Carlisle's desk. He punched

a button and the televiewer sprang to life. A mission
novitiate stuttered, then ducked his head in respect.

"Beg pardon, Monsignor. There's a messenger here.
He says he will talk to no one but you."

"Send him up," Carlisle ordered brusquely. Mo-
tioning Fr Cols to leave the room, he activated the
recording devices hidden inside the desk. It was possible Bishop Poole would ask for a record of this
meeting.

The messenger was only a boy, however. Thin, ir-
reverent, dressed in the outlandish style of the Sabbat. Without deference or preamble he handed over a
sealed document pouch.

"I'm to take back an answer."

Carlisle refrained from comment. Instead, he simply broke the seal and extracted the message.

Braganza to Carlisle: Brennan back on Duvalle.
Entered Daiist Mission with request tour of 22
LUO worlds. Suspect petition favorably received.
Answer expected within 72 hours. (Ancillary in-
formation) Forgive me, Father, for I have sinned.
I bribed a low-echelon priest. To wit: LUO list.

Below the message was the list. Carlisle scanned it
quickly, noticed similarities and discrepancies from
the "grand tour" information. He noted also that all
22 in the LUO list were under Daiist control.

"What's your answer?" the boy asked.

"My answer," Carlisle responded sourly, "is that
it's time I took a personal interest in what's going on.
Wait here a few minutes. I'm going to accompany
you to Duvalle."

Carlisle had never been to the home world of the
Sabbat. He was unprepared for the assault on his
senses. Everywhere were ripe odors and discordant
colors. The boy, who had patently refused to give his
name, vanished the moment they emerged from the
Gate.

With the Sister of Bryan close on his heels, Carlisle made for the Daiist Mission. She, he noted from the corner of his eye, accepted the hubbub and jostling with near total equanimity.

The priest manning the reception desk stared goggle-eyed when Carlisle entered the Mission, but caught himself in time. Carlisle could almost hear his mind working: *An Indexer! Is he lost—or merely insane?*

"I must talk to Dr. W. Hooker-Brennan," Carlisle stated forcefully. "Do you know where he might be found?"

"Uh." The priest saw Sister Kathleen behind Carlisle and bobbed his head respectfully. Something, Carlisle couldn't help noticng, he hadn't done for a Monsignor of the Morganite Order.

"Yes, my Lord," the priest finally managed. "He is staying at number 46 Salacia, Inner City."

The address rang a bell. Gus Pierce's sister had a small apartment there. He gave his thanks, somewhat reluctantly blessed the Mission, and as soon as propriety permitted, exited to the street. There were plenty of floater cabs, and he hailed one.

In 10 minutes' time he and Sister Kathleen were deposited before a narrow archway. Carlisle stepped within, carefully counted the doors, and knocked.

Brennan himself opened the door. If he was surprised, he didn't show it.

"Hello, Carlisle."

"Good afternoon, Dr. Brennan." The Morganite hesitated, not sure of his ground. "May I come in?"

"Sure," Brennan said without smiling. He waved a hand toward an attractive girl just rising from a cushion. "Meet Jancy Pierce. It's her brother you put inside that glass coffin."

"Correction," Carlisle said dryly. "He put himself there." He murmured a few words to the Sister of Bryan and closed the door. "She'll wait outside. What we have to talk about should not leave this room."

"We don't have anything *to* talk about," Brennan

muttered grimly. "You're a dangerous man, Carlisle—you and your damned Intuitives."

So he knows about that, Carlisle thought. He studied the archeologist thoughtfully. Something about the other man had changed. He seemed bitter, harder.

"You've asked to visit twenty-two worlds," Carlisle said, one side of his mouth drooping slightly. "Almost all of them are on the *limited access* list."

"So what?" Brennan's lean face was suffused with anger. "They're all outside Morganite authority."

"Quite true," Carlisle admitted. "Nevertheless, a formal objection from my Bishop would contravene your tour." Actually he wasn't so sure that was true. But, since it had never been attempted, he gave himself the benefit of the doubt.

"Why would your Bishop issue such an objection?" Jancy Pierce interjected at that moment. She gazed with open hostility at the priest. She was startlingly pretty, Carlisle thought, with her deep dark eyes and high-ridged cheekbones. She looked not at all like her brother.

"You're fencing with me," he said, gently but distinctly. "Your tour has much to do with the artifact Gus brought back from Corthun."

"Really?" Jancy sat down unceremoniously on one of the cushions and cradled her legs. She gave him a wicked smile. "Prove it!"

"I can't," Carlisle said. "Not just yet." He turned to Brennan. "I might suggest an alternative to the objection I described."

Brennan looked at him distrustfully. "Oh? What?"

The priest clasped his hands together behind his back and squared his shoulders a little. "The canons state you must be accompanied by a Church monitor when visiting LUO worlds. I want you to request me."

"An Indexer? Don't be silly!" Brennan stared at Carlisle with an expression of amazement.

"It is the only way I will allow you to go," Carlisle declared flatly. He stared at the other. "It *is* permitted. Many times priests from some other Order have ventured through Morganite Gates."

"And the Daiists—won't they be suspicious?"

Carlisle unclasped his hands. "When I visited your excavations on Pio-Tan, Dr. Brennan, I was quite genuinely intrigued by your skill in unearthing pre-Fugue artifacts. That, I think, is on record. It will allay whatever suspicions the Daiists may have."

"Tell him *no*," Jancy said coldly from her mat on the floor.

"There's something else, isn't there?" Brennan said with sudden insight. He gaze swept the priest's face. "Something we don't know about."

"What do you mean?"

The archeologist shrugged. "Maybe the Daiists didn't know Gus was in the Cone. Maybe they didn't know he brought back an artifact."

"Of course they knew," Carlisle demurred. "Geste is one of the worlds under their jurisdiction. They were told when Gus was admitted."

Brennan would not let it go. "Why are *you* hounding us, then? Why not some Daiist inquisitor—or one of their bloody Peacemakers?" His face was suddenly savage.

"Because," Carlisle answered with a frozen smile, "the Daiists do not know that Pierce asked to speak to *you*." He paused, watching their faces. "Nor do they know of your subsequent actions. Not yet, anyway." He grimaced faintly, said, "In the meantime, you must decide about your tour."

"Yes, then," Brennan said suddenly. "The answer is yes—you can go with us." He radiated raw anger. "That way I'll damned well know where you are!"

Chapter Fifteen

Crucis and Kapunam were hot worlds—flat, dusty, lifeless. One or two of the others—mere numbers in a chartbook to Brennan—had been forbiddingly hostile.

Masaryk was the eighth planet on the tour. *It* was simply . . . cold.

They camped their first night on a plateau amid a small range of mountains. Powdery snow with the consistency of grains of sand peppered their shelters. The wind funneling the snow through the passes sometimes gusted to gale force.

With daybreak, the winds abated. Brennan stepped out of his shelter, watched a formation of clouds as they extended themselves into fingers and then into trailing lines of base-metal gray.

"Not very hospitable, is it?" Jancy emerged from her own shelter, gave Brennan a flash of white teeth. Her hood was thrown back, revealing a wealth of platinum hair.

"Uh uh." Brennan scuffed snow with his boots, squinted down at the small patch of stone he'd uncovered. It was granite, but of a peculiar color. Mostly feldspar, he guessed. He shivered as the wind picked up again, looked over at Jancy. "Come on. It'll be warmer in the lower elevations—out of the wind."

She stared around her. "Is Masaryk a post-Fugue name?"

Brennan suppressed a grin. "Do you mean is Masaryk the new-age name for Doubab? Yes, I think it is."

"Then we'll find proof that Pan Kirst lived here."

"It's possible," Brennan admitted. Then he shook his head, frowning slightly. "Of course there might not be anything *to* find. Twelve hundred years, give or take, is a damned long time."

"There'd be traces, though, even then—wouldn't there? Metals, plastics, ceramics?"

"Most times I'd say yes," Brennan said. "But they could be buried under ice packs—I don't think avalanches are uncommon here. Or earthquakes could change the whole landscape." He peered down into a valley dark with morning shadow. "And even if we do find proof, it might not be conclusive."

"Oh, great! With that attitude, you're practically home free." Jancy's eyebrows pulled themselves into a scowl.

Brennan couldn't help laughing. "Just trying to be realistic. Actually, I think our chances of finding *something* are pretty good." He moved past the shelters to a floater covered with weather-beaten skin. Pulling at the skin, he said, "Anyway, we brought along one of the best sniffers money can buy." He lifted a suitcase-sized device out of the vehicle, patted it affectionately. "This is a state-of-the-art earth sifter. Gives basal readings down to parts per billion, has a depth range measured in tens of meters."

"Will it work on ice?"

"If it's not too settled." Brennan put the earth sifter back into the floater's crib, finished rolling up the weather-beaten skin. Tucking the protective covering away, he looked back at Jancy. "It's time we got started. Go see what's keeping Carlisle, would you?"

The girl ducked her head inside the third shelter, then stood up and scanned the approaches. "He's not there. He probably went sightseeing."

"Damn fool!" Brennan muttered under his breath. He clambered aboard the floater, lifted it off the surface, guided it gently forward.

"Yep, there he is." Jancy extended a gloved finger, pointing off to the southwest.

The Morganite was approaching the camp along a narrow swale of rocks. As he climbed up onto the plateau, his face dissolved into a rapturous smile. "The view from over there is magnificent! You can see the entire valley."

"How long have you been up, Monsignor?" Jancy asked.

"Oh, before daybreak." He looked from one to the other. "I did not want to wake either of you."

Brennan allowed the floater to settle beneath him, crunching the hardpacked snow.

"You should have," he said furiously. "Going off alone like that is just damned stupid."

"But it was light enough to see," Carlisle protested, and then stopped, two spots in his cheeks. He stared at Brennan for a long moment.

"You could have been killed," Jancy said softly then. "That's what he means."

Carlisle glanced her way, nodded somewhat abruptly. "I realize that, my child. And I hold no grudge for explicit language used with good intent."

Brennan snorted, swung out of the floater, began breaking down shelters.

"I did notice," the priest remarked sometime later, "that the mountain has a sort of natural descent—a series of staggered plateaus."

Brennan said nothing. He couldn't help hear the unfeigned enthusiasm in the other man's voice, however. If Carlisle were not a priest, he decided, he'd maybe make a decent archeologist.

The shadows were gone by the time the floater reached the mountain's base. Brennan stopped the vehicle, turned his head, stared back the way they'd come. There were ice-shrouded cliffs halfway up, and wind-devils still farther along. He watched as one swirling devil knocked loose an overhang of snow. Inexplicably, he shivered.

"Lonesome enough place," Jancy said as though she, too, felt a certain oppressiveness.

"We'll set up a base camp over there on the flat," Brennan said, snapping out of it. He maneuvered the craft across a shallow ravine and brought it to a halt. Getting out, he said, "We'll use one big shelter this time."

It was two days before Brennan found the first indisputable trace of previous occupation. He was methodically skimming the mountain's base, blocking it off into sections, trying to ignore the quickening wind. Going over a low spot, the earth-sifter's tell-tale suddenly came alive.

A crashing sound on one of the slopes drew his attention. He stopped the floater and stood beside it, canting his head at an angle to look. An ice ledge had broken off, starting a glittering cascade of crystals. The colors . . . *damn!* Unlike anything he'd ever seen before. The mountain could almost be alive, if your mind ran to that. Brennan grinned at himself, at his fancies.

After a moment he remembered the basal readings—concentrations of refined metals, worked stone, bits of organic matter. Earth movements had hidden some of it, but there was enough to be sure. Man had lived here, most likely right where he was standing. He looked down, brushed away the snow cover, picked up a handful of small stones. They crumbled into fine powder under the pressure of his fingers. The rock was old here, rotten with weathering.

"When can we start digging?" Jancy asked that

evening. Her eyes were bright, catching the light of the fire.

"Day after tomorrow," Brennan said. "I want to map the parameters first, find someplace to screen the detritus."

Carlisle had been silent during the evening meal, his round face troubled.

"This place is the real reason for your 'tour', isn't it?" he asked now, looking with steady eyes at the archeologist. "The rest of it—Crucis, Kapunam—all that was just window-dressing."

Brennan started to deny it, then shrugged and returned the other's gaze. He had had enough intrigue— he was sick of it. Besides, there was little Carlisle could do except complain. The Gate on top of the mountain wouldn't open for another 16 days.

"That's right. There was a lodge here at one time— and a sort of research station. We intend to authenticate it."

Carlisle poured himself a cup of coffee with an unsteady hand, then set it down without tasting it. He looked puzzled. "Why keep that from me? Why go to such elaborate extremes to obfuscate the issue?" His face took on a pinched look. "It has to do with Gus Pierce, doesn't it?"

"Yes, it has to do with Gus," Jancy answered almost immediately. She was seated on a camp chair, her long legs basketed in her arms. Now, looking at the priest, her eyebrows acquired a sardonic tilt. "How strong is your faith, Monsignor?"

"What do you mean?"

"Do you want to tell him, Brennan—or should I?"

She was deliberately antagonizing the Morganite. Brennan understood her anger well enough. Were it not for the Church, Gus Pierce would be more than simply a latent corpse. And were it not for the Church, Brennan reminded himself, Judd Caskell would still be alive.

"We believe," he said, watching a pulse beat in Carlisle's throat, "that Kirst was merely a man, not a god. We think there's proof that he lived here—maybe died here."

"Kirst isn't a man," Carlisle chided. "No, no . . . it's impossible!" His face paled, then regained its color. "You don't know what you're talking about."

"Holy writ says The Shining Light battles Kirst eternally," Brennan went on. "We intend to prove that there was only *one* battle, and that it happened up on that mountain." He stopped, feeling almost sorry for the priest. Then he said, "Setsen Dai lost."

Carlisle's voice went gravelly. "And you intend to find that out here . . . in these ruins you've discovered?"

"That's right."

"You will fail."

"Perhaps."

Carlisle picked up his coffee cup. "You cannot find *Good* and *Evil* buried in the ground. I'm relieved that you've told me. Now I can enjoy your efforts more fully."

"You cannot accept that Setsen Dai and Kirst were once human?" Brennan asked.

The priest was silent for so long that Brennan thought he had not heard. Then, softly, the Morganite said, "My faith has always been my bastion. Prove what you say. You will find that the Church, too, is interested in finding out the truth."

"As long as it's your *particular* truth," Jancy said tautingly.

"No, wait a minute. It may be we're not being fair," Brennan told the girl. He moved his shoulders in a shrug. "Gus said Monsignor Carlisle really believes in the precepts of his religion, and that he was a man of integrity."

"He said that of me?" Carlisle was astounded.

"Yeah, well, he didn't mean it as a compliment," Brennan said with a grimace. He scratched his head, appeared momentarily confused. "Monsignor, I'm going to be as open with you as I can. I think the Church, if it knew what we were doing, would try to stop us."

"Because . . ."

"Because it can't afford to see its doctrines challenged." Brennan paused. "It's happened before. There's an ancient pre-Fugue text that relates the story of a man punished for demonstrating that his world was round."

"Galileo. Yes, I've read that text." Carlisle sipped his coffee and returned the cup to the table. "But that religion was pre-Fugue Bf3000 or so. What has it to do with the present?"

"That religion," Brennan said in a flat, cold voice, "was inquisitory, repressive. It made men fearful to think new thoughts."

The priest held up his hand. "If you believe that about the Holy Orders, you are wrong. Some *may* think the Church is a tyranny, but if so, it's a gentle one. Go through any stargate and you will find an ordered peace. There are no more plague factories. There are no more armadas of death."

"But there *are* penal colonies," Jancy piped.

"And there *are* Peacemakers," Brennan growled between his teeth.

After Brennan had finished the mapping and picture-taking, he marked the area of the dig in a grid of rectangular squares, 10 meters on a side. The grid sections that showed concentrations of metal he marked with a flag.

He began the excavation at the upward edge of the grid, suctioning out a trench horizontal to the slope, the soil siphon riding his shoulders easily.

"How long will it take?" Jancy asked, smiling down at him. He hadn't heard her approach over the siphon's loud *snuffle*.

"The whole thing?" Brennan glanced around. "It's not a very large site. A week should do it. Maybe two?"

"What can I do to help?"

Brennan pondered the request for a moment, then shrugged. "Clean the artifacts as they come out—and preserve them. Ambient air is sometimes enough to turn organics into sludge." He grinned. "I have something called a 'macro-fine' that does most of the hard work. But after that, there's cataloging and reconstruction; that's what takes time."

"You trust *him* not to sabotage things?" Jancy pointed back toward the shelter.

"I don't think Carlisle will be a problem," Brennan heard himself saying. "I agree with Gus. Say what you will—he's got integrity."

At night Jancy tried to teach Brennan how to breathe in the Dysip style. She'd brought along half a dozen of the COmPUte cubes—friends, she called them.

"What is it exactly that you do?" Brennan asked. Pleasantly tired from his day's exertions, he seated himself cross-legged across from the girl.

"You don't *do* anything," Jancy said. "You *go away* from your body, swallow yourself, allow your consciousness to live in the wind inside your own pharyngeal cavity." She settled back, began consciously to relax. "Your breath," she murmured, "carries all the tension necessary to activate the Dysips."

"What is it, a form of Zen?"

"I guess so. There've been scientists who have tried to codify it in terms of theta waves and endocrinal chemicals. But *they* were never able to spirit up a Dysip."

"Um." Brennan stirred a little, getting comfortable. "What's next?"

"Breath is energy-carrying," Jancy said, looking at him through half-closed eyes. "You must learn to dissect each inhalation, then run each energy packet up and down the spine."

Brennan just stared at her.

"With practice you can maintain it on a subconscious level," the girl told him. She was totally relaxed now except for a twitching eyebrow. "You can't *walk* around, of course—or at least *I* can't."

"Well—" Brennan said, and stopped abruptly. A

wraith had formed at her elbo
of indeterminate age, wearing a
black silk.

"This is T'sai Li. Although the
of personality, T'sai Li has al
little bit more."

"What does she do?"

"Recites poetry. In a lovely
been able to understand. But sh
care about her audience."

T'sai Li turned her head enou
and Brennan. She bowed forma
on her lips.

Jancy banished T'sai Li after fif
sweetly in Brennan's direction. "

The only thing Brennan coul
headache.

Chapter Sixteen

The wan sun was halfway toward midsky. Carlisle felt no warmth from it. He was perhaps three-quarters of a kilometer up one of the mountain's broad slopes. From where he stood, Brennan was a foreshortened gnome digging in frozen ground, his soil siphon spewing forth a rooster's plume of earth.

Carlisle sat down on a stone. Above him the mountain groaned softly, protestingly. At first the noises had bothered him, kept him from sleeping, but after a week he had come to find them restful.

And, after a week of excavating, Brennan seemed no nearer to his goal. Still, he kept on, and Carlisle envied him. He longed to hold the nozzle of the siphon hard by the ground, feeling it vibrate as it stripped away the strata.

He had said penance for his thoughts, to The Shining Light and to his own patron saint, Morgan the Intercessor. But still, the yearning was very strong.

He thought often about what Brennan had said, and tried to picture Setsen Dai as a man. The idea was so foreign he was tempted to laugh. The archeologist meant what he said, though, as his efforts in the ruins attested.

God was a holy Light—of that Carlisle was sure. The other side of the picture, however, was a bit murkier. He had to admit Kirst sometimes seemed to share some of the capriciousness of Man. Which only proves, Bishop Poole would have said, that there is a darkness inside the human soul.

There was a click in Carlisle's ear.

"I'm going out for a while, Bren." The voice came softly over the comm net Brennan insisted the three use. Jancy exited the shelter, climbed aboard the floater, waved a hand in the archeologist's direction.

"Where to?" Brennan asked, without looking up.

"West, I think. Over toward Maylow."

"Still looking for that cave? I couldn't find it with the earth-sifter. It probably slid down the mountain along with some of those overhangs."

"Maybe there are others."

"Maybe. See you." Brennan looked up, waved his hand once, then bent again to his digging.

The floater disappeared down the long slant of a ravine, appeared again briefly, and then dropped from sight. Carlisle watched for some minutes, and saw the craft finally, on the flat between the two mountains.

That the two were lovers he was sure. They had come to it wonderfully, without effort and without artifice, drifting toward one another as surely as magnets.

Carlisle did not mind that—he was, in fact, delighted. Yet, necessarily, he found himself excluded. When Brennan practiced his Dysip breathing—and he was getting good—they sat close enough so that their knees touched.

After half an hour the stone seemed cold, and exceedingly hard. Carlisle stood up, preparing to head back toward the camp. What would he do, he wondered, if the archeologist's efforts *did* produce some hidden, earth-shattering information? CALIFUR, after all, warned of a period of great danger, a danger epitomized by this very dig. Dusting snow from his boots, Carlisle started downslope. He didn't know the answer yet, but each night he asked for guidance, for wisdom to handle such an event. And each succeeding day Brennan dug deeper, filling his artifact boxes with shards and pieces of metal.

"Brennan!" Jancy's voice came over the comm net as a triumphant yell.

"What is it?" Down below in the ruins Brennan stopped working, looked vaguely west.

"The *cave* might be gone—but didn't the Helm Maiden say something about a lookout point?"

"Um—I seem to remember that. What have you got?"

"Not sure. There's a chiseled-out cavity here—right into the rock." She paused for a moment. "Dirt's fallen in. Snow, too." There were muttered words too low for Carlisle to hear, and then an exultant cry from the girl.

"It's an earthenware jar! Pushed way back in there. There's a stone blocking it. Just a minute, I'll get it out."

"Leave it," Brennan began tersely. Then he stopped. A crashing sound boomed in Carlisle's ears, followed by a slow grinding roar.

"Oh, my God! Bren, it's slipping! The side of the slope!" The girl's panicked words were swallowed up in a rushing wave, like water going over a waterfall.

"Saint Morgan—have mercy!" Carlisle cried out. He slanted west, dread in his heart. A brief glimpse behind him showed Brennan only now tossing off the soil siphon and scrambling out of the excavation.

"Jancy! Jancy!"

The only answer was a final shudder as kilos of snow and ice slid inexorably downward.

"Carlisle, you hear me?" Brennan's voice was a strangulated cry.

"I hear."

"Save her, goddamnit! You've got a fifteen-minute lead on me." There was stark fear in Brennan's voice.

Carlisle ran, sometimes floundering in the deeper snow. It was perhaps two kilometers to Maylow, then a long easy climb on an upward-extending ramp. Three-quarters of the way up, however, the mountain steepened, and the last few hundred meters were tedious and dangerous.

"B-Bren?" The voice was halting, half choked off.

"God—you're still alive!" Brennan's words rasped in Carlisle's ears. "Are you hurt?"

"My neck," the girl answered weakly. "Can't seem to move anything."

"Lie still," Carlisle urged quickly. "Don't try to move." He tore across the flat, hit the ramp, began scrambling up.

"Feel cold, Bren," the girl murmured.

"Coming, Jancy! Goddamn it, Carlisle—*move!*"

The priest took too long a step, slipped, slid back three meters. Using hands and feet, he managed to make it to the top of the ramp. Then, panting heavily but not giving himself time to rest, he began to climb.

There were noises; he didn't hear them. The wind blew in gusts across his vision, swirling the snow, prying at his fingers.

Somewhere below him Brennan was attacking the slope. That was the only word for it; the man seemed a cursing, savage maniac.

"Um—Bren?" the girl's voice was slurred, without timbre.

"We're coming!" Brennan called encouragingly. "Carlisle will be there in another twenty minutes— I'll be there in thirty."

"Too late. I'm slipping again, a little. No way to stop it." Fear made Jancy's voice quaver.

Carlisle closed his eyes, murmured a prayer to whatever saint was listening. He was a hundred meters short of a ledge that wound partway around the mountain. He might be able to see her from there.

"Is there pain, Jancy?" Brennan's words were like open wounds.

"No. No pain. Only it's cold, and there's snow covering part of my face."

"Carlisle, damn you! How long?"

"Ten minutes," Carlisle murmured into the comm net. He leaned forward, grasped a firm hold on an outthrust rock, swung his weight upward. Grunting with the effort, he said, "The wind seems to be slackening. That's a good sign."

He made the ledge. It was narrow, but with his stomach flat against the rock face, he could advance in a steady sideways fashion. Clearing its upward reach, he could see down into several crevasses. The snow was all fresh-fallen. Jancy must be around on the other side.

"It was that stone," the girl said slowly, as though she'd thought about it a long time. "The one blocking the cavity. When I pulled it out everything above it came down." She paused for a moment and then went on. "Maybe it was planned that way."

"A deadfall? Maybe so. Kirst was supposed to be a cagey son of a bitch." Brennan chuckled hoarsely, then barked a short laugh. "He's *your* goddamn devil, Carlisle. He should be a pretty good one."

Carlisle didn't answer. He studied the terrain remaining to be climbed. He had a thought—maybe it wasn't necessary.

"Jancy?" he said tersely.

"Umm." Her voice sounded weaker.

"Look up at the mountain. What features do you see?"

There were five seconds of silence, then: "There's a knob right above me, some brush growing on it."

"How about to the right?" Toward Carlisle.

"Can't see anything. Snow's blocking me."

"Left?"

"Uh, a promontory of some kind. A giant's nose."

Relievedly, Carlisle saw it, a slanting overshot granite ledge. If he worked himself around following the ridge line, he could be there in five minutes.

He said only, "Good girl—I have you in sight."

In a tired, frightened voice, Jancy said, "Better hurry. I can feel the weight changing on my neck and head. And I can hear snow moving below me."

Carlisle was halfway there when the rushing sound came again.

"Oh God! I'm slipping again ..." The sentence remained unfinished. The silence afterwards was broken by Brennan's rage-filled cry and Carlisle's mumbled prayer.

The priest found her three-quarters down the slope of the crevasse, her neck at an awkward angle, part of the floater pinning her legs. He brushed the snow from her face, held her head tenderly. His mind frozen and his heart heavy, he began last rites.

It was afterwards that he became aware of the earthenware jar. It lay beside the girl's body, the upper half of it smashed and gaping. Carlisle reached inside, drew out nearly a dozen tapedexes, so old they crumbled even as he handled them.

He could feel his hand tremble. Was this what CALIFUR had warned against? These records from a mountaintop? Instantly he thought of hurling them further down into the crevasse, where they'd never be found.

He raised his arm and then lowered it. He sat down in the snow. For half a minute he stared down at the artifacts, sweat from his exertions stinging his eyes. *God save me*, he murmured at last. *I can't do it. I'm too much like Brennan. I have to know what's on them.*

He held them in his lap for 10 minutes, while Brennan climbed down into the crevasse. Then he surrendered them.

Chapter Seventeen

"Monsignor, they have called for a meeting of the Supreme Council!" Fr Jacc entered the monastery garden where Carlisle was laboring. The old man's face was aglow with excitement.

Carlisle put down his pruning shears and surveyed the tree branch critically. He did not speak. The penance he'd set for himself was six months of silence and humility. He'd chosen for that penance the garden within the Archivists' monastery. When he wasn't pruning trees or mulching roses, he served Fr Jacc and Fr Cols.

The tree needed balancing, and Carlisle picked up his shears preparatory to attacking the other side.

"Stop this nonsense!" Fr Jacc ordered, peering at the Morganite through the tree's branches. "They're holding a meeting of the Supreme Council. And Bishop Poole has specifically asked for you."

Carlisle felt a heaviness within him. The past three months had been peaceful, serene. He'd blanked out the outside world as neatly and efficiently as a monastery swift going after grains of rice.

"You must hurry!" The old man was nearly jumping up and down. "He wants you at the Mission on Itano."

With great reluctance, Carlisle put down the shears. He began to fear—once again—the future.

Bishop Poole looked on the verge of collapse. His lined face was haggard, drawn, his eyes no longer bright with life. The instant Carlisle saw him, he felt a sense of desolation. He wanted to hug the old man, but instead merely kissed the ring, offered himself for service.

"Come into my study," Poole said. His gait was slow, awkward, often halting. When he slumped into the overstuffed airchair before his fire, it was with a sense of finality.

"The Supreme Council has met," he said by way of preamble. "All of the Orders. On the matter of Dr. Brennan and his petition."

Carlisle seated himself on a casual side chair and tried not to see the pain in the other's face.

"Archbishop Fitterage of the Daiist Order delivered a eulogy to the Morganites," Poole said. "For informing the Church of the impending crisis."

"Yes, my Lord?"

Poole grimaced. "You could taste the sarcasm in the air."

"The Daiist movement has always been less intellectual than the rest," Carlisle said, "and perhaps more pragmatic. Maybe they can afford to be. They have the Peacemakers."

"Umm." Poole lifted his eyes. "You've been serving a penance, Charles. For what reason?"

Carlisle squared his shoulders as well as he was able. He said sadly, "Envy, my Lord—and doubt as to my place in God's plan."

"What do you envy?"

"Dr. Brennan and his work."

"Have you seen the tapedexes he brought back?"

"The contents?"

"Yes."

"No, my Lord. They were too old, too damaged. Dr. Brennan said they would have to undergo analysis and repair before they could be studied."

Poole made an impatient gesture. "They have been analyzed. And repaired, for the most part. I have read them—as has the Supreme Council."

Carlisle stared at the grave, serious face of his mentor. "Yes, my Lord?" He could feel his heart beating irregularly within its cage.

Face ashen, Poole said, "They purport to be a first-hand account of life in the pre-Fugue era." He paused, sucked in a ragged breath. "Written by someone calling himself Pan Kirst."

"*Evil Incarnate*," Carlisle muttered. He put clasped hands in his lap. No *wonder* CALIFUR had pronounced an impending crisis.

"The artifacts were registered—as law requires," Poole went on, his eyes on the flames rising from the hearth. "*You* did that."

"Yes, my Lord."

"Even so," Poole continued as though Carlisle had not spoken, "the Church has not permitted them to become public."

Carlisle could not contain himself further. "My Lord . . . surely they were not authenticated?"

"No," Poole said, still looking at the fire. "CALIFUR found it necessary to supply a portion of the content. Enough to disallow authentication."

Carlisle felt a wave of relief sweep over him. "Then, my Lord, I don't understand. If they fall below authentication standards, what is the harm?"

Bishop Poole sank back suddenly in his chair. "Because their publication would cause great confusion. It was the decision of the Supreme Council that the material be restricted."

"And what does Dr. Brennan say about that?"

"He insists upon having the originals—along with the copies CALIFUR made."

"But that's his right!" Carlisle stammered. His gaze

locked that of his Bishop. "The law is clear in matters like this."

There was a fitful silence, broken finally by Bishop Poole pouring ice water from a crystal pitcher.

"When we restricted them," the aged priest said then, "Brennan petitioned for registration of two artifacts discovered in the Cone. Do you know of them, Charles?"

"I have not seen them."

"Umm. Brennan intends to *force* us to show the Kirst records. He insists they're corroborative."

"But *he* has not seen them himself!"

"He has not."

Carlisle marveled at the boldness of the archeologist's ploy, smacking though it did of desperation. By citing the Kirst tapedexes as evidence of another artifact's authenticity, he was sticking his neck out well beyond safe limits.

"Will the petition be heard?"

"I believe so," Poole said. "Dr. Brennan is very well known and respected. He cannot be ignored."

"He believes in himself," Carlisle said. "And he will not give in."

"Charles?" Bishop Poole took a sip of water, put the glass down. He turned haunted eyes toward his friend.

"Yes, my Lord?"

"The Kirst tapes," the old man whispered softly, "they're an abomination. They *cannot* be made public."

"No, my Lord." Carlisle was confused.

"If you read them, remember that Darkness has great power. Enough to cause doubt in the weak-willed.

"I will remember."

"Then go." Poole gave him a fleeting smile. "The Council has asked that you attend the hearing."

Chapter Eighteen

The petition for registration of Gus Pierce's two artifacts took place in conference room number 12, CALIFUR mega-plex.

The petition, although properly filed and vouchered, did not follow the routine laid out for similar requests. Nine out of 10 cases required only the presence of a cadre of Churchmen, one representing each of the Orders; thus, when the the Intuitive's decision was read (in a quiet voice by a black-clad chamberlain) unanimity among the cadre was merely a matter of counting hands.

The Pierce case was different. It was decided that both the presentation and rendering should be delivered in closed hearing—*et adversatus*.

"Why?" Brennan wanted to know.

The chief chamberlain, a thin man with shaven head, regarded the archeologist coldly. "There are criminal charges pending against you, Dr. Brennan. They shall be pressed in the event your petition is denied."

"What charges?"

The chamberlain paused, consulted a sheet of paper. "Ah, here we are. A. Aiding and abetting theft of proscribed artifacts. B. Breaking into a Church Archive. C. Conspiracy against the established order."

Brennan's lips tightened dangerously. "So they're going to put *me* on trial, then. When is the hearing to take place?"

"A week from tomorrow. You may, if you wish, have someone represent you. And it's a *hearing*, not a trial."

Brennan was shaking with anger. "Do I understand correctly? If the petition *is* granted, no charges will be filed?"

The other man nodded. "That is correct."

"What would occur if I were to abandon the petition altogether?"

"It would be a wise choice." The chamberlain's lip twitched. "In that event, none of the charges would be pursued."

"So that's the *quid pro quo*," Brennan growled. He ground his teeth. "Damn it—no! If it takes a trial to clear this up, then so be it."

The chamberlain shrugged at the other's idiocy and turned away. At the very least, he thought, it should provide a moment of diversion.

The courtroom was nearly full. At the front was Ali Hong, a small man with yellow skin and blue-black hair—the Judicial Prelate. His purpose was to mediate only; all testimony would be submitted directly to CALIFUR. On a table in front of him rested the two artifacts in question—a Forster thin-gel photograph and the Helm Maiden's diary.

"Silence!"

The prelate rapped the desk sharply, and the forest of conferring whispers stilled.

"Dr. Waverly Hooker-Brennan. Do you have counsel?"

Brennan stood up. "I do."

"His name?"

"Kasim Hobbs, professor of archeology, Trospros University." He smiled and looked down at the bald head of his friend and colleague.

"Chief chamberlain—does the Church have opposing counsel?"

"Yes, my Lord. Father Maxwell Stuyvesant, of the Daiist Order. Your honor, it may be noted that Fr Stuyvesant has spent several years as Dr. Hooker-Brennan's monitor in the field. This in no way detracts from his suitability to serve as adversary counsel."

"So noted." The prelate paused, then without preamble laid out the ground rules to be followed by prosecutor/accuser and petitioner/defendant.

A. Information (exhibits) attesting to the suitability of the artifacts petitioned must be authenticated by CALIFUR.

B. Issues of legality come under the purview of the prelate, all rulings to be final.

Looking at Kasim Hobbs, the prelate said: "Professor, you may begin your case."

Hobbs stood up, turned slowly, surveyed the room. There were perhaps a score in his audience, all Churchmen. He identified Monsignor Carlisle in the row of chairs behind Stuyvesant. The priest did not look happy.

Hobbs stepped to the table, held up the Forster thin-gel, taking care that his fingers touched only the edge. "You have all seen this artifact. Amazing! Impossible to *forge* something like this, you know." He paused and smiled. "First, you'd have to find an alien."

Stuyvesant was on his feet. "Please, professor! It has not yet been proven that that *is* an alien."

"What do you think it is, then?" Hobbs asked, raising woolly eyebrows. Not giving Stuyvesant time to reply, he put down the thin-gel, picked up the second artifact. "This is a record of a young girl—who writes of a direct confrontation with someone known as Pan Kirst."

Stuyvesant half rose. "Same objection."

Hobbs laid the artifact down on the table, rested a hand on it. "By following information gleaned from this girl's account, Dr. Brennan was able not only to locate the world in question—Doubab—but find there the ruins of the lodge and research laboratory she writes about. That alone is *de facto* proof."

Stuyvesant said nothing, but busied himself with a mnemonic recorder and brief conferences with those around him.

"Further *de facto* proof," Hobbs went on, "will no doubt be determined by the several cases of shards and plaster castings Dr. Brennan managed to bring back from the site."

The judicial prelate leaned forward. "Where are those castings and shards?"

"Your honor, they were registered by Monsignor Carlisle immediately upon discovery—as the law requires. They were then submitted to CALIFUR for authentication. The Church, so far, has blocked retrieval of these artifacts."

"Is that true, Fr Stuyvesant?"

"Yes, my Lord. The Church is quite willing to allow these exhibits to be entered into the record, however—so long as no claim is made that they once belonged to Pan Kirst."

"Do you so claim?" the prelate asked, looking toward Hobbs.

"Without having seen their authentication numbers, it is difficult to tell," Hobbs remarked dryly.

Ali Hong nodded briefly. "Very well. You shall have that opportunity. Chamberlain, bring in the artifacts in question—along with CALIFUR's authentication numbers."

"Thank you, my Lord," Hobbs said quickly. He smiled his warmest smile. "But there are other artifacts as well, potentially even more rewarding."

"What might those be?"

"Tapedexes. Discovered by a colleague of Dr. Brennan's. And again—exactly where a cache might be expected."

"Have they been registered?"

"Yes, my Lord. By Monsignor Carlisle."

"Do you object, Fr Stuyvesant?" The prelate glanced toward the Daiist priest.

"Yes, my Lord. The items under discussion were 'discovered' by Jancy Pierce." Stuyvesant stopped and looked around. "She is the sister of Gus Pierce, who is responsible for *those*." He pointed toward the thin-gel and diary. "Who is to say what invention she perpetrated upon Dr. Brennan and Monsignor Carlisle?"

"Can that question not be asked of her?"

"She's dead," Hobbs put in harshly. He looked up at the prelate, then folded his hands behind his back. "Monsignor Carlisle was the first one to her side. He will attest that they are no 'invention.' "

"Monsignor Carlisle," the prelate murmured, looking out at the throng. "Is he present?"

Carlisle stood, bowed to the prelate. He did not look at Stuyvesant. "What Professor Hobbs says is the truth, my Lord."

"Then unless you have further objections, Fr Stuyvesant, I intend to allow the evidence." The prelate stared down at Stuyvesant's table.

"My Lord." Stuyvesant got hurriedly to his feet. "CALIFUR found it necessary to re-create whole sections of this material. I submit that there is insufficient left to be *called* evidence."

Ali Hong snorted. "Nonsense! CALIFUR re-creates lost and missing material all the time. That's CALIFUR's purpose. Chamberlain—bring in this so-called evidence."

Book Two

Chapter Nineteen

Tapedex one. Location Site: Masaryk. Date: AF457/1/11. 0.04% Re-creation. 0.23% Repaired. Material: 74.76% Hydrocarbon compounds. 21.05% Ferrous alloys. 00.23% Ceramic casting. 04.96% Other.
[Authentication Rating: 61.86%]

I was examining a section of friable, earthy stone when Rowan buzzed. Another tourist had arrived.

"The season is over," I said shortly. "Finished. *Ganz alles kaput*. The mountain is closed."

"I know that, sir. He will not go away."

I catalogued the stone before answering. I was in no mood for further interruptions. For eight months I was willing to play the fool, laving charm like butter from a crock. Enough was enough! The *melte* belonged to me.

"Tell him to come back in ninety days." Three

months from now the mountain would again don its white shroud. I would emerge from my lab, forelock well in hand, china-stepping my way into the hearts and purses of the curious, the poets, the seekers after grails. But not now. Not with the contents of two plaques to unravel.

I heard mumbling over the intercom. Trying to get all that straight, I guessed. Rowan was a damned fine innkeeper and a better friend, but he wasn't much use with gate crashers.

"Yes, sir," Rowan said finally. The intercom went dead. After several minutes it buzzed again. Rowan's voice had graduated into a high squeak.

"Dr. Kirst!"

"What?"

"He insists upon talking with you."

I sighed and put aside my stylus. "Once more into the breach," I said. "Okay, Ro. Tell our nice visitor I'll be up shortly."

I got a click as he cut me off.

To get from the laboratory to the lodge I had to go outside. As always, the mountain dominated everything, pocked with cancer now that the snow was rotting away. Its brown and black cliffs hung above the valley like crusts of blood. You'll pardon me if I tend to anthropomorphize—the mountain, to me, lives. And yes, suffers, bleeds.

There was a man and a woman in the lodge. Rowan stood defensively behind them, guarding I don't know what.

I had only to take a look at the man to know I wanted him to leave. Little wonder Rowan had squeaked.

He was an Earther. His hands and face were a translucent, chalky white; evidently he'd caught one of the plagues we'd sent his way. Evidently, too, he'd lived through it. Some are like that—natural immunes.

Pity.

The woman was also dressed in white. There was a caduceus on her collar: a doctor or nurse. Or, I thought uncharitably, a companion, perhaps. A lover. A whore. Who knows; she was anyway beautiful, with soft auburn hair and wide blue eyes.

"My name," the Earther said, drawing my attention back to him, "is Syl Barrister. I am, like yourself, an archeologist. I have read everything written about the *Mountain of the Crown*. In particular, I have read everything *you* have written about it. I want to climb the mountain, Dr. Kirst. I want to view the plaques firsthand."

I said, "Before the mountain was famous I took out a fifty-year lease on it. That means *I* say who comes here and who doesn't."

He gave me the briefest of shrugs. "I know that."

In the last war, the space war—the Armageddon of all wars—we had proven to Earth we meant to keep our freedom, at the cost of maybe a billion lives. And at the cost of one life in particular—a girl named Jody, whose picture sits on my desk. Don't ask why the outworlders shun Grand Old Terra.

That was a lot of years ago. They're coming off-planet again, the Earthers, and I suppose they'll be tolerated eventually—as long as they have money.

I said to Syl Barrister: "This is the season of *melte*. The snows are going, and no one climbs the *Mountain of the Crown* during *melte*."

Blue eyes, white face—the effect was startling. He managed a lopsided grin and lit a cigarette.

"I know all about the *melte*, Dr. Kirst. First, let me ask—do you think I could climb the mountain unhindered in the midst of your tourist season?"

I shrugged. "Probably not. But that's the only chance you'll have."

He named a very large figure of money, raised his eyebrows inquiringly.

"Mr. Barrister, take your money and go home. Go back to Earth."

He doubled the offer. I felt my throat constrict some. There were things I could do with money like that.

I said instead, "You can't buy me, Barrister. Don't try."

He appeared contrite. "Money means very little to me, Dr. Kirst. I am ashamed to say I thought for a moment I could use it to sway you into guiding me. Perhaps I should use another approach. Having read all that is written about the mountain, and after studying pictures of the plaques, I have arrived at certain conclusions. Would you be interested in hearing them?"

I snorted. "In a word—no! A month ago a priest tried to convince me a heavenly ascension took place here. He was looking for angelic footprints, no doubt. Before that a professor from off one of the Academy ships tried to persuade me this is *Man's* birthplace. I've been here eleven years. I've heard everything. I'll stick with my own theories."

Barrister smiled tolerantly. "That a race of unknown aliens, the only sentient creatures other than Man yet discovered, marked their passage through the ages on this mountain. And escaped the planet to seek their destiny in the stars."

My smile was not at all tolerant.

"A simple theory, but mine own. Rowan will arrange for your passage off-planet. If you will excuse me . . ."

The woman spoke for the first time. She had a husky, throaty voice. I liked it.

"Please do not treat Dr. Barrister as though he were a tourist out for a good time. He has very good credentials back on Earth."

"Then let him take his credentials back to Earth," I said. I turned to go.

"Dr. Kirst!"

I cast back one gimlet eye and stopped in my tracks. The woman was holding a little folding case so that I could see the crossed banners over spaceship that identified her as an officer of the Royal Navy.

I came back and stopped in front of her.

"Who are you?"

She snapped a salute. "Major Aleta Fields, assigned

to duty as physician and diplomatic liaison for Dr.
Barrister. We're concerned that he receive all possible cooperation."

Dandy. Just dandy.

"Well, Major. In spite of any real or implied threats,
I cannot take him up the mountain. It's not passable
during *melte.*"

"Have you ever attempted a climb during *melte?*"
the Earther asked.

"There was never a need. When the snow comes, it
is relatively easy to climb, and all the plaques are
exposed. Thousands of people have climbed all the
way to the Crown—during winter. With the spring
thaw, the passages become choked with melting ice.
There are mudslides. There is a very strong, gusting
wind. The paths I'll take my tourists on next winter
are, at this moment, covered over with skin-ice. Haz-
ardous. Extremely. Are you an experienced mountain
climber, Barrister?"

"The *Mountain of the Crown* is not high, as mountains go," he replied slowly. "And the slopes are such
that mere beginners have little difficulty in climbing
them."

"In winter, man! In winter."

"Yes. In winter. And I wish to climb during *melte.* I
do not believe it is insane, Dr. Kirst. I think it is . . .
necessary." He spoke with such fervent conviction I
was taken aback.

I pondered it. Major Fields stood straight, her back
against the bar. Barrister was a few feet in front of
her, his lips ready to invoke a smile.

"No," I said.

"We can go," Major Fields said curtly, "but we'll
come back with an order."

Barrister did not add anything, simply stood watching me. If he had said so much as a word I would
have ordered both of them out of the lodge.

"Does your offer of money still apply?" I asked
after five seconds.

He smiled an apologetic smile. "Of course."

"And does the Navy permit me to take his money?" I turned to the woman.

"He offered it," she said icily. "You may accept it, if you wish."

"It's a rotten deal," I said, just as icily, "even with the money. But I'll do it."

Barrister gave a short nod. "Excellent."

"Provided certain conditions are met."

"What conditions?"

"First, I will not be responsible if Dr. Barrister meets a fatal accident. He knows the danger."

Before the woman could speak, Barrister bobbed his head.

"I agree."

"Second, we will not stay on the mountain after dark. There is too much likelihood of mudslides. It's easy enough to have a floater pick us up at night and take us back in the morning."

"That sounds reasonable. Agreed."

" 'Kay. We'll start tomorrow. Be ready to go at six sharp."

The Earther shook his head. "I wish to do a little reconnoitering on my own. Perhaps I could rent that floater you spoke of for a day or two."

"Be my guest." I handed them the standard booklet I give out to all the tourists. It explains how the mountain came to be discovered (by accident) and the work I'm doing translating the plaques. There are pictures of the mountain and of the Crown—that mysterious impressionistic sculpture that rests on a plateau at the mountain's top.

The mountain is exactly 10,104 feet high. It is not, as Barrister pointed out, any threat to Everest or Nix or K2, nor any of the other monsters that draw restless men to them. It is not steep, it is not particularly threatening; in fact, it is not even a challenge—when the snow is packed on its slopes.

The mountain is of interest only because of the plaques. And the Crown. Beginning roughly 10 feet from the base is the first plaque, a squarish piece of alloyed steel. On it are crude symbols yet to be understood. At intervals other plaques appear, each more sophisticated in makeup. Near the top of the mountain, the plaques have mathematical content that is readily discernible—things like the electron number of hydrogen and oxygen and carbon atoms; even mathematical constants.

Approximately a hundred feet from the top is the Crown.

Think of a semi-circular wall of steel twice the height of a man. Think of birds in flight. Think of a pulsating, paralyzing vault to the stars that gleam like diamonds above the mountain.

I don't know what the creatures look like who built the Crown, and placed the metal plaques. I may never know. But I *do* know the spirit that took them on into space.

Perhaps they're waiting for us, somewhere out there.

The stone above the Crown has been tooled, as though awaiting more plaques, though none have been found. The *Pan Kirst Theory* says that space is for history yet unfolding.

I expect the aliens back.

That night there were rumblings from the mountain as rocks rolled and earth shifted. It sounded as though ghosts were walking around up there.

I have a picture in my head of what the aliens look like, based partly upon the distance between plaques, gravity, weather patterns, and the size of the symbols inscribed on the alloy. And based partly upon imagination and dreams. Sometimes I think I see them, in the valleys and ravines of the mountain, tall furred creatures busy at their tasks, ignoring the humans who struggled up the slopes in their awe-struck thousands.

At times, when the mountain talks, they seem very real and close, those voyagers of yesterday.

Barrister was gone in the morning, taking the woman and the floater. I was happy for the respite. I ate a quick breakfast with Rowan, and then dug enthusiastically into the mysteries of alien culture. There were some new approaches I wanted to try on plaque 72. Outside, it began to rain, and the slopes of the mountain growled as ice packs nudged down.

At dinner both Barrister and Major Fields were quiet, their attention absorbed by Rowan's cuisine. They didn't speak of their trip in the floater (they returned from the west) and I didn't inquire.

Ask me no questions, as the man says, *and I'll tell you no lies.*

Only afterwards, when the light had begun to fade and the first stars splashed their glory over the valley, did anyone attempt to make conversation.

Barrister lit one of his cigarettes. "I think perhaps tomorrow we can begin the climb. Does that suit you?"

I shrugged. "You're paying the freight. You get the grand tour anytime you say."

"Has the rain increased the hazard?" There was a worried frown on Aleta Fields' pretty face.

"Major, Crown Mountain—the *Mountain of the Crown*—has all the character of a dirty old man. An evil old man. If you leave your window open tonight, and listen, it will talk to you. It will say that if it can, it will crush you—brutalize you. Listen to the ice sliding around up there; you'll become aware the thing has a life all its own."

I had made an impression. Her face tightened a little, then grew hard. Her windows would probably be locked that night.

Not so Barrister. He was interested. He had followed every word with an inquisitive sidewise tilt of his head.

"Mountains have personalities, too, Dr. Kirst—I quite agree. It is so on Earth, so why not here? I have heard of killer mountains. Is this really one of those?"

Major Fields was white-faced. "Excuse me," she said. Her back was ramrod straight as she walked away.

I smiled gloomily at Barrister. "During tourist season, it's a benign old man, all ample lap and frosty white hair. In the time of *melte*, though, it feels its youth again. It becomes uncontrollable. I don't know if it's a killer, Barrister. I expect we'll all find out tomorrow."

He stubbed out his cigarette. "I expect so." He shot me a tight grin and we listened for a moment to the sick cleavage of ice above us on the slopes.

"You don't know," he said finally, "how I'm looking forward to this climb." And he gave me a last enigmatic look and wandered slowly off to bed.

I spent the next hour mulling over the situation, trying to find a pattern where the Earther fit. None came to mind. I walked down to the lab, poured myself a drink, and got undressed. I was crawling under the covers when the phone buzzed. Cursing, I swung a shoe, missed, and finally hooked the thing with a thumb. I punched receive, and heard Major Fields' soft voice.

"Dr. Kirst, I've been waiting to talk to you."

"Talk to me in the morning," I said shortly.

"Wait!"

Something in her voice made me hesitate. Finally I sighed, and half sat up. "Go ahead."

"Had you ever heard of Sylvan Barrister before yesterday?"

"No," I said emphatically, "and I hope I never do again. I don't much like Earthers."

"He's special," Major Fields said. "He was one of Earth's tacticians during the war."

I didn't answer. A tactician was one who directed battles, maneuvered whole fleets, sacrificed planets. He was a player in a four-dimensional chess match, where the rules had never been learned, let alone forgotten. In essence, the entire war had been fought by tacticians, rarefied intellects protected and pampered, locked away safe from the holocausts they visited upon others. I sat in the darkness and thought about Barrister. He could have ordered the strike that destroyed Jody. *Pawn to bishop four.*

I drew in a long breath. Time to get hold of myself. The woman on the other end of the phone had not said anything for at least three minutes. God, I thought, how I loathe tacticians. And, I suppose, with good reason.

I had been one—one of the best.

"Why is he here?" I asked. "Is he legitimate; is he really an archeologist?"

"He's been a full professor for five years," Major Fields said. "The problem is we don't know what else he is. He may be genuine, or he may be looking for something to give Earth an edge again."

"Why not just tell him to stay home?"

"When we have our own tactician right here? It's too good an opportunity to miss. We want to find out what he's after—if he's after anything."

"Why here?" I wondered aloud.

"You tell me."

"Hmmm." I hung up the phone and crawled under the covers. I didn't go to sleep for a long, long while.

In the morning, there were fog streamers hung like bunting across the mountain's flanks. The slopes looked festive, expansive. It was as though the mountain was deliberately calling me a liar, welcoming us instead of challenging us.

We moved smoothly at first, the woman just below me and Barrister farther back, roped together in a traditional intimacy none of us was comfortable with. We were also linked into a communication net that included Rowan back at the lodge, in case we needed help.

It was a strange feeling, this trespass of the mountain's slopes. It was as though I'd caught it naked, having gotten used to it in winter's clothing. I'd traversed this same route times forgotten, leading my dreaming sheep, unaware how red the stone, how very white the clay.

Expense Record		

Entertainment	Type	Date

Guests	Name	Title o

Travel	Type	Date

Allocation	Business	Perso

Additional Comments

Reminder: Always obtain itemized

	No. of Persons	Business Purpose
r Position		Company

	No. of Persons	Business Purpose
onal		Reimbursed

bill for lodgings if more than one expense included.

We stopped briefly at each plaque. Barrister looked bemused, more interested in the feel of rock and steel against his hands than the message hidden in the glyphs.

At 300 feet or so we met our first patch of skin-ice. It crackled like thin glass under our feet and we advanced cautiously, making sure our spikes were anchored securely.

I heard Barrister say, "It is my theory, Dr. Kirst, that the mountain was *meant* to be climbed during *melte*. Do you find that laughable?"

The notion had never crossed my mind. I considered it now, grasping a ledge of stone and pulling myself up.

"Do you have any particular reason for thinking so?" I asked cautiously. I was beginning to get the idea that, Earther or not, Barrister had put in some research time.

"Yes. I've studied weather printouts for the past dozen years. They are unvarying; they show a greater wind velocity during *melte* than at any other time."

"The spring mistral," I said. "We'll run into it farther up."

We climbed some more, and finally Barrister took up where he'd left off.

"The mountains west of here seem to act like giant flume for that wind, funneling it along."

"So?"

"That's where I went yesterday. I examined those mountains. They've been deliberately shaped to bring that wind."

I was silent, climbing, getting the feel of the slope. Kicking myself. I had noticed the carved mountains at least five years before, but had not tied them to *my* mountain. My respect for Barrister went up a grudging notch or two.

"Go on, please."

"That was a job of some considerable engineering. Why was it done? Since it is a warm wind, my conclusion was that it is to melt the snow on Crown Mountain."

"And by doing so make it easy for them to climb?"

Glancing downslope, I caught glimpse of a half-smile.

"Perhaps," he said. "Although perhaps not, as well."

We had climbed over 2,000 feet, and began to feel the first puffs of the mistral. This low on the mountain it left a sensual kittenish impression. Up higher, I knew, the kitten would bare her claws, and become a saber-tooth.

The plaques at this altitude were still faintly primitive, made up of simple and recurring symbols. Something resembling a skewed shield, for example, accounted for nearly a quarter of the glyphs as we approached plaque 210.

Barrister and the woman eased up beside me, and the Earther ran his hands over the plaque, examining it minutely.

"You don't know," he said, looking up at me, "how often I wished I was up here, actually *touching* these works." He smiled again, faintly. "They are a long way from Earth, in more ways than simply the physical."

I found myself grinning tightly, staring at his too-white face. A hundred-battle, billion-casualty wall existed between Earth and these alien tracings. I felt momentarily sorry for him, trapped on his tiny home like a rat in a warren. Then it passed, as I thought of Jody, and I gestured upward, where there came a rattle of wind-tossed stones.

"We have at least three good hours left before nightfall. Let's make the most of them."

"Shouldn't we stop to eat?" Major Fields asked. She looked a little tired, already. I glanced at Barrister, who had climbed the first 3,000 feet as easily as I. He appeared fresh and eager to continue.

"I can have Rowan take you off in the floater," I told the woman. "There's really no need for you to continue, if you don't choose. You there, Ro?"

Rowan's clipped tones sounded in our earphones.

"Right here, Pan. You want me to bring up the floater?"

The woman stared at me in tight-lipped silence. Unused to climbing, she was more a menace than an asset. The last 500 feet she had been dragging against my harness.

I said, "You can watch us on the telescope. We have one hooked up to a monitor unit—and you can stay in the net. You'll hear everything that goes on."

She turned to Barrister, but he only nodded a little sadly. "He's quite right, my dear. Perhaps that would be best."

She turned back to me. "Dr. Kirst, in spite of any agreements with Dr. Barrister, I must inform you he's under the protection of the Royal Navy. I will be watching you very carefully." Her eyes were chilly.

"Fine. Ro, bring up the floater."

"Yes, sir. Coming up."

While we waited, the Earther sank down on his haunches, his fingers running ruminately over the alloyed plaque.

He saw me watching, grinned self-consciously. "You know, we had several computers dedicated to these glyphs at the university. But, as is sometimes the case, our biggest breakthrough came from an independent researcher."

"Oh?"

"Yes, indeed. From your own book, Dr. Kirst. *Translations Out of Time.*"

I was startled, rather than pleased. That book had been written in a flush of youthful enthusiasm, with a new bride on my arm and a universe fresh as a flower waiting to be explored. I wrote it, and forgot it, and then the universe crumbled into ashes around me.

As I remembered, I had concentrated on a half dozen or so of the plaques, throwing away the rules and reaching for the poetic in an effort to understand them. It was a throwaway book, a teaser, a mere think-piece.

But Barrister was saying: "That work was inspired, Dr. Kirst. It was unfortunate that so many years went by with, uh, interruptions, before it came to my attention. In any event, allow me to congratulate you."

I told him to skip the congratulations and leaned against a slab of flat brown stone. Rowan arrived and took Aleta off. I saw her go with relief, mixed with something else. Perhaps she brought the war with her, even more than Barrister.

Just the two of us were linked now, and the only sounds we made as we trudged upwards were an occasional grunt or hissed intake as we fought for footing on the ice.

Above 4,000 feet the mountain was encased in a sheath of wet-glaze. It was like an iridescent jewel under our feet. Water rolled over it, forming little rivulets around our boots. Sometimes pieces of it broke away, skittering down behind us with a sound like Chinese bells.

The wind now blew in billowy gusts, plucking at our bodies and threatening to dislodge us.

"Keep moving," I said to the Earther. Above us was a plateau, a wide shelf nearly 50 feet across where we could rest and prepare for further ascent. There was even a portable comfort station set against the cliff face. For my tourists, I meant to please.

"Right," Barrister said. He seemed hardly out of breath. Perhaps he'd prepared for this climb on Earth.

"What's the height here?" he asked as we made the plateau. The wind was gusting heavily, then quieting. Our contact with the wet ice had left us soaked and uncomfortable. Nightfall was at most an hour away.

I said, "Just over 5,000 feet. Halfway."

He nodded. "Perhaps we should begin here in the morning. It looks as though it is more or less a straight run from here."

"There's a saddle at 7,600 feet. For the rest of it,

we'll be exposed on the slope. Just beneath the Crown, there is a relatively easy traverse. But there is the wind—and the ice."

"Yes," he said, "and they will both get worse."

I called down to Rowan. "You listening? Come get us. We're calling it a day."

"On my way," Rowan chirped.

While we waited, Barrister leaned against a shoulder of rock and lit one of his cigarettes. With a sharp glance at me he removed himself from the comm net.

"I know all about you," he said. "Your war record, your work here, translating the plaques. You've earned quite a reputation."

I shrugged, watched him blow streams of smoke through his nostrils. "What's the point?"

He looked out over the valley for a moment without speaking. Then he said, "The point is I envy you, Kirst. You've found something most of us hunt for all of our lives. Purpose."

"You mean the mountain?"

He nodded, his lips twitching with wry humor. "You've made it your life, haven't you? Your reason for being?"

I looked at him. His white face was ghostlike, at home with the other ghosts on this mountain.

"I've translated six of the plaques," he said. "The ones from your book. They tell an interesting story."

"Go on."

He drew on his cigarette, flipped the remains away. Watching it spin away downslope, I touched the button that cut me out of the comm net. He noticed the movement and gave me a sardonic blink.

"The aliens climbed during *melte*, or so say the plaques. When you think about it, it has a certain logic. Climbing the mountain during *melte* is not an easy thing. Upward struggles seldom are, for mountain climbers, *or* for a race of people."

I took the news badly. The plaques had been mine too long. I did not enjoy sharing them, even if my book *had* provided the key. My stomach knotted and my fists clenched. I turned my back on him and walked to the edge of the plateau. The thought came to me that he was trying to steal the mountain away from me, trying to shrink it to a size small enough to match his own small dimensions.

"What else did the plaques tell you?"

He lit another cigarette. "You were right in your assumption. The Crown is a site of Exodus. A stargate. The aliens are somewhere out there." He pointed one finger at the lowering sky.

"You haven't published?" I asked.

He gave me a buddha's smile. "No."

"Why not?"

"I had to see where the mountain would take me. The plaques reveal the way, not the destination. I had hoped ..."

I stood waiting, watching him. After a moment he completed his thought. "I had hoped we could work together. Collaborate."

I didn't even have to think about it.

"No."

"Because I was a tactician?" He raised his eyebrows; his pallid features reminded me of a clown's face I'd seen once as a child.

"Maybe."

"Or is it because I'm invading your domain? Poaching from your private preserve?"

"Maybe that, too." He was too accurate in his assessments to suit me. I saw a speck rising, far below, glimmering in the failing light. I switched myself back into the comm net. "Get that crate up here, Rowan," I croaked. "Get me the hell off this mountain."

Dinner was a dismal, a failure. When it was mercifully over, I returned to my lab, poured myself a stiff drink, and dug around in the tumble of books until I found a copy of *Translations Out of Time*.

It gave away no secrets. I could not recapture the poetic energy I'd had eleven years before, the elusive mood of naivete and creative intuition. After two hours I sagged against a bench and let an attack of nerves turn me into quivering jelly. I heard someone come in.

"Dr. Kirst, you okay?" Rowan grabbed me under the arms and lifted me up.

I managed a weak grin. "Sure, Ro. Nothing a pill or two won't take care of."

"Sure, sure," he said. He lowered me into a chair and dug a tranquilizer out of the little medicine chest in the bathroom. He watched me take it, concern written all over his face. My old and faithful retainer.

Abruptly he snorted. "Earthers! Nothing but trouble. What is he after, anyway?"

"He's after the mountain," I said. "But don't worry. He's not going to get it."

Late in the night I heard footsteps crunching on the gravel walk. They were not Rowan's—those I could identify. Not the Earther's—he had a long, even stride. The woman, then, no doubt come to tuck me in.

When the footsteps stopped I threw open the door. "You wanted to see me?"

Her face was an ivory oval. She smelled somewhat of jasmine. Her hair was combed into a dusky swirl. "Yes."

I held the door. "Come on in. Excuse the clutter."

Inside, she stood looking about, measuring me against the books and plaster reproductions of all 990 plaques, the steel desk with its nests of instruments, the rumpled army cot.

She touched one of the plaster plaques. "What have you learned from this?"

I dug out a bottle of brandy and found a glass that had been washed only a week earlier. I poured her two fingers, found another glass, poured myself the same.

"That," I said, "is plaque number 805. As nearly as I can determine, the oblong wheels represent wisdom. The curlique-like stamens indicate time. I surmise the plaque tells a story, perhaps the local equivalent to the Sermon on the Mount."

She sipped her brandy. "I'm sorry I was so ... official, today. I really do not enjoy playing nursemaid to an Earther."

I gave her my best winning smile. "Think nothing of it."

She appeared relieved. With a tilt of her head she asked, "Have you found out if Barrister is interested only in the plaques?"

"Yes. He says he's translated six of them. If so, it would be a brilliant work."

"You haven't seen the translations?"

"No." I grinned. "He wants me to work with him, share the discovery."

She took another sip, her eyes growing large behind the rim of the glass.

"That would suit us fine. We'll find out what he knows."

I shook my head. "Not even the Royal Navy could induce me to collaborate with him. Besides, I have only to study my own early work to know what he knows. He gave that much away."

"Then he's not working for Earth?"

I shrugged. "If he knew how to activate the Crown— the stargate—that would certainly raise Earth's prestige. And if the stargate opens trade with the aliens, Earth will inevitably benefit."

"How do you know the aliens would welcome trade?"

I shot her a smile. "We don't know. The only thing we can deduce is that the aliens are a very macho race. Evidently they pride themselves on overcoming severe tests. That mountain out there—it's a kind of rite of passage. Climb it during *melte*, prove yourself worthy."

"Worthy of what"

"That's what we hope to find out tomorrow."

She finished her brandy. "Don't trust Barrister," she said. "He knows more than he lets on."

I hid a smile. She was an arsenal of seduction. And transparent as new glass.

"As a matter of tactics," I said, "I shall watch him very carefully."

I did not sleep well. My dreams were peopled by furry phantoms, and above me the mountain grumbled secretively. I was apprehensive; I did not want the morning to come.

It came anyway. When the pearl opalescence of dawn wove its net above the horizon, I woke up. There was a sheen of sweat across my forehead. With foreboding I dressed, went to the lodge to wake the Earther.

Halfway there, the door of the lodge flew open. Major Fields saw me and stopped. Panic lines were etched in her face.

"It's Barrister! Come quick—he may be dying!"

He wasn't dead yet, but he was close to it. His skin had taken on a papery texture, and his temperature was through the ceiling. It was obvious he was in severe pain. I stood and watched while the woman bathed him with cold water and injected sedatives into his bloodstream.

"This is the reason a doctor was assigned to him as liaison," she said, glancing at me. "This attack is a side effect of the plagues used against Earth. It's recurring, like malaria. There doesn't seem to be a cure for it, and if it doesn't kill him this time, it probably will eventually."

I didn't say anything. I had directed those plagues.

He did not die. He hung on, fighting for breath, the fever raging through him. When he was awake his face was masklike, revealing little. When he was unconscious, the muscles around his mouth relaxed. He became vulnerable then—human, a victim of life like the rest of us.

We watched him closely. Twice he went into paroxysms of choking, and both times Aleta brought him back from the edge.

At midday, Rowan brought in a meal of steak and

potatoes and coffee. We sat wolfing it, glancing now and then at the figure on the bed. The constant tension had taken its toll of the girl. She looked tired. There were dark circles under her eyes.

"Will he make it?" I asked, sipping coffee.

She gave a little shrug, put down her own cup. "He seems a little stronger now. He might recover, barring complications."

I suddenly thought of something. The mountain. Out there waiting for us.

"Barring complications," I said, "how long before he can climb again?"

She shrugged, looked at me, brushed back an errant strand of hair. "It depends on him. Two weeks. Three at the outside."

Time enough. Perhaps.

I stood up.

"I've got to go. There's a chance I can beat Barrister to the stargate."

She took another sip of Rowan's coffee and thought about it. When she had it, she said, "Can you really translate all six plaques in that time?" She gave me an uncertain smile.

"I've got to try," I said. "Let's hope he doesn't recover too soon."

She seemed to relax. She studied her reflection in the bottom of the coffee cup.

"I won't delay his recovery," she remarked at last. "I couldn't do that."

I shook my head. "I wouldn't expect you to. Bye."

"Bye."

I hurried back to the lab. Outside its door I paused and looked up at the mountain. Ice clattered against a rocky slope, mushed lower into a valley. I imagined I saw furry movement and grinned at my self-indulgence.

Two weeks, she'd said. Three at the outside.

I used the time. I examined the plaques the Earther had translated, reread *Translations Out of Time*, and zeroed in on a few of the more comprehensible glyphs.

Aleta joined me when she could get away, those times when Barrister was asleep. She brought carafes of coffee and bottles of brandy, cleaned my pig sty into a manageable clutter, and played Capulet to my Montague.

We became lovers.

I had no objections, really. She was warm and tended not to talk too much. She never intruded on my memories of Jody, and seldom got in the way when I was working.

The plaques were a puzzle. There were times when I nearly collapsed, my mind numbed with effort. But I was making headway. The plaques were of two parts, the first evidently a preamble, a courtly welcome, like heralds trumpeting the approach of royalty. They pointed ahead. They promised the keys to the stars.

The second part was more difficult—bedrock after loam. I chased syntaxical phantoms in my dreams, awoke to black coffee and the workbench. As I chased trains of thought into dead switching yards, my respect for Barrister grew. The mind that was capable of penetrating densities of thought like these was deserving of the sincerest admiration.

The Earther had survived the worst of the attack. Though weak, he was recovering. I stopped in once, found him sleeping. I was amazed at how gaunt he had become. His cheeks were sunken. His head bore all the aspect of a whitened skull. Lesser men, Aleta assured me, would have given up long ago. The Earther, it appeared, had a will of iron.

His recovery was swift. He wasn't leaving me a lot of time. I persuaded Aleta to shoot me full of stimulants, and I didn't sleep for two days. Little use. The glyphs were an impenetrable forest, an unscaleable cliff. They defied and then defeated me.

I bottomed out.

Done.

Finished.

We sat drinking brandy, she dressed less than coyly in a sheet off the army cot.

"Barrister took solid food today," she said. She reached out a finger, traced it over the stubble that graced my chin.

"Good for him," I said. I knocked back the brandy and stood up. Getting drunk was not the answer. I felt lost and bleak and empty.

"There's nothing left to do," I told her. "He's beaten me." I hated the way it sounded, hated myself for saying it.

She didn't say anything at all. After a while she just reached out her hand, and I took it.

In two days Barrister was walking, eating huge meals from Rowan's kitchen, gaining strength, looking up at the mountain, squinting at the sliding ice.

There was one last thing I hadn't tried. In the throes of desperation I went back 11 years, kissed Aleta hard on the mouth, threw out the rules, and reached deep inside myself for whatever was left of the poet.

In this universe God is creator, Kirst (cursed) is the created.

Pun intended.

At the end of 36 hours my mind was fragmented; shadows took on life, colors swam in front of my eyes. I was on the edge of madness.

Maybe that was what was needed.

I found the threads that ran through the glyphs, ran them down, skeined them into fabric.

There was not one key. There were many.

Aleta touched my shoulder.

"Pan. Barrister wants to finish the climb now." There was sadness in her voice.

I looked into her face, saw myself reflected in the blue of her eyes. I was taken aback. What crazy man was this?

"Tomorrow," I said. "Tomorrow." I stood up, caught her arm for support, and stumbled to the cot.

"Pan, did you hear? He's getting impatient. He wants to climb the mountain."

I patted her hand. "I did it, Jody. I did it."

She lowered me, swung up my legs.

"I'm not Jody. I'm Aleta."

I stretched out on the cot, touched her cheek, mumbled on for a while, telling her about the aliens, about the key to the stargate. After a while darkness flooded in. The universe vanished.

Rowan woke me up, in the hour just before dawn.

"Pan! Barrister has gone. He's taken the floater—and the girl."

Damn!

They were visible on the telescope monitor. They left the floater on the plateau and began the last half of the climb. As we watched, a finger of light edged above the eastern rangeline. Day had begun.

The mountain had lulled us earlier. Three hundred feet above the plateau an ice slide sent Barrister and the woman scrabbling crabwise to the low shelter of an outcrop of stone. In its lee they hung on their icepicks, letting the ice sweep over them like a ragged waterfall. They had removed themselves from the comm net, and there was nothing we could do but watch.

When the ice slide stopped, they tied a rope around the stone outcrop and rested, letting their nerves recover. Barrister lit one of his cigarettes, blew smoke to the four winds. Guessing he was being watched, he swung his white face toward us. A smile touched his lips.

I told Rowan about the stargate, saw his mouth grow grim.

They climbed through the morning, and the mountain began to show its claws. The wind picked up, blowing malevolently, making them dig in their picks and anticipate each step. There were more ice slides, though none close enough to pose a threat.

Sipping a mug of Rowan's coffee, I said, "The stargate only opens during *melte*, and then only if certain key plaques are touched. If you will notice, Barrister is following a pattern."

Rowan peered at the monitor. "Isn't there anything we can do?"

I took another sip of coffee.

"I'm open to suggestions."

Once they passed the 7,000-foot mark, the mistral was a bludgeon against their backs. The rock face was torn and buckled. They crept forward, edging onto a smooth face that was cleared of snow. They were nearing the traverse just below the Crown.

I had to admit they showed courage. They never faltered, never looked back. Once the wind blew Aleta off her feet, and she dangled at the end of her rope, banging cruelly against the cliff. Slowly, Barrister began to pull her up, and finally she regained purchase. The Earther looked exhausted. The illness, I thought, must have weakened him more than he knew.

A few minutes later they disappeared over the lip of the plateau. They had made it to the Crown. They had fulfilled their own particular rite of passage. And, I had to admit, in rather heroic fashion.

"Now what happens?" Rowan wanted to know.

I heard the mountain grumble. "They'll activate the stargate," I said. "Up there on the plateau there will be a line of footprints leading to the Crown. They'll stop there."

I thought of Aleta, of Jody. The two whirled around in my head. I thought of Barrister, and found not hate but a grudging admiration.

I took another sip of coffee.

It was evident now that Barrister had never translated those plaques, only the preamble. He'd arranged this whole elaborate charade in order to make me translate them. Even to the point of nearly dying— you don't fool a tactician by doing things in halves.

He had known me so well. And known me not at all.

The memory of Aleta came back sharp and bitter-sweet. It's too bad, I thought, she nearly had me convinced. If he'd given her a little more time. . . . I shrugged. She had to be a part of it; she was a logical extension of the Earther's plan.

I wished it had been otherwise.

I don't know what made me suspect. Perhaps it was only a carry-over from the old days. A tactician has to be a cynic by trade.

I glanced up at the mountain. According to the translation I'd done, different combinations of plaques resulted in the stargate opening to different worlds. The combination I'd given Aleta opened the stargate to one particular world.

A methane-ammonia giant.

Sometime, appropriately attired, I would have to go and get them. Even being Earthers, they deserved that.

Chapter Twenty

Tapedex two. Location Site: Masaryk. Date: Af457/1/11. 00.00% Re-creation. 00.00% Repaired. Material: 74.76% Hydrocarbon compounds. 21.05% Ferrous oxides. 00.23% Ceramic castings. 04.96% Other.

[Authentication Rating: 00.00% Tapedex damaged beyond salvage]

Tapedex Three. Location Site: Masaryk. Date: Af457/1/11. 00.21% Re-creation. 00.67% Repaired. Material: 74.76% Hydrocarbon compounds. 21.04% Ferrous alloy. 00.24% Ceramic casting. 04.96% Other.

[Authentication Rating: 62.78%]

From the top of Crown Mountain I stood watching Tessler climb. He was on the last slope, a big man dressed in scarlet and black. A pacifist, a peacemonger. The irony caught my fancy—he was a man who wanted me dead.

Tessler looked up and saw me. His face underwent a subtle change, but he said nothing. He began to climb again, his motions effortless and economical.

Below Tessler the other two climbers came into view. They were struggling, even though I had cut steps and driven in pitons to make it easier for them. The large man, Haskel, wore blue, and his hood had fallen back to reveal sunken cheeks and a scrawny neck. Again the irony caught my fancy. Haskel was a man who was already dead; no doubt he'd exchange his sure death for my chances.

The smallest figure, nearly hidden by Haskel's bulk, moved slowly and cautiously, making use of every handhold. His name was Titus Wilde, though he had a host of others—among them Setsen Dai, an outworlder term that meant The Shining Light.

"Dr. Kirst?" It was Haskel, breaking in on the comm net.

"Yes," I said.

"I'd like to take some interior soundings of the mountain itself. Deep stuff. I brought the equipment with me—it's down at the lodge."

I grinned. "Fine. When you get your soundings, you can compare them to mine."

He grunted and grasped a piton. "I might have known. *Is* there anything inside the mountain?"

"Nothing like you mean," I told him. "Nothing the aliens put there."

They had chosen to climb the mountain, the three of them, though they had all been there before. Not during *melte*, it was true, and not with the mistral trying to pry them off the wall. I shrugged and turned away. It was their choice; I'd taken the floater.

While I waited for them, I turned and studied (for the ten thousandth time) the Crown, which rested atop the mountain like a tiara on a bratty princess—except the mountain was no princess. The Crown was massive, measuring almost twelve feet high and six in depth. It was a forty-foot semicircle of sculptured steel alloy. As always, it gleamed a soft iridescent pewter. And, as always, it maddened me and drew me. It made me weep for gladness and cry in anguished impotence.

Tessler came over the lip of the plateau and stood beside me.

He said, "The light from the sky, that peculiar reddish stone—it makes the whole thing seem almost surreal." His eyes, like mine, were drawn to the Crown.

I remember he'd said something like that the last time he had been here.

"It's real enough," I said.

He took a half dozen steps forward, brought his hand down hard on the silver-grey surface. It made a sound like a boy slapping mud.

"It's been here about six hundred years," he murmured to no one in particular. "More, and the stone would have weathered down around it."

I didn't correct him. Early in my investigations of the mountain I built a wind tunnel and artificially weathered several pieces of stone. The Crown had been there between a thousand and twelve hundred years.

The mechanics of the thing were simple—almost too simple. Touch plaques in different combinations (during *melte*) and you opened the portal to different worlds.

And it worked. (I humbly stand corrected. It worked —to a point.)

Three of the combinations opened the Exodus Point to uninhabitable worlds, planets that were sterile or barren or choked in poisonous gases. Eight though, according to my translations, opened the portal to lush green worlds. And it was to one of those that the aliens had gone.

Dressed in an S-suit, I visited the uninhabitable worlds. At each arrival point I found a single plaque—a method of returning to the Crown.

But the portal would not open to the other eight!

Eventually Haskel and Wilde made it over the lip of the plateau and we stood there like four worshipping Druids at Stonehenge, looking at the Crown and saying very little.

Haskel moved around the curve of the portal to the entrance and looked in. Tessler stopped him.

"Easy. It's activated. If you go inside, the Exodus Point will open."

"Will it?" Haskel asked dryly. "It's not set on one of the garbage worlds, is it?" He looked at me.

I shook my head. "No. The code says it should open on a tropical planet. Lots of vegetation." On my way up to the plateau I had leaned out of the floater and touched the proper plaques. The Gate was set for the fifth world, the one I called Verde.

"Well, then. Isn't this why you sent for us?" He glanced around the group. "Would someone like to join me?"

Tessler moved forward and the two formed an impromptu team. Together they stepped toward the portal's focal point.

I didn't wish them luck. They were unwelcome, even if I *had* asked them there. I realized I was holding my breath and let it out slowly. Titus gave me a strange sobering glance and then turned his attention again to the two men entering the Gate.

The Crown flickered as power was pumped from . . . somewhere. That was all there was. All there *ever* was. Haskell and Tessler stood inside the arc of the portal for a moment longer and then stepped out.

"I felt a slight tingle," Haskel said. He turned toward Tessler. "How about you?"

The other man nodded. "A ten-volt buzz. A tickle, really."

They all turned to me, as though I had the answer and wouldn't give it up. I returned their look with a flinty one of my own. The mountain might have beaten me, but I was damned if any of *them* would.

Titus broke the silence, his young-old face tranquil, even in this strange setting.

"Pan, do you have any high-speed cameras? I mean, *really* high speed?"

"Yes, I do," I said. "You want to try it again, see if anything shows up?"

He gave me an acknowledging smile and turned away, his attention taken up once more by the Crown.

The wind had begun to pick up, and eddys of left-over snow coiled and uncoiled around our feet. The three seemed oblivious to it, busying themselves with measurements and black boxes. Bloodhounds, I thought, on an alien scent. Scholars, sifting the unknown through porous sieves of intellect.

Ah, hell!

They were doing nothing I had not done. And done again and again.

I had tried, God knows. All through the previous *melte*, until the snows came and the Exodus Point refused to work at all. Then eight frustrating months again, until again the wind blew warm against the mountain's flanks. Warm enough to melt the snow and activate the portal mechanism.

When the light began to fade, I gathered up the gear and stowed it in the floater. There was not a lot of conversation. There had been nobody shouting Eureka!, no breakthroughs, no solution of elegance.

As we descended, the valley below sought to engulf us, spreading out into huge ink-blot hollows between the cliffs. I kept my eye on the little row of lodge lights where Rowan would be waiting, his table set for four, and with at least one bottle of 10-year-old brandy sitting on the sideboard.

After the meal, and after the brandy, and after the intolerable hashovers of the day's events, I got up and went outside. The air was cold but clear, and this low in the valley it was still. I could hear the mountain shucking off tons of ice, freeing itself from the sheath of snow and mantle of winter. I looked up. The mountain was a black shadow against the stars, so close I could feel its weight.

There was movement behind me and Titus Wilde said: "How do you see the mountain, Pan? Is it a man . . . or a woman?"

I didn't have to think about it. "It's an old man," I said. "Gnarled and cantankerous and secretive."

"An adversary, then."

"An adversary."

We were both quiet. Titus Wilde had been my teacher, back in the days before the mountain, before the war, before . . . well, before everything. He'd taught me languages, and he'd pointed me in the direction of the glyphs.

He'd been gnomelike then, and he had grown even smaller in the intervening years. He was a mystic. He'd invented a philosophy of sorts, and had even founded a religion—or rather, a religion was founded around him.

He touched my arm. "*I* am not your adversary, Pan. Nor is Haskel, I think." He peered up at me in the gloom, his face round and smooth and capped by snow-white hair.

I nodded, agreeing. "Tell me about Tessler," I said.

"Shall we walk?" he suggested instead. He started down the graveled path to the laboratory I'd built below the lodge. He slowed a little, waiting for me to catch up.

"Tessler is a misfit," he said a moment later. "Brilliant, though. Like you, he graduated at the head of his class. He has always been a most resourceful scientist." He paused a moment before continuing. "You should understand, Pan, that he is also a passionate man. And a uni-directed one."

"You mean he's obsessed," I said bluntly.

"If you must. He is dedicated to pacifist causes, and during the Space War, he had to be restrained—he disrupted the war effort."

I grunted. "I met him once, before the war. The

first year I spent here. His politics were noticeable, even then."

We reached the lab. Titus opened the door and went in. He looked around with interest at the piled jumble, glyphcasts and stacks of books. With a grin he brushed off one of the two available chairs and sat down.

Then he looked at me soberly. "In some ways, Pan, you and he are polar opposites. He sought to end the fighting; you directed the fleets. Tacticians, both of you, at opposite ends of a spectrum."

"The war has been over for six years," I said shortly.

Titus shook his head. "For some, the war will never be over. But you haven't allowed me to finish. I've been watching Claude. He hates you, and if he thinks you are getting close to solving this puzzle (he indicated the mountain with a nod of his head) he may try to kill you."

I gave him a sidelong look and sat down in the other chair, propping my legs up on the cluttered end of the desk.

"Why would he do that? He's a pacifist."

"Because he considers you a sort of monster," Titus said simply. "He holds you responsible for the deaths of millions. It transcends pacifism—he cannot allow you to spread your kind of influence to other worlds."

"My evil, you mean?"

"Yes."

"He tell you all this?" I went over to the window and looked out, seeing nothing but myself in the black, reflected surface. Long pale head, dominant nose, hair in a kind of apostrophe: a monster.

The mystic shook his head. "He didn't have to *say* it. It was evident after talking to him for a few hours. You must be aware of it. Why did you send for him, Pan? Surely Haskel and I would have been enough."

I turned to look at him. "He's qualified," I said. "There's Tessler, you, and Haskel. The three leading authorities on the aliens and their work here." I shrugged. "He's paid his dues, he deserved the opportunity."

Titus stood up. He touched my arm again. Lightly. Affectionately. "Think, Pan," he said softly. "You are also a brilliant and resourceful person—*and* a man of passion. Your passion is that gnarled and secretive Old Man out there. Are you also uni-directed?"

When he was gone I prowled around the lab for a while, adding to the clutter, thinking about the mountain. It was possible, I decided finally, that the thing up there did have a better than skin-deep hold on me. With that in mind I turned off the lights, slumped down on the army cot, and drifted off to sleep.

In the morning, as usual, Rowan woke me up. His voice sounded bright and cheerful over the intercom.

"Good morning, Pan. It's just after seven. Breakfast in a half hour. Hotcakes, sausage, and biscuits."

I never *could* turn down Rowan's hotcakes. I stirred myself enough to take a shower and depilate my face. While I was dressing I thought some more about what Titus had said. The essence of it had been that Tessler and I were a lot more alike than we were different. I frowned. I *knew* I was dangerous. I had to suppose that Tessler was.

The first person I encountered was Haskel, already dressed for the mountain. He was standing outside the lodge on the decking, looking up, watching the fog streamers catch at the scrub.

"Dr. Kirst, do you have a moment?" He gave me an appraising look and leaned against the railings.

I said, "Certainly. And we like it informal, here. The name is Pan."

He nodded, smiled briefly. "You were aware, were you not, that I have a rather serious bone disorder?"

I didn't hide it. "Mutated tubercule. Very, very nasty, I'm told. There have been a few cases of it. I understand it can be very painful . . . toward the end."

In answer he reached inside his coat and produced a

small rectangular box. It had a dial on it and a row of tiny lights. He gave me a lopsided smile.

"This is the treatment of choice, Dr. Kirst . . . Pan. The other end of this is set inside my head at a pleasure locus. When I need to neutralize pain I simply adjust the dial."

I didn't say anything. He put the control away.

"I don't want to be morbid, please understand. The truth is simply that in a few months I will be dead. I would like to request that if there is any dangerous work to be done, any seemingly suicidal mission, that I be the one selected."

I looked at him for a long moment, then turned away. I felt a cold anger eating my insides. Why ask *me* to take the responsibility for his life—for his death? After all, what was one more, where there had been millions? So tiny a thing, this last little part of himself; surely I wouldn't mind disposing of it. No thank you!

The dial on his unit was already more than halfway around its face.

I mumbled something, and went in to breakfast.

We set up three high-speed cameras, two of them looking through the portal entrance, and one peering down from a promontory.

In pairs, we tried each of the eight combinations, resulting in muscular cramp and chilblains from standing in the freezing meanders of the mistral.

Titus and Haskel wanted to see one of the garbage worlds, and I dug some S-suits out of the floater's crib.

"I'm sending you to the first one I visited," I told them. "I needed a name for it, so I just called it Stopover."

They were gone for 10 minutes, then the Crown flickered and they were back.

"Not much there," Haskel remarked affirmingly. "A burnt-out cinder with craters, and mountains the color of anthracite. A garbage world."

The film we'd taken covered the light spectrum pretty thoroughly. We were able to see ourselves freeze in ultraviolet through to infrared. The single trip to Stopover showed instantaneous transfer. One moment waiting, the next *blip*—goodbye. Then 10 minutes later, *blip—hel*-lo!

We called it a day halfway through the afternoon.

Drinking Rowan's brandy, Tessler said: "It's got to be in the translation. Kirst's missed something."

We were sitting at a table in the lodge's common room. Outside, the twilight hit the top of the mountain, changing the colors to gun-metal. We watched the transformation through the open window, heard the bass-viol of the wind working on the scrub.

Haskel looked up, his cheeks deeply-hollowed. "Have you studied it, Claude? Have you taken it apart piece by piece and put it back together again?"

"What do you mean?"

Haskel shrugged. He looked at Titus. "*He* knows. There isn't a false step anywhere in that translation. Kirst's a genius—a goddam genius!" He broke off and stared past Tessler at the fire roaring on the hearth.

Tessler bit back a reply, shrugged, and refilled his brandy glass. His eyes found mine and burned with their overload of hate. He didn't say anything; he raised his glass in a mocking toast, drank off half of it, hurled the remainder into the fireplace.

"To tin gods!" he said. He stood up, towering and strong, sure of himself. "We'll see about that translation." A little unsteady on his feet, he turned and strode out the door.

The weather next morning was ominous. Colder air had moved in and banner clouds hid the mountain peaks. The wind velocity up at the Crown would be nothing to scoff at.

Haskel wanted to test the electromagnetic field strengths all the way up the mountain, and Titus had a theory that the Crown itself might provide an answer to the puzzle. After breakfast I loaded the floater with their equipment and we began our ascent. Tessler did not join us, and Haskel said the light in his room had burned throughout the night.

"He's trying to prove you misinterpreted the glyphs," Haskel said with amusement. "He's a fool."

I shrugged, and lifted the floater carefully through the first raw currents of the mistral. Anything was possible. And contrary to what Haskel thought, Tessler was no fool. If I had made a mistake, he would find it.

According to my translations, the aliens welcomed others to use the stargate. The instructions for its use were clear. Precise. The keys to the stars were laid out for whomever could divine their use. And the Mountain of the Crown was a beacon few visitors could miss. Wherever they were, the aliens *wanted* to be found.

Our upward progress was slowed by Haskel's efforts to measure the EM fields generated by each plaque. It was nearly an hour before I guided the floater over the lip of the plateau and set it down a few feet from the Crown.

This far up, the wind was a caterwauling tiger, awesome in its strength. I linked lifelines with Titus and Haskel before letting them leave the floater. I had once clocked the mistral winds at 110 miles per hour, and I was taking no chances of losing my charges over the edge of a 10,000-foot mountain.

"Pan?" It was Titus's voice, shrill against the storm.
"Yes?"

"It occurs to me that the portal may be closed at the *other* end—and not necessarily by the aliens who built this," he pointed to the Crown.

I thought about it while he took his readings.

"I don't buy it," I said when he clambered back into the floater ahead of Haskel. "One planet, perhaps. Two, even—or three. Eight stretches the theory too far."

He glanced up at me. "It could be the descendants

of the original builders. A few centuries can make a large difference in world views. Consider Mankind."

Lifting the floater up into the wind, I considered.

It was morning ... it was *a* morning. I sat up groggily and listened to a cascading rain pelt against the windows. The intercom buzzed insistently.

"Good morning, Dr. Kirst. It's seven o'clock. Breakfast in a half hour."

"Rowan?"

"Yes, sir?"

"You're fired."

I heard a chuckle as the intercom clicked off.

There was a calendar on my desk, and I looked at it as I dressed. Nine weeks. Nine weeks, and we had done everything but dismantle the stargate. In another three or four the snows would come, and we could forget the whole project for eight months.

Damnation!

I stepped outside the lab and looked up. The mountain was a patchwork of browns and grays and reds. The rain and dim light lent it a dignity it didn't deserve. Squinting against the pelting droplets, I could just make out the line of plaques zippering up its face. I felt an old seething anger. It was as though the mountain was laughing at me, hiding its secrets in plain sight.

Because of the rain, I went into the lodge through the rear. I was entering the common room through the kitchen when I made out two voices. Haskel and Tessler. They were talking about me.

"... a murderer, Joe!"

"No, he was a tactician. If it had not been for him and others like him, the Earth would own everything now. Earth had tacticians, too, don't forget." Haskel's voice sounded slurred, distant.

"Why do you insist on sticking up for him? Do you want to see him pollute an alien race with his ... his ... *infection?*"

"Stow it, Claude! That's pretty strong." Haskel had

roused himself, though he still seemed curiously insular. His illness, I guessed.

There was a brief silence, then Tessler said: "Do you actually think he'll find a way to make the stargate work?"

"Sure. He's not just smart, you know. He's mule stubborn, too. He'll keep worrying it until it gives or he does. It might not be *this melte* cycle, or even next, but he'll do it. You can make book on it. Look at that translation he did—impossible, right? Eleven years, it took him, but he did it. He'll lick the stargate, too."

I didn't stay to hear more, retreating instead back through the kitchen, where I took the opportunity to steal a sandwich and a quart of milk.

It wasn't true. I *had* given up—I'd sent for help.

Three days later Tessler tried to kill me.

This late in *melte* the wind's velocity had dropped considerably, though squalls still swept across the Crown. When they *did* hit it was with the force of waves crashing against a cliff. And they gave no warning. It was early afternoon; I was laying down cables for another camera run.

It occurred to me that there might be more than one locus of departure. One locus for garbage worlds, one (or possibly more) for the other eight.

I was getting the proper angle for number two camera when Tessler came over the lip of the plateau. He had obviously climbed all the way; the floater was parked a dozen feet away in the lee of an outcrop.

"You're just in time to lend a hand," I said amicably.

He stood up. He was wearing his scarlet and black coat, and he looked awesome silhouetted against the sky.

He said, "I didn't come here for that." He was carrying a piton gun in one hand. As he spoke he swung it up to cover me.

A piton gun is used by climbers. It drives a ten-inch magnesium alloy spike five inches through almost any kind of rock. I didn't care to think of what it would do to me.

"Stand up!"

I stood up, easing my legs. Tessler's face was bleak, empty, void of all expression.

"You won't contaminate *them*," he said stiffly. "I'm going to make sure you don't."

I remembered Titus's warning. Tessler must think I was getting close; he'd come to kill me. I activated the comm net. At least there would be a record of what was happening.

He motioned with the gun. "Over there!" I moved slowly along the curve of the Crown and he followed, his eyes never leaving my face.

"It won't stop with me," I said as evenly as I could. "Someone else will find the key."

He nodded shortly. "Of course. And then Mankind can meet with the aliens. But on even terms."

I stopped. I had gone as far as I could along the arc of the Crown. I was at the entrance, and I knew suddenly what Tessler was planning. I looked back at him and anger flared inside.

"Which garbage world did you set it for, Tessler?"

He shook his head and his mouth drooped a little. Apparently he was not enjoying the act as much as he thought he would.

"Go on," he said. "Step inside."

I waited, and he shoved the piton gun at me, holding it rock steady just inches from my chest. Titus had been right—he hated me enough to put aside his beliefs. Those millions of deaths were mine to answer for . . . and he was to be my executioner.

Damn!

No ideas, Pan? And you call yourself a tactician. Hah!

Maybe. . . .

I suddenly grinned at him, a mocking expression that made his eyes narrow. Loki baiting Thor.

"Do you want the secret of the stargate, Tessler? I'm close enough to guess the answer." I took a half-step back. "I know the way to the stars. Shall I tell you, or shall I take the answer with me?"

It stopped him. We stared at each other for perhaps a minute, and then he shook his head.

"No. You may be close, but you don't know . . . not yet. Goodbye, Kirst."

I had held him just long enough. The squall struck with all the fury of an angry tiger, whirling him partly around. He braced himself against it. I aimed a kick at his wrist and missed, and felt the rush of air as a piton swept over my shoulder.

There was no grace to it. I tackled him, and we rolled back and forth in front of the Crown. He was strong, and he fought with a desperate intensity. I managed to knock the piton gun away from him and we both staggered to our feet.

I said, "Don't be a fool, Tessler. I don't want to hurt you."

"No," he said. "It's you! You kill everything you touch. You're Kirst . . . you're a *disease*." He leaned to one side and picked up one of the camera tripods. Holding it in front of him, he rushed me.

As he closed, I ducked under the tripod and grasped his coat, let myself fall, got my legs under him, and catapulted him over my head. He landed inside the portal. For an instant the Crown flickered, and by the time I managed to straighten up the Gate was empty.

I waited. It was no more than 10 steps to the return plaques on any of the garbage worlds. Even without an S-suit he could have made ten steps—it was possible.

I waited. . . .

Haskel said, "The engineering part of it—it doesn't make sense. There's so little energy given off, the Gate wouldn't power a flashlight."

It was the tenth month of *melte*, and so far we had solved nothing. We had lost one of our number, and were in danger of losing a second. Haskel's features had thinned beyond the point of emaciation, and his skin had acquired an unhealthy yellowish color. I thought it was unlikely he would ever climb the mountain again, as he had on that first day.

"What if the Gate gets its energy from the other side?" Titus inquired gently.

Haskel shook his head. "There's nothing on the garbage worlds that could generate energy."

I looked at them both. "We're casting at shadows. We don't know the amount of energy required. It could be very little."

Titus stood up, walked to the fireplace, and stared at the ashes with his hands clasped behind his back.

"You still think they *want* to be found?" He glanced around at me, his pixie face worrying something.

"Don't you? It's not as though they were hiding anything. The mountain, the Crown—it's all there in plain view."

Haskel got up slowly, hands grasping the arms of his chair. He gave me a ghost's smile. "When you figure out a new plan of action, call me. I'm going to lie down for a while." He moved on leaden feet into the darkness of the hall.

"The passing of the spirit can be a troublesome thing to watch," Titus observed. He sat down again, facing me. "You knew he was dying, yet you sent for him. And he came."

"I gave him a choice," I said. "Don't judge me."

He gave a little twitch to his shoulders. "I don't. Perhaps he's found some meaning here to his final months."

"Not *much* meaning," I countered hollowly. "The mountain has licked us all so far."

Titus smiled. "But you haven't given up. You won't let him beat you."

"Him?"

"The gnarled old man you spoke of," Titus said quietly. "The mountain."

Later, walking down the path toward the lab, I looked up and watched starlight glitter off what remained of the ice sheets. Titus was probably right, I reflected. It was either me or the Old Man, and who got in between didn't matter.

Inside the lab I poured myself a drink and sat down on the edge of the army cot. I stared at the floor. Inspiration didn't come. I refilled the glass and sat some more.

When the phone buzzed I was on my third glass, and it was well after midnight. I set the glass down carefully and lifted the receiver off the hook.

"Pan . . . Dr. Kirst. I'd like your help." It was Haskel, and he sounded tired. Not in pain, just tired.

"Can't it wait until morning?"

"I don't think so."

"All right, then. What is it?" I was suddenly wide awake.

"Come up to the lodge," Haskel said slowly. "I doubt if I could make it to your laboratory."

I found him standing at the lodge entrance. His body was bowed and his face was a white wedge against the dark.

"I'd like to go up the mountain," he said. His voice was reduced to a whisper. He tried a small smile but gave it up as a bad effort.

I took his arm. "Look, let me put you to bed. We'll take you up the mountain in the morning. You can't see anything now anyway—it's dark."

"Please." He held out the rectangular box. The dial was all the way around to full. He had no more tomorrows; they were all used up.

"Wait here," I said without expression. "I'll get the floater."

As we began our ascent, Haskel touched me gently on the shoulder. "I never did ask: What are the names of the two garbage worlds?"

"Charon. Aleta."

"Charon, I understand. Who was Aleta?"

"A woman I knew," I said. "It doesn't matter."

"Do they have stars overhead?"

I thought for a moment. "Charon does. It seems to be located right in a cluster."

"Then please—that's the one I'd like to visit." He gave me a skeleton's smile.

When we reached the Crown he didn't hesitate at all. He simply walked forward until the portal swallowed him up. At the last moment he looked back, as if to say something, and then he was gone.

Blip!

I found myself wishing there *had* been stars over Charon.

Melte was ending. On the mountain the ice was gone. The plaques stood out in stark relief against the ochre stone.

Time dragged, but the season raced.

"What are you going to do now?" Titus asked.

"I don't know. Survive the winter, try to generate a new plan of attack." I looked at him and shrugged. I didn't like to think of it.

Outside the lodge the sunlight was failing. The wind, once proud, barely riffled the mountain scrub. Titus stared at me in tranquil sobriety and sipped tea from a plastic mug. For the past week, he had been researching my translation of the plaques. He'd found nothing major to disagree on.

"Pan," he said as he put down his mug, "do you see the aliens as adversaries?"

"What? Yes, I guess I do." His face in the gloom resembled that of an owl, round and wise and somehow nocturnal.

"Isn't that a paradox? As adversaries, they would hardly invite other races, other *life forms*, to use the stargate. Yet the instructions are clearly defined, and strangers are welcomed."

"There isn't any paradox," I said, grinning at him. "They're adversaries because they're a problem—as the mountain is an adversary. As it will be until I defeat it."

"Perhaps," he paused, and then went on softly, "*we* are the adversaries."

"What do you mean?"

"I'm not sure yet. It will require some thinking." He stood up and prepared to go. "Will you get a new team for the coming *melte?*"

I shook my head. "No point. They'd all be second-raters."

"I see." He touched my shoulder. "Good night."

"Good night," I said, and sat in the gloom until Rowan came in and found me.

In the morning I made coffee on one of the burners in the lab. I didn't feel like going out. Besides, I had no plans, no expectations; I had no abiding hopes. I laced the coffee liberally with brandy and sat sipping it, watching the colors emerge up on the mountain.

So I lost the fall. Two out of three?

The intercom buzzed.

"What is it?"

"Sir, Mr. Wilde said I should inform you that he has taken the floater to the top of the mountain."

"Well, he can bring it down again when he's ready," I said. I sipped my coffee, wondering what he was up to.

It was an hour before I wandered up to the lodge. Rowan set out breakfast and handed me a tapedex.

"Mr. Wilde said you would be interested in this."

Munching a slice of buttered toast, I dropped the tapedex into a playback unit. The screen cleared and Titus looked out at me. Tranquil. Wise. At peace with himself and the world.

"Good morning, Pan. By the time you see this I will be up at the Crown. I think I know now what makes it work."

I dropped the toast and didn't notice the smear of butter on my lap.

"I wondered why the aliens would invite us to use the Gate," Titus continued, "and then shut the door so firmly. Why would they welcome us with one hand and deny that welcome with the other?

"I think the answer lies in simple self-preservation. The aliens want badly to make contact with other beings, but not at the risk of being attacked. Think,

Pan—the lighted windows of a farmhouse welcome the traveler, but the doors are closed to wolves.

"The Gate must have a filter, a sensor, that picks up latent predatory instincts. Instincts that Man has in full measure. The windows welcome us, Pan, but the doors shut us out. *We* are the adversaries. *We* are the wolves."

Titus was silent for a moment, his round face peering solemnly out at us from the tank. Then he spoke again.

"I'm going to go up on the mountain. I'm going to meditate, and clear my mind, and try to be deemed sufficiently civilized to pass through the stargate. To Verde, I think. Wish me luck, Pan."

The tapedex stopped. I sat staring at the empty tank.

Kee-rist!

It was afternoon by the time I reached the plateau. The floater was parked by the outcrop, but there was no sign of Titus. There was a damp wind blowing. A south wind, heralding the end of *melte*.

With something akin to ... what ... trepidation? Anger? Jealousy? I followed the arc of the Crown around to the entrance.

It too, was empty. Except, I thought, for ghosts. I stepped in and looked about. There was a small branch of green at the locus point, with a small blue flower on it. The petals were already curled, wilted from the cold.

I stayed up there for a long time. Hours. Until darkness came.

Until I could grin again.

A wolfish grin.

On my way down the mountain, the first snows of the new season began gently to fall upon my shoulders.

Chapter Twenty-One

Tapedex Four. Location site: Masaryk. Date: Af457/1/11. 00.00% Re-creation. 00.00% Repaired. Material: 74.77% Hydrocarbon compounds. 21.24% Ferrous alloy. 00.23% Ceramic casting. 04.96% Other.

[Authentication Rating: 00.00%. Tapedex damaged beyond salvage]

Tapedex Five. Location site: Masaryk. Date: Af457/1/11. 00.00% Re-creation. 00.00% Repair. Material: 74.71% Hydrocarbon compounds. 21.10% Ferrous alloy. 00.33% Ceramic casting. 04.86% Other.

[Authentication Rating: 00.00% Tapedex damaged beyond salvage]

Tapedex Six. Location site: Masaryk. Date: Af4571/11. 00.21% Re-creation. 06.97% Repaired. Material: 74.56% Hydrocarbon compounds. 21.25% Ferrous alloy. 00.19% Ceramic casting. 04.91% Other.

[Authentication Rating: 60.87%]

Far to the west, Verde's sun diffused the clouds in orange and crimson. Twenty degrees above the equator, it was windy and warm. Late afternoon. With a sense of foreboding, I watched the vegetables tumble out of the stargate and sprawl all arms and elbows in the deep-piled grass.

"That's all of them," Colonel Shagata said. He stood ramrod straight, his gray hair close-cropped, eyes glinting coldly. Not a pleasant man. Not a man you would want to meet in an alley.

I had been counting the vegetables. There were 30: the famous Panther Platoon. In the meadow below the stargate they shuffled like sleepwalkers, their progress marked by an unpracticed infantile bonelessness. Power weapons, sufficient to reduce a city, hung uselessly from their shoulders.

They were, Shagata assured me, the cream, the elite, of the Royal Naval Marines.

Well, maybe . . .

Twin dots of color appeared in Shagata's cheeks as he watched. He opened his mouth, then closed it again with a snap. Finally he strode forward, sunlight catching the metal of his epaulets, the mirrorlike shine of his boots. A modern conquistador, I thought bleakly; a Japanese Pizarro.

He came to the nearest soldier, took him forcibly by the collar, turned him around. He slapped the flaccid face, his own registering an acid contempt.

"That won't help," I told him. "It takes at least half an hour for the drug to wear off."

He looked at me with unconcealed distaste. "It was your idea, wasn't it, the drug?"

I returned his hostile look, then shrugged. "Of course. There isn't any other way through the Gate."

He let the soldier go and watched him slouch off, muscles slack, coordination gone, brain all but disconnected. A disgrace to the uniform, even if only temporarily.

Shagata surveyed his army of imbeciles and stood even straighter. His face went white—he'd had a thought. He said, "For God's sake, Kirst. Did I behave like ... *that*?" His expression clearly conveyed what he was thinking. He was thinking that his own iron faculties had faltered. He was thinking of himself floundering helplessly, eyes glazed. He was imagining me watching—that last, perhaps, most of all. I would have seen him in weakness.

I looked at him and grinned. "If you had not been ... *like that*, Colonel, then you wouldn't be here. Simple as that. It's the fare you pay when you use the stargate."

"Then the fare is too high!"

"I didn't invite you here," I said with heavy sarcasm. Then I shrugged. He had been on Verde an hour; I had been there a year. There was no fare too great; he was wrong, but now was not the time for debate.

He gave his men another glance, a punitive one, then looked at me. "I'll want to talk to you when our camp is set up," he said abruptly. He strode to the return plaque, then, and examined it. "You use this often?" he asked.

The steel-alloy artifact came to Shagata's chest. It was a foot thick at the base, slightly less than that at the taper. It shone in the sunlight, coldly, with the translucence of old pewter. Touch the surface in the proper pattern and the stargate operated in reverse. It whisked you back where you came from.

"I've used it on occasion," I said, answering his question. I walked over to him and pointed out the pattern. Simplicity itself. Place your hand here ... and there ... and there. Wave goodbye. You had maybe half a second to complete the gesture.

"You don't need drugs for the return, do you?" Shagata demanded.

I shook my head. "I brought some with me on my first trip, but I didn't need them. The sensors work only one way, apparently."

He nodded, then folded his arms and looked around at the towering trees, at the savannahs that stretched to the horizon, at the vaultlike sky and countless lakes. As near to Eden as he would ever come, I thought. I wondered if he saw it that way.

He looked at the glowing sky a moment longer and then dismissed it. He put his hands down flat on the top of the plaque and raised his eyebrows.

"Where are the Verdeans?"

"They have a village three or four miles from here," I said. "That's where the Sachem lives."

"Ah, yes," Shagata said significantly, "The Sachem."

A meticulous soldier, Shagata wanted his camp close enough to the stargate to defend it if necessary. The nearest high ground was a tree-covered hill a mile away. He marched his men there, and an hour of feverish activity followed. Before night had fallen, the area sprouted a small sea of tents.

Three of Shagata's Panthers, moving with the easy motion of conditioned athletes, laid a rope around the top of the hill.

"That is a *kele* ring," Shagata said. He gave me a look of amusement. "Have you heard of it?"

"No."

"It is a tradition in my command. It is an arena for challenged and challenger. To leave the ring you may step across the rope as victor—or be carried across it as vanquished. No man of honor leaves the ring while he may yet stand and fight."

He abruptly clapped his hands. Two Panthers, armed with wooden staffs, stepped across the rope into the ring. Faces expressionless, they bowed to Shagata, then to each other.

Shagata clapped his hands once more.

They sprang at each other, the staffs moving almost too fast to follow.

It lasted for less than a minute. One of them executed a spin and thrust that caught the other lunging the wrong way. There was a loud sound of wood striking bone. The victor looked down for a moment at the man he'd beaten, then bowed again to Shagata and stepped back across the rope.

"You'll stay for dinner, of course," Shagata said, turning away.

He introduced me to his subordinates, a long-jawed captain named Yamada, and a lady second-lieutenant named Noriko. Like all the Panthers, they dressed in one-piece uniforms the color of wet seal. Like all the Panthers, they were lean and brown and competent-looking. As I shook their hands I caught the impelling odor and sizzling hiss of grilling steaks. It had been a year since I'd had steak. I had intended to refuse Shagata's invitation, but now I found myself grinning. Salivating. Blackmail, I decided, could be an art.

We ate at a small table set up in Shagata's tent. One of the tent walls was raised to give us a view of Verde's lush twilight.

For a period of perhaps a minute, just before darkness settled in, there was a golden haze as light suffused the clouds. The wind picked up and flowed around us silkily. Shadows around the big trees turned pale jade and turquoise before melding into background. I held my breath. It was magic—yet it happened every day on Verde.

Shagata wasn't watching. He spoke into a comm unit on his collar and a moment later there was a furious hissing crackle. The trees could still be seen, but only in outline. The night sounds had vanished.

I looked across the table at him. "Is a repulsor bubble necessary, Colonel? What can attack you here?"

The repulsor field was a development of the Earth war. It was a passive system, useful against energy weapons. Its greatest disadvantage was that it could not be moved without setting up ripples in its energy field. When the ripples got big enough, it turned itself into a bomb. Repulsor fields were also prodigious consumers of oxygen, turning the molecules into unstable allotropes of ozone and souring the air with resultant ozonides. Twenty-four hours under a repulsor bubble and you literally stank.

Shagata merely shrugged and continued eating.

"It's habit, Kirst. I always err on the side of safety. I don't know this world as well as you do."

No. Not now, not in a century.

There was a moment's silence and then the long-jawed captain put down his fork. He gave me an earnest look. "Excuse me, Dr. Kirst. I've read a little about the stargate, of course ... but I don't understand why we had to be drugged before we could use it."

I nodded and explained as briefly as possible. The Gate was an alien artifact, the builders as yet unknown. The coin of their cosmic turnstile seemed to be of one metal only: a civilized mind, sophisticated enough to be void of predatory instincts. Mankind, with a single notable exception, failed that criterion. Hence the drug. It served to dampen instinctual drives. It permitted Homo sapiens to use the Gate without tripping the sensors the aliens had build into it.

Captain Yamada thought about it. After a moment or two, he worked his long jaw and laughed. "What've you've done, then, is invent a cosmic lead slug."

I nodded agreement. That was close enough to a one-sentence explanation.

Shagata permitted himself a small smile and changed the subject.

"I understand you were against this expeditionary force, Kirst. 'Unwanted, unneeded, and unnecessary' was your phrasing, I believe. Have you changed your mind?"

I shifted in my chair. "If you've read that much of my report, you've read the rest. I see no reason to change my views."

Shagata finished eating. He lit a small cigarette, inhaled deeply, blew smoke into the air. At length he said slowly, "The rest of your report, Kirst, described the sort of force *you* had in mind."

Yamada and Lieutenant Noriko looked at us in mystification; I finished my meal. It was good steak. I had no way of knowing when I would have another.

Shagata looked at his cigarette and then up at me. Delicate skeins of smoke drifted in the air.

"Lieutenant Noriko," Shagata said at last. He turned his head a little to take her in. "You're familiar with Kirst's reputation, aren't you?"

She gave me nervous half-glance. "Yes, sir. Dr. Kirst was one of the leading tacticians in the fight against Earth. Some theoreticians believe that without him we'd have lost the war."

"That's much too strong," Shagata murmured, "but go on."

"Well, we studied two of his texts in college. *Strategical Techniques* and *Modes of Attack*."

"Were they enlightening?"

"Yes, sir."

"Well, then," Shagata said, "you might be interested in his recommendation for an expeditionary force on Verde."

Noriko swung her head toward me, then back to her commanding officer. "Yes, sir. I would."

Shagata settled back in his chair. "His recommendation, Lieutenant, was that all expeditionary forces using the stargate be composed of philosophers and poets. No military presence at all. What do you think of that?" He raised his eyebrows and stared thoughtfully at his junior subordinate. Immediately to her left, Yamada extracted a cigar from a hidden reserve and used the time to examine it carefully. His long face hid any expression.

The girl frowned. "I don't understand."

"Neither did the Navy," Shagata remarked dryly. He poured himself a cup of tea from a carafe and sat sipping it. His eyes, the blackest I'd ever seen, stared at me over the cup's rim.

I shrugged. "My views haven't changed. I can still see no reason for a military outpost here. What are you guarding?"

Shagata put down his cup. "The stargate, of course— and our representatives here."

"*I'm* the only representative here," I said. "And you can guard the stargate at the other side."

Shagata looked at his cigarette, which had developed an inch of gray ash. Then he gave me an ironic smile and refilled his teacup.

"The stargate was never intended as a military launch point," I said tiredly. "A military force here could have disastrous consequences. I told them that in my report." I stopped. I was wasting my breath; Shagata had no intention of turning around and going home.

"We're not here to start anything," Shagata said abruptly. "We're here only to observe."

"How many times have military men said that?"

He shrugged, and we all fell silent. Several moments later he broke the tension by grinding his palms together and putting out his cigarette. He looked across the table at me.

"Tell me about the natives."

I told them. The Verdeans were small creatures, the largest no more than four feet tall. They had long skulls and small, even teeth. They were olive-colored, their skins covered by a downy fur. There were about a half million of them on Verde.

"They're friendly?"

"Yes."

"And the Sachem?"

Same description, but scaled up by a factor of two. About eight feet tall, with a broader, more flattened skull. The teeth were small sabers. The fur was the color of unripe apples, and made a thick, close-napped pelt.

"This big one—he is intelligent, is he not?"

I stared at Shagata. I wasn't much used to being cross-examined, and found I didn't like it very much. I shut my mouth and waited to see if he would repeat his question.

"Is he as intelligent as we are?" Shagata's finger rotated in a small circle.

"It's likely," I said. "Maybe more. There's no measuring stick for intelligence above a certain level. Nor is there one for certain *kinds* of intelligence."

"I see," Shagata said. "Point taken. Why are there half a million of the small Verdeans and only one Sachem? Don't you find that intriguing?"

"It's one of the peculiarities of the species, Colonel. One of many. There has always been a Sachem— though exactly what formula is followed in producing him is still a mystery. As to function, apparently he's there to look after the others, give them guidance. There aren't any large predators, so he's seldom called upon to defend them."

"Some insects select one of their number to serve as queen," Yamada pointed out. "Maybe that's the case here."

"Maybe," I said. But I didn't believe it. Too many things didn't fit.

Shagata got to his feet and paced, his face set in flat planes, his movements short and jerky. He paused after a moment and turned toward me.

"Kirst, I want Lieutenant Noriko to accompany you when you go back to the Verdean village. She will act as liaison between you and this command. She can keep your records, do whatever duties you assign her. You'll find her a very intelligent woman. Very thorough."

"I don't doubt it," I said dryly. I held tight to my teacup and looked at him. Then I gave way to a deepseated anger. "You have any idea of your arrogance, Colonel? Are those orders, or merely suggestions?"

The line of his mouth tightened microscopically. He took two steps and stared sightlessly through the repulsor bubble. An inflexible man, I thought. Iron brittle, iron tough. He'd break before he would bend.

"Take it as a suggestion," he said without turning.

"Then, thanks, no. With apologies to the lady, I don't need a spy in my camp."

"And if it had been an order?" He turned his head and raised an eyebrow.

"I'd have ignored it. I hope you understand, Colonel, I'm not part of your command. I won't obey your orders."

Shagata sat again. He withdrew a fresh cigarette and looked at it critically.

"Your prerogative. Of course, your refusal to cooperate means I'll have to set up a liaison team of my own. Likely a squad of marines and a sergeant. That could be unfortunate. They would probably lack your . . . finesse. It's your choice, Kirst." He gave me a bland smile.

Blackmail can be a bludgeon, too.

I considered my options. Correction, it was singular: option. I looked intently at Shagata. He wasn't an enemy—not yet, anyway. But he *was* an adversary, and it would not do to underestimate him. After a moment or two, I shrugged my shoulders and gave him a nod.

"Lieutenant Noriko it is," I told him.

"Fine." He touched fire to the new cigarette and pocketed his lighter. "She can be ready in an hour. Is that suitable?"

"Quite suitable," I said. I looked at the girl. "I hope you like native cooking, Lieutenant."

The village was scarcely large enough to warrant the name. It consisted of a dozen leaf-thatched huts and a grassy common. Surrounding it were high bluffs and towering, thick-limbed trees, Since the only light came from Verde's low-albedo moon, everything was steep in shadow. To someone not familiar with the terrain, the village would have been invisible.

I grasped Noriko's shoulder and stopped her in front of one of the darker mounds. "This is my hut," I told her. I switched on a portable light and showed her where to stow her gear.

The hut was large enough, about ten feet by twelve, but nearly all the interior space was taken up by equipment I had brought through the stargate. Noriko looked around at the stacks of books and tapedexes, the camp table overflowing with rock specimens, the survey-computer in its shrine of duro-plastic. Hugging one wall were the sole concessions to domesticity, a rumpled army cot and a battered footlocker. She completed her inspection and gave me a lopsided grin.

"If it's the same to you, Dr. Kirst, I'll sleep outside. I'm used to that."

There was a single chair by the camp table. I swung it around and slumped down on it, then gave her my full attention. She wasn't cute—she was street-wise tough, and a different sort of animal from her commander. Spring steel rather than cold iron. She wouldn't break, she'd bend like a buggy whip. She had a thin oval face that bore a continual sardonic expression. Shrewd, I thought, rather than merely intelligent.

"Brandy, Lieutenant?" I opened the footlocker and dug out a half-empty bottle and two glasses.

"No thank you, Doctor." She looked faintly apologetic. "I don't drink."

"Since we're going to be together for some time, call me Pan," I said. I put one of the glasses back and filled the second. Then I took a drink and looked up at her.

"What has Shagata told you about me? That I'm anti-military? Anti-Navy?"

She stared at me uneasily. "I would rather not discuss what Colonel Shagata did or did not say. He gave us a briefing, but it was in confidence."

"Since you won't say, it couldn't have been complimentary," I said. I gave her a bleak smile. "He would have been right, though. I *am* anti-military."

She shifted her feet and stared at her hands. At last she put them in her pocket.

"I would think," she began, and then stopped.

"You would think what?"

"Well, that you would be *pro*-military, if anything. After all, you were a tactician. You and one or two others virtually directed the war against Earth."

I kept my eyes focused on her face. Inside I could feel the old anger building. I finished the brandy and worked at keeping the emotion from showing in my eyes. Sure, I had been a tactician. I had directed the fleets against Earth, and all along lay the waste of that effort. Earth herself I'd blanketed with plague, and those who survived did it in spite of me, not because of me.

Pan Kirst—death bringer!

Once the war was over, when I was sure we had won, I was foolish enough to think I could forget all of it, bury myself in research, lose myself in work.

It wasn't that easy, of course. It never is. The war followed me, put its brand on me. There were some, a handful, who held me accountable for my actions, for all those millions of dead—for the dreams that would never be fulfilled.

Unfortunately for my peace of mind, I was becoming one of *those*.

"Tell me about Shagata," I said more sharply than was meant. "Is he really made of stone or is that just an impression I get?"

She laughed. "You've heard of the Panthers?"

"Yes. Stories."

She nodded. "They're true, most of them. Colonel Shagata took the sweepings, the empty husks, the human garbage thrown out by the other services of New Nippon, and molded them into one of the most renowned fighting units in the outworlds."

"And Shagata, he leads them by example?"

"That's right. He is a master of the martial arts. Have you heard of samurai, Dr. Kirst?"

"Yes."

"Colonel Shagata considers himself a modern version of that ancient warrior. He believes in *bushido*, the samurai code of honor."

"Why does he dislike me so much? You would have had to be blind not to notice."

She gave another nod. "You sent men to their deaths, but did not fight yourself. You lack honor, in his eyes."

"And the Panthers," I said. "What of them?"

She smiled. "They are extensions of his arms. They would do literally anything for him."

"I see. And what about you, Lieutenant? Would you do anything for him?"

She gave me a challenging look. "I'm a Navy officer, Dr. Kirst. That first. And then . . . I'm a Panther."

And that, I thought gloomily, said everything.

In the cool brightness of morning, things seemed a little better. Outside the hut, rain fell lightly. Droplets glistened on the leaves of the trees. Birds chirruped. The morning fog had gone.

I turned and directed my attention toward Morge, who stood watching me with a dour kind of patience.

Verdeans were not human, though there were certain superficial resemblances. They were bipedal and had opposed thumbs (though only three fingers). Their bony heads rotated birdlike on long, thin necks. Running horizontally above their noses was a dark bar of chitinous material—their organ of vision.

Morge's fingers moved in practiced motion, talking to me in pidgin sign-talk.

"Your friend does not stay with you?"

"She preferred to sleep outside," I said. "I hope she did not get wet." Though they could not speak English, Verdeans had excellent ears, and a few of them had mastered a smattering of the language. Morge's vocabulary topped three hundred words.

"She did not get wet," he signed. "She slept beneath a Tobuk tree."

I nodded and went toward the door. "Let's go see the Sachem," I said.

We found him in front of the largest hut, squatting by the communal food dish. With him, leaning against the hut's support pole, was Noriko.

"Good morning, sir ... uh, Pan." She looked up long enough to give me a smile, then switched her gaze back to the Sachem. "He hasn't moved in almost an hour," she said. There was no mistaking the awe in her voice.

I shrugged and settled into a cross-legged posture just to the left of the Sachem's splayed feet.

"I've known him to stay in one position for days on end," I said. I studied the living mountain before me and, as always, felt an impelling awe of my own.

His Verdean name was Cirlos, which meant "He Who Teaches." Seated before him, in his broad shadow, I felt like a pygmy visiting a sequoia. The Sachem was huge. More, he was tranquil, monumental, a living creature that somehow bore the stamp of godhood.

We waited. Cirlos breathed in and out, shallow but even. From time to time, like a metronome, air ruffled through his nostrils.

"Cirlos gone," Morge signed. To the right of Noriko, he had assumed his patient waiting stance.

"Yes," I said.

Noriko caught the exchange but could not read the gestures. She squatted by the pole and took up a handful of dust, let it trickle through her fingers.

"He know we're here?"

"He knows."

Behind us several other Verdeans appeared, as if from the ground. They began an animated conversation, the sound range far too high for human ears.

Another hour crept by. There was no movement on Cirlos's part save the breathing. After fifteen more minutes, the girl began to squirm.

"You sure he knows we're here?"

Morge signaled a reply and I translated it for her.

"Sir, Cirlos knows. He sees. He hears. He pays you brief notice. Like flowers. Like grass. Like me . . . like Bof here." He broke off and touched another Verdean.

"Christ!" Noriko said explosively. She gave me a quick glance out of her tough-guy face, took up another fistful of dust, let go of it, and rubbed her hands together. "Tell me again how they see," she said. "Not being able to look them in the eyes has me bugged."

It had me, too, the first time I'd encountered it. So much of human expression is transmitted with our eyes that their absence is disconcerting.

The Verdeans were unaware of light wavelengths. The chitinous bars that served them for eyes focused another energy entirely. Life-quanta. Their sense of sight was an acute awareness of the life forms surrounding them.

Verde's biosphere seethed with living organisms, a thick soup of life. The Verdeans were aware of microorganisms as a background against which the larger animals (including humans) moved as brightly burning forms.

It was an interesting evolutionary adaptation. The Verdeans couldn't see through ordinary window glass, but they *could* move in pitch darkness as casually as they did in daylight.

There was sudden movement. Cirlos straightened his shoulders and turned his head a little, angling it down at me. Banana-sized fingers moved with sure dexterity.

"What is he saying?" Noriko asked. She left the support pole and seated herself beside me.

"He's simply greeting us," I said. " 'Hello, good morning,' that sort of thing."

"He's buddha-like," she whispered softly. She stared up at the broad green form.

"He is, very," I said in agreement. I wondered briefly if her comm net was open. Was Shagata listening? I shrugged then and turned to the Sachem. We began our usual discussion. As we talked, I translated his hand movements so that the girl could follow along. As always, our conversations had many lines of approach—and as many avenues of retreat. We tread lightly, with caution and a sense of mutual respect. There was no sense of hurry.

For both of us, it was unexplored territory.

I wasn't sure what Cirlos wanted from me, but I knew full well what I wanted from _him_. Simply put, he had a secret, and I intended to ferret it out.

I already had an inkling.

Verdeans communed with ghosts.

There had been a time when Man defended his cave and his woman by using fire—and all manner of tools—against his enemies. What developed was his ability to think in a logical fashion. He became sophisticated. He developed ever more useful tools. Space ships and hunting spears, after all, share a common ancestry.

The Verdeans had chosen a different path, but one that had proven equally effective. They formed an alliance with a sort of energy creature, much as Man and dogs formed an early alliance. The difference was that dogs are not invisible quasi-intelligent flying energy clouds.

They were not invisible to the Verdeans, of course. Since they had life-quanta they showed up in the Verdeans' peculiar field of vision. To them the Symbiotes must have seemed like giant birds, darting here and there through the biosphere.

I called them Symbiotes for lack of something else to call them. Few in number, they varied considerably in size. Some were large as battleships, great undulating masses of swirling energy. Others were tiny by comparison, a foot or two in diameter.

Not for the first time (or even the second), I wondered what kind of teeth they had.

*   *   *

In the days that followed, Noriko learned sign-talk. She built herself a hut across the common and spent her spare time helping me analyze rock samples.

I hadn't tried to hide my interest in the Symbiotes and my in-residence second-lieutenant took the ball and ran. I hadn't been told she was an electronics whiz. She rigged up an energy screen that ran off the computer's power supply and scanned the biosphere for Symbiotes. She didn't find any, but she didn't give up, either. She was as hooked as I was.

How hooked I didn't find out until some time later.

One morning I was shaken awake rather rudely by Morge. While I sat up groggily and tried to get my brain functioning, he talked with his hands. Shouted, if that was possible.

"Sir, lady needs help!"

"What's wrong?" I reached for my pants and shoes while keeping Morge's fingers in view.

"Hurry, please! She fight with Sachem!"

Oh, brother!

Fighting was not the precise term for what was going on. I had visited a zoo once, and watched a gorilla (all 500 pounds of him) hold his errant child over his head and shake it for some real or imagined wrong. *That* was what was going on.

I stopped running and looked up. Lieutenant Noriko was approximately twelve feet off the ground, held in the rigid vise of Cirlos's tree-limb arms. He looked angry, disturbed. They both did. Noriko's face was a curious color fast approaching puce.

"What happened?"

"Never mind—just get me down!" She glared at me, then transferred her anger to Cirlos. She tried to kick him. Without apparent effort, the big Verdean lifted her higher, shook her harder: I could hear her teeth rattle.

I got her down eventually, spitting mad. Cirlos ignored us both, settled himself in a meditative posture, and was gone. For all intents and purposes, we no longer existed.

"So what happened?" I asked.

She glowered at the Sachem and shook her head. "I don't know. I was just talking to him, asking him about the Syms—the Symbiotes."

"That's what I thought," I said. I looked at her. She hadn't been hurt; only her dignity had suffered. "The Symbiotes are a taboo subject."

"What do you mean? *You* talk about them."

I shrugged. "Cirlos and I have established ground rules. When a question gets too close to the quick, we back off, try another approach."

She smoothed her hair in impatient thought. "What makes the Syms taboo?"

"Beats me." I gave her a crooked grin. "What makes a subject taboo for us?"

"I didn't know we had any. Name one."

I named one.

Late one afternoon, Noriko put down the fossilized coprolite I'd given her, stopped punching numbers into the survey computer, and gave me a long, meditative stare.

"Pan, we've always questioned the meaning of life ..." She stopped, then continued on hesitantly, "I wonder what Cirlos thinks about it."

I had pondered the same thing long before. "You can be sure it has a meaning for Cirlos—for all the Verdeans—that it doesn't have for us," I told her. Take away the rich broth around us and they would be blind. They could never, I thought with dim regret, ever journey into space. Nor would they ever see the stars. They were caged, forever constrained, by the boundaries of this single world.

Trapped.

In Eden.

Of course no road runs just one way. What might the Verdeans see that we could not?

Occasionally Noriko went hunting, her only weapons a set of five ornamented knives. Small game was plentiful, and her skill bordered on the magical. We ate well.

"Have you ever used *luado* knives?" Her eyes, almond shaped, looked the question at me.

"No."

"They have exquisite balance." She handed me a fistful of bright sharp steel and pointed out a block of wood fifty feet away. "You need not throw them hard; a simple snap of the wrist will suffice."

I tried, missed, tried again, hit. I hefted the next one and admired the working of the steel.

"All Panthers carry *luado* knives," Noriko said with some solemnity. "They are a tradition."

"Colonel Shagata seems fond of tradition," I said.

"That may be." She recovered the two thrown knives, handed them to me. "These are yours, Pan. My gift to you. That also is a tradition." She looked at me and laughed.

They brought the dying Verdean in at twilight, carrying him carefully so that his arms would not drag. When they reached the Sachem they put him down gently on the ground, smoothed his fur, and seemed to converse among themselves. Other Verdeans appeared from nowhere, and these, adults and children together, pressed in around the common.

Under the trees it was dark, quiet. Too dark to see clearly. There was a fire burning, and it threw shadows that flickered eerily over the massed throng.

Noriko touched my shoulder and spoke in a whisper. "What is going on?"

"Watch," I said. I had seen a similar occurrence once before, the second month of my stay on Verde. Then, as now, Cirlos had rendered last rites.

He put both palms flat on the ground beside the small twitching form. Then he lifted them and began to pound the earth, each blow striking with more force than the one preceding it. The dying Verdean jerked and stiffened, and the sound of the pounding throbbed in the air.

Abruptly Cirlos stopped. His head lifted and he stared tensely at the emptiness before him. Then he rose and his arms strained upward in their effort. Firelight flickered over him, turning him briefly into a statue of hollows and points—a demon this time, not a demi-god.

Then, as quickly as it had begun, it was over. There was a faint rustling as the Verdeans turned and vanished among the trees. The body was quickly removed. Night settled full, blackening the shadows, turning the sky into a bowl barely discernible, the moon just beginning to rise.

"What was *that* all about?" Noriko asked. She turned toward me and I could make out the oval of her face.

"Where does light go when you turn off a switch?" I asked. "Where does life-quanta go when a Verdean dies?"

"Please tell me of storms," Cirlos said. He was seated in his favorite place at the end of the common. His fingers moved expressively and his massive head turned to stare at me. He seemed restless, almost agitated.

I studied him for a moment before answering. For weeks and months I had been trying to read expression into the apple-green of his face. I thought now I detected something. What, though? Sadness? Resignation?

I gave it up. I described a thunderstorm for him, but that wasn't what he was after. His fingers moved in a new pattern.

"Are there other storms?"

I nodded (he would see my life-quanta sway toward him) and told him about hurricanes and cyclones, then expanded my lecture to take in typhoons and tornadoes. Tornadoes seemed to interest him briefly, then he dismissed them as well.

Toward the end of our discussion he did something he had done before, though rarely. He reached out one hand and placed it over my head, so that the green spatulate fingers formed a cup. If he had closed them he could have crushed my skull like an eggshell.

"Energy builds ... energy discharges ... in these storms," he said with his free hand, his head held still and cocked a little to one side. I thought of an inquisitive grizzly bear.

"Yes."

"How is that done?"

I explained as best I could how electrical charges build and dissipate, always following the shortest path between cloud and ground. I told him about lightning rods.

He was quiet for a long time, his hand gripping my head like a melon. Then he took it away and drew a deep breath.

"I think ... you must be ... a lightning rod," he signed. He lifted his head then and stared at something invisible in the air. He looked at me again. "Such energy as you describe builds around you, friend Pan. Builds and breaks ... and builds again." He moved his fingers in a slow methodic fashion that expressed sadness.

Goddamn! What did *Verdeans see?*

That evening Noriko came into my hut in a somber mood. She flung herself down on the army cot and looked dispiritedly at the ceiling.

"I've just talked to Colonel Shagata," she said without preamble.

I looked up at her and shrugged, then bent again to study the laminations of a fossil. Royal Navy business, not mine. I was aware, of course, that she reported daily to Shagata on the comm net, but I wasn't interested enough to find out the contents of her reports. Simply enough put, I wanted no part of the Royal Navy, no part of Shagata and his command. Not so long as he let me alone.

She swung her legs over the edge of the bunk and sat up. "He wants us to come back to command headquarters," she said.

"You go," I said shortly. "You're his subordinate; I'm not."

She looked around as if trying to find something she'd misplaced. She frowned and shook her head.

"He wants me to bring the Sachem."

I put the fossil aside and stared at her. "Are you serious? Or rather, is *he* serious?"

Noriko nodded.

"He won't go, you know."

She nodded again, looked at her hands. "I know, but I'll have to ask him anyway. Those are my orders." She gave me a plaintive look. "Will you come if he does?"

I thought about it. Verdeans were not curious creatures, or if they were, they satisfied it by means other than Man. In the year I'd been on Verde, the Sachem had never left his village. I felt safe enough.

"All right," I said, picking up the fossil again. "If Cirlos decides to go, I'll tag along."

Which proves something, I guess. There's no such thing as a sure thing.

Cirlos agreed to go.

Shagata's camp had been transformed. He'd cut down the thick-boled trees and turned them into buildings. The hillsides were stripped of concealing brush, and while straight from the manual, it was effective enough; he'd provided himself with some excellent fields of fire.

He seemed suitably impressed by our approach, though Noriko must have told him what to expect. What he could not have been prepared for were the hundreds of small Verdeans who pressed around on all sides.

He did not let it bother him. He advanced on our straggling line, saluted, looked with a frozen face at Cirlos's immensity, then led the way to a small pavilion set up on the bare slope.

"I have gifts for you and your people," Shagata told Cirlos. He indicated a stack of boxes on a table.

I was watching him closely. If he wasn't lying, he at least wasn't telling the entire truth. Traditionally, gifts would have been taken to the Sachem's village, not the other way around. No, Shagata was a man who dealt from strength; he understood the uses of power. Well, I thought gloomily, so did I. It was clear to me he wanted us here for reasons other than gift-giving.

Captain Yamada was standing by the table, his long face immobile. He examined the Sachem with wide eyes. Then he saw me watching and gave a friendly nod.

"I understand Verdeans are fond of Tobuk-root tea," Shagata said abruptly. "We've prepared some. Captain Yamada, see that it's given out, will you?"

While Yamada was supervising the dispersal of tea, Shagata turned, smiled, and indicated half a dozen chairs set under a canopy. "Please be seated," he said. Cirlos ignored the chairs and sat instead on the ground beyond the pavilion's roof. Forced by circumstance, Shagata bowed to the inevitable and sat down across from him, crossing his legs, keeping his spine ramrod straight. Grinning inwardly, I joined them. Lieutenant Noriko was the last to be seated, settling herself familiarly between me and Cirlos's large feet.

Gifts were brought and duly presented. Surprisingly, they were good choices. Since Verdeans did not see, in any human sense, it would have been useless to give them brightly colored cloth or mirrors or any other commonly thought of trade goods. He'd chosen instead music boxes and incense and vials of spice.

I sipped my tea and kept my eyes on Shagata. He was not a particularly subtle man. When the other shoe fell, I thought, it should be evident enough.

Then he spoke softly into his comm net and the Panther Platoon marched smartly out onto the slope. Sunlight sparkled off polished metal, carved dark shadows beneath the bowls of their helmets. They executed several maneuvers with a drill team's precision. Any parade sergeant would have been proud of them. At last they drew to a halt, saluted, then went to parade rest. It was very nice, but I was sure Shagata had something else in mind.

He spoke into the comm net again. Then he glanced speculatively at the big Verdean. His final, unblinking stare was directed toward me.

"We're building a new headquarters, Kirst. A permanent Navy HQ. I thought the Verdeans might appreciate seeing how we do that." He removed a cigarette from his jacket pocket, put it between his teeth, and grinned at me.

I stared back at him. "Oh? And how *will* you do that, Colonel?"

He lit the cigarette and squared his shoulders. Even smiling, he had managed to look menacing. "We're doing the excavating right now," he said. "A nuke of just the right size is already in place. Take a look." He made an abrupt gesture with one hand and the marine troop swung around. They faced a small hillock halfway to the stargate.

I followed his gaze. So, I thought—the other shoe. And a damned big shoe it was! If Shagata was out to impress the locals, he'd likely succeed. As a demonstration of raw power, a fusion bomb's a real grabber—even a vest-pocket model like he'd be using. Precisely, of course, why he *was* using it. Most excavations were done by simple shaped charges.

Then I thought about it a moment longer and felt the blood drain away from my face. I grasped Shagata's arm.

"For God's sake—call it off! You don't know what you're doing!"

He shrugged my hand away. "On the contrary, Kirst. I know exactly what I'm doing. I'm showing the Verdeans how the Navy digs a hole." He smiled coldly and turned around, his face rigid in profile.

I wanted to say something—anything—but it was already too late. The hillock vanished in a sudden gout of upward-churning plasma. A column of incandescent gas burned its way into the heavens. We felt the shock waves, a little of the heat, and then an aftermath of shocking silence. No fallout, minimal radiation. They make very small, very clean bombs these days.

The effect on the Verdeans was little short of paralysis, They watched with a mounting horror that left their limbs stiffened. Then they turned as one and ran, blundering straight into Shagata's line of marines. Two of the Panthers went down, one of them struggling with his weapon.

Seen through human eyes the explosion was spectacular enough. Through Verdean eyes it must have seemed as though the world was coming to an end. A hole, black and yawning, would have opened suddenly in front of them—a crack in the sky. The column of fire (firestorm!) would have stripped away part of the biosphere, leaving an emptiness, a void—*the first the Verdeans had ever seen!*

The fallen Panther recovered his rifle and struggled to stand up. A Verdean landed on his chest and bounced off. Angered, the soldier swung his weapon in a short powerful arc. It caught the alien across the neck and he went down, his small body quickly buried beneath the stampeding feet of his fellows.

In the same instant Cirlos lurched erect, every muscle outlined beneath the green pelt. His mouth opened in anguish, in silent rebuke. He took four strides and flattened a handful of Shagata's marines. Then he reached down, searching for that small, quiet form.

Silence. That was the worst part. The sound of their terror was a mute aphonic resonance, a stillness that shrouded the slope and haunted the awareness.

Shagata was on his feet and moving toward the Sachem. He began to rap orders into the comm net, his face flinty hard but showing the effects of shock.

"Yamada! Noriko! Get the men moving back toward camp!"

"Yes, sir!" Noriko called out. She skirted the melee and ran toward a knot of separated Panthers. To her left, Captain Yamada grabbed a man and shoved him upslope toward the Navy camp.

One of the marines Cirlos had struck down rose up on one knee. He swung his rifle in a half-circle that left its muzzle pointing at the Verdean's broad middle. Cirlos had bounced him hard; his helmet had been ripped off, and along with it his comm net receptor. He could not hear Shagata's bawling commands. His weapon tilted slightly and a bright flash of fire burned a hole through the Sachem's promethean shoulder, nearly amputating his left arm.

The Sachem stood for a moment, looking blankly around at the rapidly vanishing Verdeans. His face gave up an expression of sadness, of pain not physical. Abruptly he turned, walked, fell.

"Shagata!" My throat burned from screaming. I caught up with him and banged him on the shoulder. I pointed. "Get his legs! We have to get him to a medic!"

Two Panthers halped me lift the burned head and shoulders. Noriko joined Shagata, lifting one leg like it was half a tree trunk.

"Careful," I yelled at them. I began a sliding run upslope, hoping my grip on the bloodied shoulder would not slip before we got him to a medical unit. Even for five the Sachem's weight was extreme, and the necessity of protecting his injured arm made the task more difficult.

Something was happening to the Panthers still behind us, but I couldn't afford the luxury of looking around. Shagata did, and his face went a slack, slate-colored gray. Then he mumbled something into his comm net and the sky suddenly darkened. With a start I realized we were inside the camp. Shagata had pulled down the repulsor curtain.

The Sachem was alive, but barely. His pulse was feathery, a trace that wandered across the med unit's screen like a minnow fighting upstream. Nothing to do now but wait. I turned around and fixed my gaze on Shagata.

"What did you see out there?"

Shagata had grown old in the minutes the incident had taken to develop. His eyes had the glazed look of a steer in an abattoir.

"The Panther command is dead," he said dully.

"What do you mean—dead?"

He made a gesture and seated himself tiredly in a chair. "Only the five of us and three or four others made it back to camp. The rest are . . . out there." He jerked his thumb toward the slopes.

"Yamada?"

He shook his head.

I turned toward Noriko. She gave me a dim mockery of her old grin.

"Did you see it?" I asked her.

She gave a short nod and said carefully, "Have you ever watched somebody touch the bus bars on a power station? I did. This was worse. Much worse." She stared down at the floor between her feet and, for the first time I'd known her, she looked vulnerable.

Shagata was recovering. He looked at me sharply, his eyes haunted.

"What happened, Kirst? Do you know?"

"I can guess," I said. "When Cirlos was attacked he sicced the Symbiotes on us."

They considered it, then Noriko said, "Maybe the nuke stirred them up."

I shook my head. "Nothing happened until after Cirlos was hit. Think back."

Shagata started to speak, then his gaze flickered past me, came to rest on a small goblin-like figure tugging without effect upon Cirlos's good arm.

"How did *he* get in here?" Anger made his voice tremble. He flung himself out of his chair and took a long stride forward.

At his approach the small Verdean cowered, though he did not leave the Sachem.

"Colonel!" I took a step and put myself between them.

"He says he wants to help," Noriko said from her chair. Her eyes followed the small green fingers. "He wants to stay here. With Cirlos."

"How did he get in?" Shagata demanded again. His brows lowered heavily over his eyes.

"He came through the bubble," Noriko said shortly. "His name is Morge. I know him, Colonel. He understands English."

"Then ask him what happened to my men."

Fingers flashed. "Symbiotes," Noriko translated instantly.

Anger flickered like lightning across Shagata's face.

"Cirlos! The bastard deserves what he got!"

I held up a hand. I had read the Verdean's signals, too, and I had seen ... *something* ... that Noriko had not.

"Morge."

The Verdean swiveled his head. He stood by the Sachem's shoulder in an attitude of defeat. By the way his cheeks puffed in and out I suspected he was wailing, though I could not be sure.

"Morge, how does the Sachem control the Symbiotes?"

The fingers moved. "Pan, I cannot break the faith of my Sachem and tell this thing." There was pleading on the small face.

"I know," I said. "And I'm sorry to have to ask. But it is the only chance we have. And it's the only chance the Sachem has, as well."

He thought about it for a space of seconds. Then his fingers moved again, and behind me, I heard Noriko suddenly gasp.

Shagata looked from one of us to the other and his eyes snapped fury.

"Well, what is it?"

"I've been wrong about the Symbiotes," I said sourly. "Dead wrong. I thought they were domesticated, partners with the Verdeans. I wasn't even close."

"You mean they're not?"

I shook my head. "They're sharks, or the closest things to it. They follow the Verdeans constantly, stalking them."

Shagata looked puzzled.

"They're afraid of the Sachem," I told him, and there was a bitter taste of accusation in my mouth. Shagata sensed it and said nothing.

"Put a dolphin in a tank with a shark and he'll kill it within minutes," I said. "The Symbiotes—imagine calling them that—dared not attack as long as Cirlos was around."

Noriko stood up and glanced over the readouts. Cirlos was holding his own, barely.

Shagata grappled with it. "And when he fell ... out there?"

"Feeding frenzy," Noriko interjected somberly. She sat back down in her chair.

The three of us stared across the eight or so feet separating us and each thought our own thoughts. I suspected that Shagata was just beginning to realize the consequences of his actions. Not only was his command decimated, but outside the repulsor field the Syms were hunting, and it was my guess they found the hunting good.

Twelve hours later I stood outside examining the repulsor field, seeing through it the dim gray light of dawn. I hadn't slept well, and the reek of ozone had given me a headache.

Cirlos had survived, though the ordeal left him weakened and in a coma. His physiology was strange to the med unit, and it had overcompensated when it amputated what was left of his arm.

He had broken out of the coma four hours later, then drifted back into a deep but normal sleep. He would live, no thanks to his human guests. I sipped from the flask of brandy I had brought with me from the village and thought about Verde. Here, too, I had brought death. First Earth, with her tall cities and blue oceans—and now Eden. What was it the Sachem had said? I was like a lightning rod, drawing down energies of destruction. I laughed grimly and finished the brandy. My scythe was vast, it seemed. It reached all the way to the stars.

I heard gravel crunch behind me and turned that way. Noriko gave me a sober look and then stared over my shoulder at the bubble.

She said, "You were right after all, weren't you?" This was a place for poets, not soldiers." She placed her hand on mind in a gesture of understanding.

When I didn't say anything, she turned around and looked at me directly. "You blame Colonel Shagata, naturally. But don't judge him too harshly. Despite what you think he is a man of honor, a samurai. Fighting is all he knows."

I gave a hoarse laugh. "True enough," I said, and then smiled in spite of myself. Who was more to blame, the lightning or the lightning rod? I turned away and studied the pale dawn light again.

"I don't think it matters very much," I said. "Not any more. I was with Cirlos when he came out of coma this morning. We talked for a time. He thinks only a new Sachem can stop the Symbiotes now. They've broken any hold *he* might have had on them."

"How long will it take to find a new Sachem?"

"Weeks. Months. Years." I shrugged. "Too *damned* long."

She stood still and studied my face, and whatever light was in her eyes died a little. After a moment she smiled, that old sardonic tough-guy smile of hers.

"And in the meantime, what will happen to us?"

"In the meantime," I said brusquely, "we can sit and wait—until we run out of oxygen, or we can go out and fight the Syms."

Exiting a repulsor field is not unlike pushing through soft asphalt. It is possible only because the field's purpose is to keep out high-level energies, not a body

measuring its forward velocity in feet per minute.
Don't lean against it—you'll fall through.

Thirty-six hours later Cirlos was not only standing—
miracle enough—but standing and walking. The left
side of his body was swathed in synthetic skin and
antibiotic jelly.

Beside his tall form Morge seemed little more than
a child. Together, the Sachem's hand firm on the
small Verdean's shoulder, they passed through the
field.

"Cross your fingers," Noriko said from my right.
She gave me a wan smile. Should the small Verdean
live, it meant Cirlos retained his power. It meant life
for those inside the bubble. If not . . .

Three feet to my left, Shagata stood with his hands
clasped behind his back. He said nothing. What was
left of his command stood behind him in a loose
semi-circle—five privates and a sergeant. They looked
lean, disciplined, ready. Hell, maybe they *were* the
elite.

I looked ahead. The two Verdeans paused for a
moment on the other side of the bubble, then moved
a few feet out onto the slope. They turned and stopped.
That far from the field they were blurred, discernible
only in outline, and seemed more a single figure than
two.

"Pan!"

"I see." I let out my breath. It *was* a single figure.
Cirlos. He stood alone on the slope for a long time,
unmoving, a statue lacking substance. Then he lowered himself to the ground and, with his single hand,
began to pound upon the earth.

"Last rites," Noriko murmured softly. Her face was
drawn, lip muscles tight.

After several minutes Cirlos abruptly rose, turned
to stare back toward the bubble, then was gone,
swallowed by distance and the blurring of the field.

"The Sachem, where is he going?" Shagata asked.

"Back to his village."

"And what the hell are we supposed to do?" The knuckles stood out white on his clenched fists.

"Breathe shallow," I muttered. I turned away and entered one of the log buildings. Let him get the story from Noriko. I'd had enough of bitter, driven men.

Now if I could still smile at that . . .

Six feet above the ground the air was almost unbreathable. The intense Verdean sun had made the inside of the bubble a foul-smelling sauna, swelling the stinking gases, forcing them lower.

We had taken refuge in the lowest point of the camp, a shallow dip that cut across the plane of the slope. Shagata's Panthers spent their time cleaning their weapons, staring at the repulsor wall, silent, waiting for Shagata's orders. Sweat formed black patches on their uniforms.

"We're going out," Shagata said suddenly. "While we can still fight. There is honor in that. They're good soldiers. They deserve to go out fighting."

I gave him a croaking laugh. "That's suicide, Colonel. The Syms will have you for lunch."

He looked at me contemptuously. "*We* are not afraid to die. What do you prefer to do? Stay here and turn belly-up when the air gets too foul to breathe?"

I shook my head. "Not that, either. There is one last chance—the drug we used to come through the Gate. I have some of it in my footlocker. Cirlos is bringing it back here. The Syms don't harm the lower animals, Colonel."

The contempt was still there in the look he gave me. "What are the odds of that working?"

I shrugged. "Hundred to one. More, maybe."

He thought about it. He didn't like the idea of the drug. And even if it should prove workable, he didn't care for the notion of Cirlos herding us along to the stargate like wayward cattle. He didn't like the idea of being thrown out of Verde.

I watched him. I knew the man, knew what his

answer must be. I had known it hours before, when I'd first prepared for it.

"We're going out. I prefer to die with some dignity, Kirst." He made a preemptive gesture with one hand and the Panthers stood as one.

"You're not going anywhere, Colonel." I took the pistol out of my pocket and pointed it at him. It was one of his own weapons, a very efficient needlegun.

He gave a short laugh. "You're going to stop me? *You*—with *that?*"

"I'm going to try."

He turned so that he faced me, and his mouth drew down in a deliberate curve.

I said, "I will *not* kill you, Colonel. I will shoot to injure, to maim. The kneecaps, the ankles, the wrists. No dignity will be left you."

It stopped him.

"If you would fight like a man," he growled, and then stopped, staring at me with raw hatred.

I laughed at him. "Is that a challenge, Colonel? Are you challenging a tactician?"

"As you will."

We locked eyes and the war of wills went back and forth with no apparent victor. Finally I tossed the needlegun aside and gave a lopsided grin.

"You win. I accept your challenge. Are you carrying your *luado* knives, Colonel?"

He gave a short nod, his body relaxing ever so slightly.

"Very well. I'll see you in the *kele* ring." I turned on my heel and walked past him up the slope. I didn't wait for him, didn't give him time to think it over. A moment later I heard his footsteps behind me.

The higher we went, the more difficult it became to breathe. I walked steadily, reaching the *kele* ring and striding to its far perimeter. I turned then and showed Shagata the five knives I carried.

"Ready, Colonel?"

He had stopped on the other side of the ring. His

face showed no expression, but his chest labored. He produced five identical knives and held them up.

"I'm ready, Kirst."

"Then let's begin."

He had no chance, but then I'd intended giving him none. His first knife caught me directly under the breastbone and slithered off to the right. I gave him a grin and threw one of my own. It missed him by six inches, bounced off a stone, and skittered ten yards downslope.

Honor is nice when you can afford it. To a tactician, honor is a weapon, to be used and discarded as the need arises. Honor had made Shagata follow me to the *kele* ring, was now starving his body of oxygen.

He didn't make it easy, though. His second knife struck me over the heart, slicing through the shirt and furrowing the battle armor I wore beneath it—armor stolen from his own supply room. I grinned again, tapped the tiny valve at my throat, increased the flow of oxygen across my face. I had prepared the rig the night before, cannibalizing one of the emergency units from the med station.

I missed my second throw and watched as Shagata underwent a fit of coughing. He straightened finally, his movements leaden, his body bathed in sweat.

"Damn you, Kirst!" He took a single step forward and brought his arm up and down, the knife leaving his grasp in a flickering curve. It caught the meaty part of my arm, tore through muscle, exited off to the left. I kept my grin, but it was an effort.

Abruptly he had another fit of coughing. This time he did not straighten up. I watched him fall, then waited two minutes, watching him writhe. When I was sure it wasn't a ruse, I crossed to him, leaned near enough for him to draw a breath or two of pure air. Sure that he would live, I lifted him across my back and started downslope.

*　　*　　*

We waited, and our throats burned. Afternoon heat, cumulative even through the bubble's field, pushed the gases lower and set up convection currents.

I glanced at my watch. Giving us the benefit of the doubt, we had maybe an hour.

As if reading my mind, Noriko left the slight protection offered by a curve in the shallow trench. She sat down beside me and gave me a long, searching glance.

"What if Cirlos doesn't come back? What if he *can't* come back?"

I made a grimace that might pass for a grin. "I forgot to ask for a guarantee."

We waited, and outside the Syms waited, too. Sooner or later and in one way or another, we would have to go out and meet them. The alternative was not worth thinking about. Maybe Shagata was right, after all, I thought bleakly. Go out with a gun in your hand, with a curse on your lips. Sweat dripped into my eyes and I wiped it away with the back of my hand. It was beginning to hurt to breathe, and beyond the circle of buildings there was a fog of grayish air.

"Look there!" Noriko grabbed my arm and pointed at the shimmering wall. I looked that way too, stood up, and waved away a feeling of giddiness that threatened to swallow me whole.

Cirlos had returned.

He was stooped now, his teeth bared in an unconscious snarl of pain. He was at his own gargantuan limits.

I went to him, got him seated, his head out of the fog and breathing the slightly less polluted air in the trench.

"What happened at the village?"

He was clutching a small stoppered bottle. He put it down in order to talk.

"Gone. Those who are not dead . . . have run to the hills." His fingers moved slowly, listlessly. Feeling some of his pain, I reached out and put a hand on his good shoulder. I didn't say anything. What was there to say?

Sometime later I asked, "How many Syms are there—outside the bubble?"

"Many, but one would be enough. I am sorry, Pan."

"You know of what we talked, this morning? The stargate, and the pattern there?"

"I remember."

"Do you have the strength to do it?"

"I have the strength."

I turned away and picked up the stoppered bottle.

I drugged three of Shagata's Panthers first, doubling the standard dosage. When I was done Cirlos looked at them closely, observing their quantum levels.

"They seem different," he signed at last. "All the peaks have leveled out. They seem flat, unformed."

"Let's hope that is how the Syms see them," I said. I glanced at Shagata. "That's as good as we're likely to get. You ready to try it?"

He shook his head and took his hand out of his pocket.

This time *he* had the gun.

His eyes burned at me. "Be careful, Kirst. Don't try me. Put the bottle down, then step back."

"What are you doing, Colonel? This your way of getting even?"

"In a way." He gave me a cold smile that never reached his eyes, then gestured with the gun. I put the bottle down and backed up a step or two.

"Fine," Shagata said, and when Noriko picked up the bottle, he pointed toward me. "Drug Dr. Kirst."

I stood stoically while she administered the dosage. When she was done I looked at her and then at Cirlos. I wanted to remember that apple-green face, wanted to take that much away with me.

"Banzai," I thought I heard Shagata say. He gave me a look of curious respect.

Then my senses started to waver and the universe went away.

*   *   *

I woke up and immediately wished I hadn't. The wind was howling, trying to break me in half. My head felt like a giant drum. And I was freezing.

I was no longer on Verde.

I looked around and saw six Panthers. About thirty feet to my left was a rag-doll form I knew must be Noriko.

I looked for Shagata, but he wasn't there. I hadn't thought he would be.

The stargate was closed, too—at least the one leading to Verde. No one would be going there while the Syms were loose.

Someday, though . . .

"He ordered us out," Noriko said later, nursing a scalding cup of tea in the lodge below the Gate. She stared past me into space. "The last I saw of him he was putting on battle armor."

"The final gesture," I said, sipping brandy. "He went out to face the Syms, after all."

She managed a tiny smile.

"He was samurai," she said. "A man of honor."

I thought about Cirlos, and Shagata, and honor. I tried hard to feel cynical, but somehow it didn't work. Was *bushido* alone a human trait? It was all, it seemed, a matter of definition.

I thought about it, and after a while I raised my glass, and toasted the samurai.

Chapter Twenty-Two

Tapedexes seven-twelve. Location site: Masaryk. Date: Af457/1/11. 00.00 Re-creation. 00.00 Repaired. Material: 74.76% Hydrocarbon compounds. 21.03% Ferrous alloy. 00.25% Ferrous casting. 04.96% Other.

[Authentication Rating: 00.00%. Tapedexes damaged beyond salvage]

Tapedex thirteen. Location site: Masaryk. Date: Af457/1/11. 09.34% Re-creation. 06.71% Repaired. Material: 74.97% Hydrocarbon compounds. 20.85% Ferrous alloy. 00.38% Ceramic casting. 03.77% Other.

[Authentication Rating: 58.23%]

I didn't make the mistake—he'd have cracked my spine without changing expression—of trying to sneak past Slovik to go up to the lodge. So, instead, I sat upright on the hard edge of one of the laboratory chairs and thought about an Indian I'd known when I was fifteen. *You choose your own oblivion,* Ijira Waden was fond of saying. *You, me, humankind—each in our own way, going willy-nilly to our own dark door, peering within, nodding at shades abiding in that place.*

An adventuresome man, Ijira Waden. He'd done his share of peering within, nodding. And they'd found him one day wrapped around a jacaranda tree, a look of purest terror on his face. I wondered always if he hadn't opened that door too wide, gone too far, seen too much.

I wondered if Ijira Waden hadn't perhaps encountered a Slovik all his own.

The lab window stood open, revealing an oblong square of slowly lessening light; it grew dark quickly in the shadow of the mountain. I stared out past Rowan's tourist lodge, now long unused for tourists, past stands of scruffy underbrush, and felt against my face the leading edge of night currents falling off the slopes.

"Pan."

The voice came out of gloom, from the intercom over the steel desk. Rowan's voice. Friendly, concerned.

"What is it?" I asked. I rubbed my chin, felt a two-day's growth. Outside there were patches of blackness, widening geometric absurdities that filled crevices and hollows, making of the mountain a thing in mourning. Here, then there, winked silver eyes as the failing light caught the angle of the alloy plaques.

"I thought you would like to know," Rowan said. "Something is happening on the mountain."

"So?"

"I've been listening on the comm net. They're using the Gate."

I grinned in the darkness, pictured Roger Morgan playing God.

"Pan?"

"I heard. The man doesn't want to admit defeat. That much is apparent."

"He's not trying to get out," Rowan replied. "This is something coming *in!*"

That stopped me grinning and sent a writhing snake of electricity up my spine. Impossible, I thought, and knew it wasn't.

Damn Morgan! What trick had he come up with?

When I opened the door, the creature with Inca eyes twisted around in the shadow and looked at me, then motioned me back inside.

"I want to go up to the lodge," I said.

The thing didn't say anything, only hunched forward in a crouch that made him appear smaller than he was. At my next step he would uncoil, then batter my brains against the sides of the lab.

"Morgan has found something important," I told my guardian. "He won't mind if I watch."

Slovik shook his head. Then he advanced a half-step and my stomach muscles formed a knot the size and shape of a cannonball. Light spilling from the lodge revealed spikey eyebrows, excessively long, muscled arms. He'd have been worshipped in ancient times, when stone knives were in fashion. He was a caricature of Man—a genetic devil.

Morgan's watchdog.

I grinned at him, but all the same I took a half-step back and closed the door. I was sweating. I thought: *There is a man up there on the mountain tearing the guts out of me. And there is this thing (call him a man if you will) outside my door to make sure I don't interfere.* And, in some ironic mental admiring whisper, the thought: *He is* exceedingly *good at his job.*

There was some brandy left; Morgan was nothing if not humane. I opened the bottle, found an empty coffee cup, filled it halfway. As I drank I felt a sudden surge of anger, and counted it a good sign. Too long had I felt hollow, neutered.

The anger lasted until the drink was gone. Then I

sat down in the chair again and stared out at the approaching night.

Convention has it that Man must take the low road to the stars, traveling at some substantial subtraction of the speed of light. Convention is wrong. Up there on the mountain was a stargate, a point of exodus that an alien race had built, then used to bootstrap themselves the hell away from there.

Talk about your high road.

There was a hitch, of course, to Man using it. The aliens had put a lock on the Gate, a screen to keep their enemies from following them. An old teacher of mine named Titus Wilde figured that out, and beat it because he was such a benign old gent.

All of that happened a long time ago. Seventeen years. A lifetime.

When Roger Morgan had first shown up he asked about Titus, but he used the name Setsen Dai. That name, freely translated from the original, bastard outworld Burmese, means The Shining Light.

There was no hint, that first morning after landing, that Morgan was other than what he seemed, a scholar come to see the portal firsthand. His entourage had not yet arrived, would not for another day.

He had a commission from Laerdes, one of the lesser academies, to study the principles of sub-space transfer, whatever that was. But he seemed more interested in Crown Mountain, looking up at it with the same hunger I still feel at times. It can get hold of you, that mountain.

"We don't even know what they looked like, do we?" he asked, glancing my way. "The aliens, I mean— the ones who built the portal."

"No," I said wryly. "They didn't leave statues. The only thing they left behind was the mountain." After a pause I said, "But maybe that's monument enough."

He bobbed his head, understanding. "The mountain," he said musingly, "and its portal. How many have gone through it, Dr. Kirst, since that first day?"

I said, "Three hundred and twelve," and stopped,

aware of how sharply I had bitten off the words. The
stargate accepted only those drugged enough to elude
the sensors—a finesse that resulted, temporarily, in
brain-numbing autism. There were eight worlds in
the alien's network. All eight had been probed. Beyond
a handful from a world called Verde, there had been
no returnees.

"Wasn't the Navy interested for a time?"

"They were," I said. "Still are, in fact. But there's
always a war to fight somewhere else—and this *is*
pretty far off the beaten track." I stopped, clasped
my hands behind my back. "They send a liaison man
every few months, to see if I've made any progress."

Morgan turned and studied me for a moment, his
eyes flickering over my graying shaggy hair, over the
frayed collar and tunic shiny with age. If he had
harbored any illusions, they were shattered before
now; he was simply consolidating his findings. But
that didn't mean I had to like it.

I said, "I make no apologies, my young friend."

He flushed, then raised his head and smiled in
chagrin. "Sorry," he murmured. "It's just that you
don't fit the picture I had of you."

"And what might that have been? A tall, hawk-
nosed recluse whose powers don't dim with the passage of time?"

He nodded. "I'd seen pictures of you, taped inter-
views. You always seemed so incisive, so *alive*."

"And now I'm a ragged old soak," I said grimly.

"Well," he shrugged, embarrassed. Then he grinned
engagingly and gave his attention again to the mountain.

There was a brief silence then, until he broke it.

"There's a poet on Laerdes," he said quietly, "who
insists that mountains are only slightly lesser gods.
He would like it here." He broke off, looked at me
briefly, then studied the high bluffs. Almost, but not
quite, he managed to suppress his excitement, his . . .
anticipation.

We talked that evening, over brandy and beer and

thick slabs of beef, about Titus Wilde and transcendentalism and the manner of things in the universe. Heavy stuff. Heady stuff. Sub-space transfer, it seemed, was a method of short-circuiting something called Stern's Loci, bending the fabric of space back upon itself like a blacksmith with a rubber horseshoe. It was only a theory as yet, but it showed promise. And then, of course, there was the portal. It might be that up there on the mountain Morgan would find a working model of his transfer station.

I looked at him. He was short, with fair, freckled skin and a shock of carrot-red hair. His eyes were blue, his whole manner open and friendly. It was impossible not to like him. "And if you do find that model?" I asked. "What then?"

He grinned. "No more sleep-ships. Step through at one locus, emerge at another. We'll be able to go anywhere in the galaxy—or in any galaxy."

After three brandies it all sounded reasonable enough. But then what did I know, I'd taken my last physics class ten years before Roger Morgan was born. Still and all, I meshed it through the gears. It took some time.

"It sounds too simple," I said finally. "You try that theory out on anyone else?"

He looked a little less happy. "I read a paper on it," he said after a pause. "At a symposium at the Academy. They were pretty skeptical."

"And so you're here now to prove your case."

He nodded, then refilled his beer stein from a pitcher on the table. His eyes were clear, but something about them troubled me. He had been hurt, and he meant to amend that hurt. Something inside my head went *bong*.

Engarde, mon ami . . .

We lapsed into silence then, our ears tuned to the eternal night song, gods of wind and mountain fighting their ancient battle. Could be Morgan's poet had a point.

"What if your observations don't prove anything?" I asked finally. "What will you do then?"

Morgan looked up, shook his head as though to clear it. That moaning basso *te guello* takes some getting used to. "I don't intend to fail, Dr. Kirst. If I have to, I will dismantle the stargate piece by piece."

I jerked my head up. He meant it.

... *te guello* ... *te guello* ...

Long after Morgan had gone to bed I remained awake, thinking. The after-dinner conversation had taken some unpredictable turns, and it disturbed me more than I cared to admit. Morgan must know that if he attempted to dismantle the portal I would stop him. On the other hand, he did not strike me as someone who acted on impulse. He would have a plan. I hoped he would not become an adversary; I'd had my fill of fighting.

"I understand Mr. Morgan's friends will be here in the morning," Rowan said. He was standing just outside the kitchen doors, waiting to clear away the dishes.

"There are three of them," I said. "Keep an eye on them, will you, Ro? Something tells me Morgan is going to require my full attention."

Rowan's eyes widened. "Trouble, sir?"

"Could be," I said.

I've always had a flair for understatement.

"I know about you," Morgan told me at breakfast. "You were a tactician in the Earth-wars. Very skilled. There's a computer file on you at the Academy. Typed out, it comes to 116 pages."

There was ham and eggs, freshly baked biscuits with new butter, and a carafe of specially blended coffee. Rowan's satisfactions are not mundane. I filled my plate and thought about it and wondered if Morgan had been touched at all by the universe beyond Laerdes Academy.

The war happened. Like countless others it had

taken me, used me, thrust me aside. I had killed and I was afraid of killing. I had grown old with killing.

"When are you going up to the portal?" I asked, changing subjects.

He picked up his coffee cup, took a sip, raised his eyebrows appreciatively. "The equipment is coming down this morning," he said. "We've even brought our own floater. We'll start first thing in the afternoon."

"Will you climb or use your floater?"

He smiled. "I know that climbing is the best way, the *alien* way, to view the plaques. And it's recommended in all the guide books. But it's the kind of ritual I can do without. I'm only interested in the portal."

"The two are tied together," I said. "The plaques provide the patterns for the Gate."

Morgan looked at me between bites of ham. "I brought along slave units. I'll attach them to the plaques and set whatever pattern I choose up at the portal." He shrugged. "I'm surprised you hadn't already thought of it."

"I had," I said. "It seemed . . . too mechanistic."

The grin again, boyish, friendly, easy to underestimate. "You're an anachronism, Dr. Kirst, you know that? Time has fled you by. I get the feeling you want the mountain to remain just as it is, forever."

Close, but not quite true. The mountain and I had grown to know each other, our moods, our seasonal vacillations. Leopards both, whose spots can change. The mountain was an honored adversary. I wanted to understand it, to dignify it . . . *and dignify myself, perhaps, thereby*.

"You can use the slave units," I said. "But don't even think of dismantling the portal. You'd have to cut it apart with torches to do that . . . and what if you were wrong?"

He shrugged. "Then I would find out where I was wrong. Are you sure you won't change your mind? Observations may not be enough."

"I'm sure," I said.

Morgan glanced at his watch, pointed overhead, gave me a hesitant grin. "We can talk about it while we're off-loading our gear. Why don't you come along, meet my associates?"

I shook my head. "I'll be in the laboratory. But bring them by. We'll have a toast to your success."

"Fair enough." He rose and gave me a mock salute, then turned and exited through the lodge door.

The laboratory was squat, ugly, part of it built on stilts, part of it buttressed against the slope of the mountain. I'd built it in years past, added to it as needed. I'm told it reeks of fog and rain and something indefinable. The smell, perhaps, of eons of time. It's there in the plaster casts and hewn stone and ancient scratchings that make the aliens one with Man.

I was thin-slicing a fragment of petroglyph when the gravel crunched outside. It was idle work, habit only. A moment later Morgan put his head in, then ushered in his colleagues. I got impressions of brownness and blondness. They were young, probably students. There were two of them.

"Shields," one of them said.

"Finney," the other one said.

I put down the petroglyph and got out a bottle of ten-year-old brandy. As I doled out the liquor I shot a look at Morgan.

"I thought there was another one."

"There is," he said, nodding. He took a ritual sip of his drink and sat on the cleared edge of a table. He seemed to have lost the grin somewhere. "Do you remember," he asked after a moment, "that computer file I put together on you?"

I nodded.

"Well, it made you out to be pretty formidable." He looked at me as though he'd come to other conclusions since. Given the circumstances, I couldn't blame him. He tried the grin again, gave it up. "All the work you've done here, translating the glyphs, your war record, your whole reputation—" He stopped and let his eyes rove around the lab. Finally he continued. "The computer said you were smart, Pan. Too smart. It said you would find a way to stop me if I tried dismantling the stargate."

I set down my glass, didn't say anything. It was his game.

"Will you give your word to stay out of it?" He looked at me, eyes pleading.

"No."

"I didn't think so." He stopped and took another sip. "It's a pity, because the computer coughed up a lot else. Your family tree back to the first twig, your schooling, your first peccadilloes." He paused and took a breath. "It gave me a complete psychological profile on you. Clear back to the cradle."

"So?"

He gave me a blank stare and shrugged. "I took that information and built a neutralizer out of it. I hired a person at the genetic center to program some DNA, and I grew the fetus to maturity in an experimental rapid-growth chamber. I made a golem."

I picked up my glass again, knocked the brandy back. I tasted nothing, felt nothing. "And where is it?" I asked. "This idiot *doppelganger* of mine?"

"Outside," Morgan said. He stood up. He wasn't looking at me anymore. He picked up a petroglyph, put it back down. "His name is Slovik," he said. "And as long as you don't interfere with our operations, he won't bother you."

"And if I do?"

He shook his head. "Don't. He's a compendium of all your childhood fears, your terrors, your private phobias. I've been told the calculus is exact." He paused and glanced up. "If you want to know the truth, he even scares me."

He was coming for me, clenching his fists, his face the color of old pennies. Damn you, Morgan—call him off!

I sat up straight in bed, sweating, furious with myself.

I picked up the phone, dialed.

"Morgan?"

"This is Shields."

"I want Morgan!" I gripped the instrument too tightly; it was slippery with sweat.

"What is it?" a voice said. It was Morgan, his words still slurred with sleep.

"You know what—Slovik!"

"Oh," there was a muffled yawn. "Don't bother him, he won't bother you."

"Goddamn you, Morgan! You've had seven weeks up on that mountain. Haven't you found out *any*thing?"

"Sure. We found out observations aren't getting us anywhere. We'll have to cut. I know, I know," he overrode my protest, "I promised that would be a last resort. But the sooner we dismantle the Gate the sooner we'll be out of your hair. Think about that— I'll leave it up to you."

I thought about it.

"Don't cut," I said.

"What about Slovik?" Morgan asked into the following silence.

"Lock him up somewhere."

Short and emphatic. "No."

"Thanks for nothing," I yelled, and slammed the phone down. And sat. And after a while reached for the brandy bottle.

Now, outside, it was dark. Up on the mountain, things were happening.

I said, "What's going on, Ro?"

"I don't know, sir. They've cut themselves out of the net."

Damn!

Fifteen minutes later Rowan said, "I have them on the telescope monitor, Pan. They're coming down."

"Can you see anything?"

"Too dark. All I see are floater lights."

"Okay," I said. "Get Morgan for me as soon as he comes in."

"Yes, sir."

I waited, my mental clock ticking away seconds. It takes a floater maybe five minutes to negotiate 10,000 feet. Give Morgan's crew another five to walk from the dock to the lodge. There was plenty of time for another coffee cup of ten-star.

After seven minutes the intercom sputtered into life.

"Pan!"

"What?"

"They're just getting out of the floater. *Sir, it's Titus—he's returned!*"

"You don't look at all well," Titus Wilde told me some minutes later. "Isn't Rowan feeding you properly?"

Despite the seventeen years since his disappearance, Titus had not changed at all. He was slightly built, gnomelike, with a close-fitting cap of white hair. His eyes were deeply hooded. In years past he had been my teacher, my mentor—my best friend. He was, in fact, charismatic—many regarded him as a saint.

But where does even a saint go *not* to age seventeen years?

I said, "Hello, Titus. It's been a while."

We found chairs and sat. We were in the lodge, fire burning cheerily on its hearth, tankards of ale before us, something soft playing in the background. J.S. Bach, I think. This once Morgan had relented. Slovik's purview was extended to include the lodge.

"Mr. Wilde refused to say anything until he saw you," Morgan said. He took a sip of ale and hooked a leg over the arm of his chair.

I looked at Titus. "You've met the aliens?"

He nodded, picked up his own drink, studied the brown liquid for a moment, then put it down. He said, "They have many portals like this one, Pan. The universe is a big place, and they have a yen for travel."

"Oh? What are they like?"

"Big. Furry. Long-boned. Much as you pictured them in your imagination." He gave me a smile and sipped at his drink.

"Have you come back as their ambassador?"

"Not exactly." Titus's young-old face registered a kind of ironic amusement. "Seventeen years is a long time, Pan. I came back because I wanted to hear a human voice again."

"And to put up the plaque," Morgan put in. He grinned when my eyes widened. He liked surprises.

"Yes, there's that," Titus said. "The aliens asked me to place a plaque for them while I was here. A kind of capstone, you might say."

"Where is it?"

"At the portal. Morgan and his friends have agreed to move it for me—it's too heavy for a single man."

"And, speaking of portals," Morgan interjected smoothly, "what can you tell me about the principles underlying them?"

"Not very much, I'm afraid," Titus said, laughing. He folded his arms and relaxed, his face serene, owlish with wisdom. The years fell away. It was good to have him back.

"Morgan has a theory," I said, and then shut up and let Morgan take over the conversation while I listened and drank my ale and took mental notes. The rest of the evening slid away from us, full of eager talk about transfer stations, furry aliens, and limitless space. I saw that Titus had caught Morgan in his charismatic fold, as he had once caught me.

Shortly after midnight, when the fire had burned itself out and the ashes gone from black to gray, Morgan told Titus what he was planning to do with the stargate.

"Dismantle it?" Titus asked. He raised his eyebrows and stared first at Morgan, then at me. He caught the sense of discord and pursed his lips. "You're allowing this, Pan?"

I grunted, drained my mug. "Not by choice," I said, and told him about Slovik.

We fell silent, then, until Morgan got up and stirred the ashes. I shivered. It was getting late, getting cold.

"When will you be leaving?" I asked Titus.

He said, "In a day or two," and then he smiled. "That is, if Roger will delay that long in dismantling the Gate."

Morgan put away the poker and sat down. He gave Titus a sharp glance full of question marks. "Pan has said he'll stop me if he can," he said. "I believe him. How about you—where do you stand?"

I stopped lighting a cigarette and waited. It was a very good question.

The little mystic considered it, said finally: "As far as I can see, you're doing nothing to actually harm him. In fact, the humility may do him some good." He grinned a little, drawing Morgan into his aura. "I won't interfere, but I *will* remind you, Pan is a tactician. Press him too far and he'll find a way to beat you."

Morgan gave a deprecatory sigh and finished what was left of his third tankard of ale. And I sat, and stared at The Shining Light, and wondered what I was missing . . .

When I awoke in the morning I remembered back, saw the sweat-soaked sheets, knew Slovik had spent the night pursuing me. I looked out the window, saw his sticklike silhouette against a granite cliff. Momentarily I wished I had a high-powered rifle with a 20X scope, but then the thought came to me . . . *what if I missed? Oh, God! If I missed* . . .

I was stepping out of the shower when Titus called through on the intercom.

"Morning, Pan. How about having breakfast with me?"

I toweled myself and grunted. "It will have to be

here in the lab. Morgan's familiar will have *me* for breakfast if I try to leave."

"Very well. Sausage, scrambled eggs, toast, and coffee. Toast on the dark side but not burned. How does that sound?"

"That will do nicely," I said.

Fifteen minutes later we were sharing a meal on the uneven top of the laboratory table, gazing out at the dizzying sheer cliffs of Crown Mountain. Titus had had a good look at Slovik on the way down from the lodge, but his only comment had been a fractional lift of his shoulders.

I buttered a slice of toast and said, "Is Morgan right? Are the portals sub-space transfer points?"

"I don't know," Titus said. "It's certainly possible. But the actual construction of such a stargate is several orders of magnitude beyond Man's present capabilities."

"Even if Morgan is successful in dismantling this one?"

The little mystic shrugged, started a reply, then jerked his head around. There came a rattle of stones, brief, surreptitious. He looked at me. "Slovik?"

"Yes," I said. I was sweating again, though the morning was cool.

Titus put down his fork and looked at me soberly. "Sorry to sound tactless, Pan. But there's something inherently ironic about the outworld's leading tactician being held in thrall by a bogeyman. Hope you can appreciate the black humor in that."

"Sure," I said. I gave him a pasty smile. "I'm splitting my sides."

He took a sip of coffee, put the cup down. "I meant it when I said I wouldn't interfere, Pan. This struggle is between you and Morgan."

"Aren't you concerned he might destroy the stargate?"

A head shake. "No. Not much." Then his expression of nonchalance flickered for an instant, and I sensed beneath it a warmth remembered from past associations. Part of his charisma ... he really did care. That was why I loved the man, I guess. But then why, I wondered, was he working so hard to conceal it?

He finished his coffee and stood up. He gave me a sere look. "The portal, the mountain—all of this," he said, waving his hand to take in half the continent, "doesn't mean to me what it must mean to you. You've made it your career, your life."

"Morgan means to take it from me," I reminded him.

"Then fight him," Titus said, and peered out the window in the direction of the sounds. "But Pan ... be prepared to lose sometime. Nothing goes on forever."

"Sounds like an epitaph," I said, and poured myself a second cup of coffee.

Slovik didn't like Brahms. I spent the day playing Brahms.

Spite hath no fury ...

Morgan announced himself stumped that evening, his gaze off in the twilight, his eyes not meeting mine.

"We're going to start dismantling it tomorrow," he said. "I'm sorry."

It would have done no good to hit him. Behind Morgan stood Shields and Finney, eager shadows. They wanted action, and a brawl would suit them fine.

"Maybe you've missed something."

"Maybe not, too." He flicked me a glance that said he had sidestepped as much as he was going to.

"It means that much, does it, being able to go back and rub their noses in it?"

He flushed, but didn't say no. And then they were gone and I heard the wind rustling up on the mountain. Their mountain, mine no longer.

When it was fully dark I poured myself three stiff fingers of brandy and sat by the window. I sat, and watched the heavy darkness where the lodge was, and the heavier darkness beyond that was the mountain.

Titus came down from the lodge an hour later. I turned on the lights and he sat on the unmussed edge of the army cot.

"I wanted to say goodbye now," he said. "I'll be leaving at first light."

He sat in relaxed silence, and his smile, when it came, was fleeting. End of a road. I knew that when he went through that portal I would never see him again. The sense of loss was suddenly overwhelming.

I swirled the brandy around in my glass and tried to think of something lighthearted to say. Something else came out instead. In a shaky voice, I said, "Stop him, Titus. Please."

He looked at me, startled. Then he shook his head. "No, Pan. I'm an outsider. This is between you and Morgan."

It was as I knew it must be.

Hell!

The gravel crunched . . . he was creeping up on me. I lay paralyzed, heart pounding. Unpitying he came, hair like black hemp . . .

I awoke then, and the darkness fell back a little. I turned on the lights, looked at the clock, lit a cigarette. Four hours until dawn.

I spent one of them putting together the shards of a petroglyph. Under the magnifier it was easy, just like putting together a jigsaw puzzle. Then I stopped and had another cigarette and thought about another kind of puzzle altogether. Not so easy, this one—the pieces were locked up inside my head.

The answers didn't come suddenly, but they came. The stack of cigarette butts had grown into a small pyramid, and the night was a lot older. I sat staring into my hands as though I'd never seen them before. It was like being hit by a hammer.

The first answer was simple, straightforward, much

as I might wish otherwise. Morgan was right; I was wrong. My ambivalence in reacting to him underscored that truth. I had had years to study the stargate, yet I had not discovered its method of function. I had left the mountain as I had found it, content in its mystery, helping to build the legend that surrounded it.

The second answer wasn't so simple, nor so sure. And it required doing something I didn't want to do, maybe couldn't do . . . *fight Slovik*..

There is a word for how I felt—*terrified!*

It was still dark outside, though there was grayness in the eastern sky. Light from the open windows pushed back the shadows, illuminating the immediate area.

I stepped outside and to my right, keeping the building at my back. My stomach muscles were in a vise, and I couldn't stop my hands from shaking. I saw a gray blur move between two rocks, step suddenly out into the light.

We stared at each other, Slovik and I.

In my right hand, folded, was a weighted net. Hung down my back was a leg off the laboratory table. I took a step away from the building, my eyes carefully on his middle. If I met those eyes I was dead.

He waited until I had taken a second step and then he sprang at me.

It happened too fast for me to use the net. I ducked, fell under him, rolled. I came up fast, hurling the net as I turned.

He was already in the air, arms extended, fingers clawed and reaching . . . *oh god* . . . *oh god!* The mesh fell over him then, but only partially, leaving one arm free.

I ducked again, rolled left. He was tearing at the netting, strands of rope popping like champagne corks. I tore the table leg free, brought it down, smashed it against the side of his head.

It hurt him. He looked at me through the net's

webbing and I knew fear that no man should live with. Hell must surely be filled with such as he.

I brought the club down again and he caught it this time, using his free hand. He ripped it from my grasp and hurled it into the darkness.

He said, "Pan-n!"

There was a rock there, big around as a small suitcase. Under normal circumstances I could not have lifted it, but circumstances were not normal. I raised it halfway over my head, sent it crashing down.

Slovik grew still. He didn't look at me anymore.

I leaned then against the side of the lab. Reaction slapped at me, turned my muscles to jelly. I felt my insides turn over, and I emptied up my breakfast back to the previous Tuesday.

When I felt well enough, I followed the path up to the lodge, the sound of my footsteps on gravel curiously reassuring. The gray light had turned to pearl with a touch of green. There was no sound but the wind.

Rowan was awake, his kitchen bright with light, his coffee perking, his mixing bowl full of waffle batter. He looked up when I came in, did a double-take, and stood there grinning.

"You beat him." Like he'd known it all along.

I said, "It was a close thing. Where is Morgan?"

"Sleeping. Breakfast isn't for another half hour."

"And Titus?"

"You just missed him. He's gone—up to the portal."

I turned then and sprinted out of the lodge, up toward the floater dock. There was one dark mound there where there should have been two.

Thirty seconds later I was rising, lights off, up the side of Crown Mountain. It was tricky, a little. The winds kept wanting to smash me into stone overhangs. I fought, though, and lifted, my eyes on the pearl nimbus at the mountain's top.

I brought the floater over the top of the plateau too fast, overshooting the landing dock. I countered for it and switched on the lights. I had time enough to see

Titus standing above the stargate and then there was no time at all. The floor of the plateau came up with a rush, the other floater directly in my path.

I struck and the world went dim for a few seconds. When it had cleared again I got out of the floater and stood there, watching Titus climb down from his perch.

"That was one hell of a landing," Titus said. He dropped the final few feet and peered at me. "You do know you'll have to walk down, now."

I realized he thought I was Morgan. I took a step forward, so that one of the landing lights pooled at my feet. I said, "Hello, Titus."

"Pan!"

"Don't tell me you're surprised."

He came close, touched me lightly on the arm. He gave me a worried look, then one of admiration. "Of course I'm surprised. But congratulations. I truly thought Morgan had defeated you."

"*He* had," I said. "*Totally. Unequivocally.*"

"Then how . . .?"

I laughed harshly. "Morgan was only going to dismantle the stargate . . . you intended to *destroy* it." I pointed to the niche above the Gate. In the glowing light there was a faint metallic glimmer. "Is that the plaque the aliens asked you to place for them? The capstone?"

"Yes."

"Let's go look at it. I want to see what it says."

He stood without moving, assessing me. Then he relaxed and permitted a faint, ironic smile. There was pain in it, for both of us. He said, "What for, Pan? You already know what it says."

"That the aliens don't want us." It hurt, saying it.

He nodded. "Not verbatim, but close enough."

A sadness descended like a balloon. "And that was why you weren't concerned when Morgan said he was going to dismantle the portal. You were going to destroy it permanently, before he had the opportunity."

"That's right."

I stared at him. "It's set now, isn't it? All you have to do is step inside, activate the portal."

He didn't answer, but he didn't have to. I looked above him, at the spears of light bouncing off the tops of the mountains. The aliens had come back after all, across the lightyears, down the centuries. They had looked and found us wanting. And sent their emissary, this poorest angel of their Olympia, to close the marble doors.

To hell with you, Jack!

Titus shuffled his feet. "Never match wits with a tactician," he said ruefully, then gave a little shrug. "Will you try to stop me now?"

"I'll stop you," I said.

"Why?"

"You said it yourself . . . you're an outsider. You would deny us . . . the stars."

We stood still in the midst of growing light. There were shadows, though, to hide our faces from each other. Reluctant participants both. Saint and sinner.

He moved backward and fell into a crouch. I had learned martial arts from him in the dim days when I had been a student. I had never beaten him.

He said, "I'm sorry, Pan."

"Me, too."

Afterwards, in the cold light that presages day, I sat with his head in my lap and watched as the shadows melted away on the slopes. There was sudden movement there, a bloodied head that rose and fell and came on very fast. Slovik, still alive—and on his way.

What if, after all, Titus had been right I wondered? Maybe Man was not yet ready to join those . . . others. Perhaps Man is the alien . . . eternally—alien even to himself. I wasn't sure, but . . . *goddamn* . . . I wasn't *not* sure. There was a leaden feeling in my gut.

Up on the mountain the only sound was the wind.

And I sat there, in the growing light, and waited for what was to come.

Chapter Twenty-Three

Court had been recessed for a day and a half.

Kasim Hobbs, his round face haggard from lack of sleep, stood peering out the hotel window at a lenslike layer of thin white clouds. It was past noon, and hot; the concrete below the hotel shimmered with heat risers.

"We've got to be prepared," he said, turning away from the window. "There's no telling what Stuyvesant and his lot will come up with."

"They can't deny Kirst's tapedexes *exist*," Brennan said grumpily, slumping down on a divan.

"But they *can* deny their relevance," Hobbs shot back. "Thank God for Ali Hong. I've looked up his record. He's got a reputation for not being in anyone's pocket."

"When does court convene?" Brennan asked. He eased himself off the divan, helped himself to a cup of coffee from a carafe ordered three hours earlier. He spat out a mouthful of it and cursed.

"Tomorrow morning, promptly at eight o'clock,"

Hobbs said. He looked at his friend worriedly and straightened his shoulders. "I'll order some more coffee. I think we're going to need it."

All rose when Judicial Prelate Ali Hong entered the courtroom. They seated themselves upon his nod, waited while he conferred briefly with the chief chamberlain. The functionary turned, addressed the crowded room.

"Silence!"

When all rustling had stopped, Ali Hong leaned forward in his chair, addressed both benches. "I have examined the evidence presented and am going to allow it in court. Fr Stuyvesant, do you have objections beyond those already given?"

Stuyvesant rose. "My Lord, the purpose of this hearing is to ascertain if two artifacts may be registered *after illegal removal from a site.* We do not see that this new evidence, unauthenticated as it is, provides any reason for so doing. We have no objections, however, beyond those stated."

The prelate turned to Hobbs. "You may continue your case, Professor."

"When this information goes to *CALIFUR* for final judgment," Hobbs said, standing, "we request that the Kirst tapedexes be authenticated again, this time *en toto.*"

Brennan, seated behind Hobbs, could see the reaction on Stuyvesant's face. The Daiist grimaced, started to rise, and then sank back. Hobbs and Brennan had decided upon the strategem upon discovering that the four undamaged Kirst 'revelations' had an authentication number of 76.43 percent when evaluated together. This welcome fact was tempered somewhat by the realization that the Church would have the same information. Still, each tapedex held a portion of the truth. And they corroborated each other, giving teeth to the old adage that said 'the sum is greater than the parts.'

"Fr Stuyvesant?"

"The Church has no objection, your Lordship."

Hobbs shot a quick glance at Brennan. The expectation had been that the Church would object strenuously to such a proposal.

"So be it, then," Ali Hong said. "Continue, Professor."

To Carlisle, the hearing was nightmare. He had read the revelations with a deepening sense of despair. When he was done, he could not find it within himself to doubt that Pan Kirst had been a living, breathing human being. An exceptional man, perhaps, but a man with faults and strengths and longings—like any other man. Like Carlisle himself. If that was so, then so must it be with Titus Wilde, whom he had worshipped as Setsen Dai.

Thy God whom ye loved is but a man. The devil whom ye feared is the darkness within thyself ...

Satis superque ...

He watched numbly as Hobbs prepared a series of plaster casts. The archeologist pointed out that hieroglyphs discovered in the laboratory ruins matched precisely glyphs currently on display in several museums. The dates of these glyphs correlated favorably with that of Kirst.

So far as the Morganite was concerned, none of it mattered. During the three-day recess, he had visited Bishop Poole. The old man had been weaker than usual, his eyes without spirit.

"How goes the trial?" he'd asked Carlisle.

"The Daiists insist it's a hearing. But they intend to prosecute Brennan if CALIFUR does not authenticate the Kirst documents."

"You have read these ... documents?"

"Yes."

Pain flickered across Poole's face.

"Are you all right, my Lord?"

"Yes. Fine." Poole eased his body somewhat, filled a glass of water and sipped at it.

"Where is God, my Lord?"

"Where he always was, my good friend."

"In the light?"

"Yes. In the light—The Shining Light."

"You can still believe that?"

Poole placed a hand on Carlisle's shoulder. "It is the meaning of the word *faith*, Charles."

Faith—a word that lately had stuck in Carlisle's throat. . . .

The hearing ended midway through the third day.

Kasim Hobbs had meticulously pointed out each corroborating piece of evidence. Fr Maxwell Stuyvesant had rebutted several of the points, but in the main let them stand. The Daiist's philosophy bothered Hobbs, and his discomfiture communicated itself to Brennan.

"What do you think he has up his sleeve, Kaz?"

"I don't know what it is, but I expect we'll find out soon. CALIFUR is due to take the evidence this afternoon."

Prelate Hong squinted down from his bench. "Is that the total of your evidence, Professor?"

Hobbs stood up. "Yes, my Lord."

"Fr Stuyvesant, you have been unusually reticent. Do *you* have anything further?"

So, thought Brennan, Hong's noticed it, too.

Stuyvesant gathered his robes about him and stood. "The Church has nothing further, your Lordship. However, we draw your attention to the request made by Professor Hobbs—that the Kirst tapedexes be evaluated *en toto*."

"What of it?"

Stuyvesant inclined his head, smiled faintly. "The Church has agreed to that request. We simply want to be certain that the evaluation includes *all thirteen tapedexes*."

"Oh come on, now!" Kasim Hobbs bounded to his feet, stared with a disbelieving eye at the Daiist. He turned to look up at the prelate. "Surely your Lordship will not permit such a ... a ... sophomoric trick."

Ali Hong looked pained. "*You* requested evaluation of the tapedexes as a whole, Professor, not the Church. They have simply pointed out, and rightly so, that an incomplete evaluation—that is, leaving more than half the tapedexes out—will not be acceptable. All *thirteen* must be evaluated."

"But my Lord, the other tapedexes show nothing. They would serve only to dilute an already rendered authentication."

Hong shrugged, looked sympathetically at both Hobbs and Brennan. "I am aware that zero values reduce high averages. Nevertheless, I must rule for the Church."

Brennan, looking on, knew at that moment he had lost.

CALIFUR returned a decision less than an hour later. The Church could restrict the Kirst material—petition denied.

Epilogue

Chapter Twenty-Four

Life along the Zacatal Wall was slow. The afternoons were drowsily hot and dusty. What pedestrians there were traveled at a snail's pace. Beggars, half a hundred strong, sat in the shadow thrown by the Wall, sitting on their bowls or using them to chase away the flies.

One or two lonely jugglers, playing to the occasional knot of tourists, stirred themselves enough to smile and exhibit their skills.

A man dressed in a loose white tunic came down the avenue toward the Wall. He was short, but with a broad chest and powerful arms.

"Where is the Dysip Breather that works this Wall?" he asked, addressing his question to a beggar with one leg and one eye.

The beggar answered by waving toward the far end of the Wall.

"He here, now?"

The beggar gave a grunt, studying the man covertly. He didn't look like a man who was overly wealthy. But perhaps a coin or two . . .

"I said," the man began again, staring intently at the other, "is he here now?"

"He's *always* here," the beggar said. He averted his eye. The short man seemed to look right *through* a man.

Ignoring the jugglers and beggars, the short man trudged along, seemingly unmindful of the heat. As he neared the far end of the Wall, his stride slowed.

The Dysip Breather was sitting on a loosened block of stone, his back braced against a crumbling column. His legs, extended beyond the Wall's shadow, were dappled by sunlight.

He was talking to an apparition sitting on a stone across from him. The apparition was tall, gangly, with shoulder-length black hair and black, black features. *His* legs, also extended beyond the Wall's shadow, were summarily missing.

The short man stopped, watched for a moment, then moved forward again.

"I don't know," the apparition said, in an answer to some question posed to him, "I think, as they say in Latin, *non liquet.*"

" 'The case is not clear,' " the Dysip Breather supplied with a nod. He noticed the short man at that moment and fell silent.

"Hello, Brennan. It's been a long time."

"I guess so," Brennan responded without feeling. "Where's your cassock?"

"I returned it to the Church. Almost a year ago."

Brennan studied the other man. Carlisle seemed surer of himself, more at ease with the world. Maturity, he supposed, was the word that came to mind.

"May I be introduced to your friend?" Carlisle asked.

"Okay. Jutis Frieman, meet Charles Carlisle. Jutis was a scholar back in Bf679," Brennan added for Carlisle's benefit. "He taught linguistics, history, and a little bit of religion."

Carlisle made a formal bow. "How do you do?"

"Fine, thanks," Jutis said. His ink-dark face defied

scrutiny, but Carlisle caught a glimpse of white teeth as the man smiled.

"They say you're always here at the Wall," Carlisle said, turning to Brennan. "Is this by any chance where Jancy performed?"

"Down there by that tumbled stone," Brennan replied, pointing farther along the Wall. "It's too hot, just now."

There was a brief silence, then, as Carlisle tried to find a seat out of the sunlight. He eventually turned over a block of masonry and propped it up across from Jutis. Seating himself, he said, "Did they allow you to practice Dysip Breathing at the penal colony?"

"I wasn't allowed any Dysip cubes," Brennan said, giving an eloquent shrug, "but they couldn't stop me from practicing."

"It's too bad," Carlisle began, and then stopped.

"About my sentence, or about my being blacklisted from the Archeological Society?"

"Both."

Brennan shrugged again. "I should have known better than to take on the Church. Gus was right about that—the establishment always wins."

There was an ironic twist to Carlisle's lips. "Not always. Certainly not in your case."

"What do you mean?"

"CALIFUR predicted a crisis," Carlisle said, wiping away a rivulet of sweat. "Everyone thought it was hinged to the Kirst revelations."

"You mean it wasn't?"

The former priest shook his head. "It was hinged to the Church's own *response* to those revelations. The Church chose to restrict the evidence—using a technicality. That was the wrong response. What they've set in motion is the beginning of their own destruction."

Brennan had a scar along his jaw that hadn't been there when last the two had met. He rubbed it meditatively, eyeing the other with a look of incredulity.

"You've checked this out?"

"Ran it through CALIFUR three times. It will take

a while, of course; the Church is awfully big. Sooner or later, though. . . ."

"Is that why you tracked me down . . . to tell me about it?" A sudden spark of anger appeared on Brennan's face.

"No. Not that."

"What, then?"

Carlisle leaned forward on his block of masonry. "I ran some other calculations through CALIFUR while I was about it," he said, a grin breaking through. "The Church can't stop the stars in their travel, much as they'd like to think they can. Corthun will be fully out of the Cone in six month's time."

Jutis Frieman suddenly crossed his legs, drawing the attention of both men.

"I was asking him about God," Brennan murmured, nodding toward the black man.

"What *about* God?" Carlisle inquired, tilting his head.

Jutis smiled broadly. He quoted: *"Deus ignotum per ignotius est—hinc illae lacrimae."*

" 'The unknown God is explained by the still more unknown,' " Carlisle interpreted. " 'Hence these tears.' "

"Exactly," Brennan said, making a sound like a raspberry.

"So what about Corthun?" Carlisle said. "The aliens must have a stargate near there somewhere."

"You think we're civilized enough to use it—*if* we found it?"

Carlisle examined the fingers of one hand. "I think so. The aliens couldn't keep Man out of their starlanes by force—we were too devious. They put a lock on the Gates and we picked it."

"So they sent the Fugue."

"How would *you* have kept the heathen away?" Carlisle asked rhetorically.

"And now?"

"They've changed us," Carlisle said, looking at the archeologist soberly. "Softened us, I suppose you'd say. There hasn't been a war since the Great Awakening. I don't think *they'd* think we're wolves any longer."

"We're still plenty dangerous, though," Brennan said.

"Maybe." Carlisle repositioned his chunk of masonry a little and looked at Jutis Frieman. "What do you think, Mr. Frieman?"

The black man's lips twitched. "What do *you* think? You're the one who's alive."

"I think the aliens are in for a surprise."

The black man basketed his legs, stared searchingly at them both. "I do, too," he said, and after a moment added like a benediction: *"Cave homo."*

After perhaps five seconds, Brennan took a deep breath. Jutis Frieman ceased to be.

"Before I go anywhere, there's something I have to do," Brennan said. He stood up, dusted off his trousers, picked up the Dysip COmPUte.

"What?"

Brennan paused, squared his shoulders. A grin tugged at his mouth, puckering the edges of the scar.

"Go see Gus. Maybe he'll have a word or two to say to us."

"I'm sure he will," Carlisle returned, letting the masonry block fall back into its depression. He managed a rueful smile. "More than we'll want to hear."

Somewhere along the Wall, a member of the Sabbat began to carol. It was going to be a long summer that year.

THE GREATEST GAME OF ALL...

POUL ANDERSON

THE GAME OF EMPIRE

WHO WILL STAVE OFF THE LONG NIGHT
WHEN DOMINIC FLANDRY NO LONGER CAN?

INTRODUCING...
DIANA FLANDRY

in the first new
Polesotechnic League/Terran
Empire novel in years!

She'll do her old man proud!

Distributed by Simon & Schuster Mass Merchandise Sales Company
1230 Avenue of the Americas • New York, N.Y. 10020

BAEN BOOKS

HAVE YOU FOUND YOURSELF ENJOYING A LOT OF BAEN BOOKS LATELY?

We at Baen Books like science fiction with real science in it and fantasy that reaches to the heart of the human soul—and we think a lot of you do, too. Why not let us know? We'll award $25 and a dozen Baen paperbacks of your choice to the reader who best tells us what he or she likes about Baen Books. We reserve the right to quote any or all of you...and we'll feature the best quote in an advertisement in _American Bookseller_ and other magazines! Contest closes March 15, 1986. All letters should be addressed to Baen Books, 8 W. 36th St., New York, N.Y. 10018.

PATRICK TILLEY
CLOUD WARRIOR

"Reminiscent of Stephen King's *The Stand*." — *Fantasy Review*

"Technology, magic, sex and excitement. . .when the annual rite of selection for the Hugos and Nebulas comes around, CLOUD WARRIOR is a good bet to be among the top choices." — *San Diego Union*

"A real page-turner!" — *Publishers Weekly*

Two centuries after the holocaust, the survivors are ready to leave their underground fortress and repossess the Blue Sky World. Its inhabitants have other ideas....

352 pp. ● $3.50

BETWEEN THE STROKES OF NIGHT
Charles Sheffield

"JUST WHEN YOU THINK THERE CAN'T POSSIBLY BE ANYTHING MORE YOU REALIZE HE'S JUST GETTING GOING!" —Analog

2010 A.D.:

Only a remnant of humankind escaped the Nuclear Spasm, in primitive orbiting colonies safe from the war below. But when the battle for mere existence was won, the exodus began...and Man found new worlds far from the ruined Earth.

27,698 A.D.:

To these worlds come the Immortals, beings with strange ties to ancient Earth, beings who seem to live forever, who can travel light years in days – and who use their strange powers to control the existence of ordinary mortals.

On the planet Pentecost, a small group sets out to find and challenge the Immortals. But in the search they themselves are changed: as Immortals, they discover a new threat – not just to themselves, but to the galaxy itself.

352 pp. • $3.50

"FASCINATING...A STRONG CONTENDER FOR NEXT YEAR'S AWARDS"—LOCUS
"WILL APPEAL TO FANS OF SF AND INTRIGUE ALIKE"—LIBRARY JOURNAL
"CONVEYS THE EXCITEMENT OF A CONCEPTUAL BREAKTHROUGH"
—PUBLISHERS WEEKLY

VERNOR VINGE
THE PEACE WAR

"FASCINATING...A STRONG CONTENDER FOR NEXT YEAR'S AWARDS"
—Locus

"CONVEYS THE EXCITEMENT OF A CONCEPTUAL BREAKTHROUGH"
—Publishers Weekly

"WILL APPEAL TO FANS of SF and INTRIGUE ALIKE"
—Library Journal

"...SUPERB. IT REMINDED ME OF LUCIFER'S HAMMER."
—VOYA

55965-6 · 400 pp. · $3.50

BAEN BOOKS